IF YOU FALL

S. E. LUND

ACADIAN PUBLISHING LIMITED

COPYRIGHT

Join the S. E. Lund Mailing List and get free eBooks, updates on new releases, upcoming sales and giveaways as well as sneak previews before everyone else.

She hates spam and will never share your information!

Join here http://selund.com

BECKETT

BEFORE...

THE PLAIN MANILA envelope was tucked under my torn and bloody camos at the bottom of the cardboard box holding my gear. Sent back after the accident, the box sat unopened in the old brownstone I owned for almost eleven months. The envelope had been folded up several times and secured with a thick rubber band. The edges of the envelope were frayed, and the paper torn where the rubber band dug into it. The name *Dan* was scrawled on the outside.

I assumed it was short for Daniel – Daniel Beckett Tate-McNeil.

My quadruple-barreled name.

Curious, I opened it only to find a stack of letters written on thin airmail paper, folded up and fastened with some blue foil ribbon. The letters and photos had been stained with blood. I untied the ribbon and tucked in the folds of several letters, I found photographs of a beautiful young woman with long auburn hair and freckles on the bridge of her nose. Wide hazel-green eyes

1

were framed with thick eyelashes. The photos must have been of the woman who wrote the letters.

There were no envelopes – just several dozen letters, the script small and regular. A woman's handwriting.

I opened up one of the letters, holding the photo in my hand.

My dearest Dan...

I was at a loss. The letters clearly weren't written to me since I had no girlfriend while I was in Afghanistan. No girlfriend really, not since Sue.

No one called me Dan so how the *hell...*

I hadn't gone by Daniel since I was a child and my parents went through a very messy divorce. When my mother separated from my father, she took me with her to Louisiana and then California. We left behind our ties to my father and his family, name included. I was named after my grandfather, who had been part of the old Westies gang in Hell's Kitchen in the 50's and 60's – Daniel "Danny Blue Eyes" McNeil. A small-time thug in the infamous Coonan family. So Daniel McNeil was a name associated with the side of my family my mother wished to escape.

After my mother cut all ties with my father, we moved just outside New Orleans where I began using my middle name and my mother's maiden name Tate. Beckett was my other grandfather's name, on my mother's side. So, at the ripe old age of ten, I became Beckett Tate and never looked back – not until I had to join up and use my legal name again. No one except my closest family knew my first name was Daniel, and only my father's side of the family called me Dan so I had no idea why the envelope would be addressed that way.

I sorted through the letters, organizing them by date to see what the woman had written, laying out the photos that went along with the letters. There might be clues to the identity of the real owner inside.

The first letter was dated over a year earlier and included a photo of the woman in an antique wedding dress overlain with lace, like something you'd see in the roaring twenties. She sat on a park bench in Central Park, a bouquet of wildflowers in her hand and twined in her long dark red hair. On the back of the photo was a date of the wedding – May 5th of last year.

The first letter was dated only a week later.

May 12

My dearest Dan,

I miss you already and it's only been an hour since you left. I knew when I agreed to marry you that you'd be taken away from me almost as soon as the ink on our marriage certificate was dry, but I didn't really understand what that meant. Our week together on our 'honeymoon' was far too short and now I won't see you again for months...

I know you said not to write too often, since you're never sure where you might be sent on a mission, but I remember finding my grandmother's letters to my granddad that she wrote back during World War II and how much she treasured those letters, so I want to write you as much as possible. I'll only send one letter a week like we agreed, but it will be seven letters rolled up into one longer letter. It's really no trouble and makes me feel like you and I are having a conversation, even if it is one sided. Please, don't feel pressure to respond – I know you and your team are very busy.

I wanted to give you time to get situated back in Afghanistan before I wrote but this letter and the others should be waiting for you once you do arrive. I did what you suggested and am going to stay for the summer with your family in Topsail Beach, to take my mind off your leaving me again and get some work done. I have to finish up some revisions to my final paper in criminal psychological assessment. Being out here will be a nice vacation from the bustle of Manhattan. Your mom and I plan on spending time in the garden, now that the planting season is underway and the flowers are beginning to bloom. I may even pull a few shifts as a bartender at Oceanside. Your dad's back is bad and he isn't able to pitch in when a shift needs to be covered. He needs the help.

We're all really proud of you making the Special Operations Forces and hope that your tour of duty is easy and that nothing too dangerous happens while you're there. One day, I hope this war will be over so you won't have to leave me again, but I know it's probably not going to end any time soon. Maybe this will be the last time we have to be separated, if you do decide to get out once this deployment is finished.

I miss your touch, your smile, and most of all the fun we have together. You make me brave.

All for now,

Love, me

I checked out the second and third letters, and they were pretty much along the same lines. She didn't sign her letters except *Love, me*. She wrote of her time with 'Dan's' parents in Topsail Beach, about the flower garden, about the restaurant his parents owned, about the characters at the bar where she worked, and about her paper.

I quickly googled Topsail Beach and saw that there were far too many restaurants for me to know which one was attached to the woman who wrote the letters. I'd have to find some other way to discover her identity so I could return her letters.

The letters were from a young bride to her bridegroom, who had gone away to war only a week after their wedding. He was in Special Operations Forces, so I had my first clue about the identity of the mysterious Dan. Armed with that information, I might be able to dig a bit, contact a few people I still knew in the service to find out why, other than the name we had in common, these letters were sent to me instead of to his family. By the blood on the letters, I had a suspicion that Dan was killed in action but other than that, I had no evidence.

The last letter was dated August 15th, and then there was no other. That final letter was sent less than a week before *my* incident – the incident that got me my only scar from my time in Afghanistan, other than incidental cuts and scrapes that are part of everyday life on deployment in a war zone. I thought it might be a coincidence, but the date and the blood stains on the letters was too much to let go. The connection nagged me, so I read through the letters, noting down everything she wrote in case there was any other clues to her identity.

I felt incredible sympathy for the beautiful young woman I knew only as *love, me*. The letters might be all she had left of her new husband, judging by the blood on the thin airmail paper.

I knew what I had to do. I had to find her and return her letters. I'd do some sleuthing, find out who the young SOF was who lost his life, and FedEx the letters to his beautiful young widow.

It was the right thing to do.

The mysterious young woman, whose letters I was reading for clues to her identity, seemed ethereal to me. I imagined her with flowers woven into her long hair the way it was in her wedding portrait. For all I knew, she might be a tall Amazon of a woman, but she didn't come off that way in her letters to her new husband nor did her photos suggest height. She came off as someone who needed him, his strength, his fearlessness – as someone who fought her fears, wanted to confront them, and was glad to have a husband who was brave.

After reading her letters, I had an image of a stalwart young man named Dan, with a square jaw and whitewalls, who towered over her protectively in his military camo. From what I read, he took her places that she would never go on her own. Mountain climbing in the Rockies. Parasailing on the Gulf Coast of Texas. Flying in a small plane to a secluded mountainous area in Peru to explore ruins. Fly fishing in the Montana wilderness.

Without you, I'm a chicken. With you, I'm brave. Please be careful over there. Don't always do the bravest thing. Do the safest thing. Stay safe, please. Come back to me...

It's impossible to do the safest thing when you're in a war zone. You do what keeps you alive, if you can, or what saves your brothers-in-arms. You need quick wits and fast responses when you're in a firefight or on a dangerous mission. Sometimes, there's no time to think. You just respond, using muscle memory and routines drilled into you so that they become second nature. Sometimes, there's not even time to respond.

Like when an IED blows up your supposedly mine-resistant armor protected vehicle, or MRAP. I'd learned that all too well during my last trip to Afghanistan, when I got my scar and almost lost my life.

LATER THAT NIGHT, I sat in my office and tried to recover after the business meeting from hell when I had to tell half my team that the other half had just been fired, explaining the half-empty boardroom.

Graham McKenny, my business partner and best friend forever, had been killed in Malaysia on a job two weeks earlier and as a result, half the capital we relied on for collateral was gone to his estate and to his brother. Not to mention the lawsuit we faced by the widow of one of the customers who was killed along with Graham. Despite the waiver he signed, I might add.

We had business insurance on Graham because he worked in dangerous places as a war tourist guide, but it was his collateral that kept us afloat and helped fund our projects. Along with my other friend Brandon, Graham and I were in the same Marine Recon unit over in Iraq during the last year of the surge. Then, Graham and I had been in Special Operations Forces, deployed in Afghanistan.

Short and pugilistic with a shaved head and a southern twang that he cultivated despite living in Hell's Kitchen for most of his adult life, Graham was the best friend I had on earth. His death hit me hard.

Real hard.

Not only did I fire half my staff as a result of the sudden drop in our financial worth, I cleaned out their offices myself, and then sat alone in the darkened office space after everyone else left, wondering how I was going to hold it all together.

So, despite the fact it was the week from hell in which I tried to patch up the holes left in my business from Graham's death, I had to find out who wrote the letters.

About seven thirty, my cell rang. When I checked, it was Terry, a contact I had in the Marines Special Operations Command and the only person I could trust to tell more than the most basic of details of the incident. I was with MARSOC in Afghanistan, testing out our prototype comms system I'd developed for the CIA's Special Activities Division. I'd put in a call earlier to Terry to try to find out who sent me the package of letters.

"Hey," I said when I answered. "Thanks for returning my call."

We exchanged pleasantries, called each other old bastards and giant pricks as Marines are wont to do. Finally, we got down to business.

"Hey, Beckett," he said, his voice finally serious. "It's great to shoot the shit and all but why did you call me, anyway?"

"I need help tracking down who sent my stuff back from Afghanistan. I was embedded with a Special Operations Forces unit last year testing a prototype Brimstone developed under a DARPA contract." When he said nothing, I continued. "I was with that Marine Special Ops team that went down in a chopper crash last year."

I waited for his response. He must have heard about it through the grapevine even though the nature of our mission had been kept out of the headlines. It was in August. We were embedded with a Recon team that hit an IED while testing my prototype in enemy territory. A Special Ops team came to our rescue and then the chopper crashed in a sandstorm.

"Holy shit," he said finally. "You were part of *that*? Oh, *man*. I had no idea..." He paused for a moment. "I remember hearing some talk about it, but it was pretty hush-hush," he said, his voice hesitant as if he was trying to decide whether to admit he knew of the event.

"Yeah," I said. "I thought maybe someone from the team might

7

have sent my kit back. I found something that doesn't belong to me and I'm trying to return it, but I have no idea who it belongs to."

"I don't remember hearing your name mentioned."

"You wouldn't. Our mission was classified. I was with SAD at the time."

SAD – the Special Activities Division of the CIA. Black Ops, off the books, operating in enemy territory, doing things that would break international law. Our little 'incident' was recorded as an accident due to weather *inside* Afghanistan. Two Marines and a Navy hospital corpsman were killed when their chopper went down in a dust storm during a routine training mission. That was the official story, anyway. I was one of the five who got out with our lives.

I had an eight-inch scar on my neck to show for it and a month-long gap in my memory surrounding the whole event due to a brain injury.

He clicked his tongue. "Then I can't help you. SAD stuff's black. You'll have to go to your original contacts. How did you get with SAD anyway?"

I laughed. "I'd tell you, but then I'd have to shoot you. But like I said, we had a DARPA contract, so…"

"Yeah, yeah, yeah. I get it. Burn before reading." He paused for a moment, thinking. "Why don't you contact your SAD handler?"

"He's no longer with SAD. They're kind of sticky about forwarding addresses."

"Good luck finding out. If you were with SAD, they're pretty closed to your casual enquiry. I can ask around discretely but I doubt anyone will talk if you were with SAD and especially if you were part of *that*."

"Thanks anyway," I said. "Next time you're in Hell's Kitchen, look me up." We said our goodbyes and I hung up, turning the envelope containing the letters over in my hand.

My call with Terry got me thinking that perhaps, in the

mayhem that ensued when a Marine team came to recover us, my things and one of the team's personal effects were mixed up after the crash. Because I was with a SAD team, it would be next to impossible to get names. I only knew my primary contact and the first names of the rest of the team – all former spec ops from various services – SEALs, Rangers, MARSOC.

I needed to know who was involved in our rescue so I could track down the owner of the letters. I was beginning to realize that it would be very hard to find out through official channels. So I turned to the news, and read back issues of *Marine Corps Times*, the Corp's news source on any Marine deaths. I went back to the previous year's archives and checked each issue from August on.

Then I saw it.

Hospital Corpsman Daniel Lewis, Wilmington, N.C. Training accident.

Left behind was his new wife, Mira Lewis, (nee Parker) of Queens, NY and loving parents, Scott and Jeanne Lewis of Topsail Beach...

Mira... I picked up the photo of her in her wedding dress, her hair braided with wildflowers. She must have been named after Mira the star, also called Omicron Ceti, a red giant located in the constellation of Cetus. About two hundred light years from Earth, Mira was a binary star and one of the only non-supernova variable stars known.

How do I know all this about Mira?

I was that geeky kid with the backyard telescope who spent my nights trying to chart all the major stars in my science notebook instead of staying inside to play whatever video game was the latest amongst my peers. I often considered going into astronomy instead of computer science, but my love of building things – mostly computers – was stronger than my desire to sit in a lab in front of a computer screen and look at numbers. Which was what I ended up doing anyway, studying computer systems at Stanford.

Life is funny that way.

I read the obit and the family forum entries offering condolences. There was an article in the local paper about Hospital Corpsman Lewis, and how he was a medic with Force Recon...

I read the obituary and some of the forum posts about Lewis. Friends wrote that he was wild man, fearless and heroic. He'd become one of the most highly trained medics, deploying with Marine Special Operations Forces. They did other duties, including going deep behind enemy lines.

I looked at the photos of Lewis. Tall, strong, heroic. Going into the most dangerous places and saving lives.

Now, at least I had a name.

After reading her letters, I knew one thing for certain. No matter how busy I was trying to save my company from bankruptcy, no matter how long it took, I'd find her and return her letters.

It was the least I could do.

MIRANDA

I KNEW the first moment I laid eyes on him that he was trouble.

The door to the bar opened, emitting a bright swath of light into the otherwise dim interior. A man stood in the doorway, framed by the light. Tall and strong, his shoulders were wide, his hips narrow. He clutched a motorcycle helmet under his arm.

A biker.

When I caught a look at his face, I felt a stab of desire. Despite the rugged exterior, he was beautiful. Dirty blond hair below his collar, blue blue eyes, and a neatly trimmed beard on a jaw so square you could practically cut yourself on it.

He reminded me of a bad boy biker, or maybe a Viking warlord looking for his next conquest. Dressed in some faded well-worn jeans, a white turtleneck despite the warm weather, and a black leather jacket, he was something to look at.

I'd spent the previous year in Topsail Beach and with the exception of tourist season, there weren't many new faces – especially none as gorgeous as his. To keep myself amused, my best friend Leah and I spent a lot of time imagining who the strangers were, concocting fabulous identities for them to pass the time. For Mr. Viking God, I imagined that, instead of a biker, he was a secret agent, maybe an assassin, newly in town looking for his target. Or a Calvin Klein model on location, having spent the day doing an underwear shoot.

I knew one thing for certain: any woman who laid eyes on him would fantasize about him that night while her man pounded into her. Any man who saw him would imagine bashing in his handsome face, just to take out the unfair competition.

Now, as the daughter of a career FBI Special Agent, I knew that spies and assassins weren't the way they were portrayed in movies and novels, but it was fun to imagine. Spies looked like anyone else. That was their goal. Blend. Fade. Become invisible.

This stranger could never blend, no matter how scruffy his jaw or faded his jeans.

He was just too pretty.

When his eyes came to rest squarely on me where I stood behind the bar, a bottle of bar lime in one hand and tequila in the other, a shiver raced down my spine. I stood there, arms poised in mid pour, and gaped.

In that moment, he reminded me so much of Dan, I had to blink twice. It wasn't that he looked like Dan. Dan had slightly darker hair, had been clean shaven and was leaner. It was the way the man held himself so tightly in control. Despite the wild exterior, his eyes were assessing. He had that *'ready to wreak havoc'* look about him that Dan developed during several hellish tours of duty in Iraq and then time in Special Operations Forces in Afghanistan during the last year before his death.

This man had that same sense of stiff-backed power held in check that Dan had. There was also just a hint of sadness in him. I couldn't tell you where I saw it, but it was there. Maybe in the way he held his mouth, his full lips pressed a bit too firmly together. A bit too much pain in his gray-blue eyes, which were the color of stormy seas.

Gramps always said that if you turned a man into a killer, there would be consequences. If you gave him wide-open terms of engagement, his kills would haunt him the rest of his days no matter how justified they were. At least, that's what Gramps told me when Dan returned on leave once and I felt as if I didn't recognize him.

War changed men.

Gramps said it was the crucible that tested a man's character. Only the true psychopaths could get away with being a killer with no effects on their souls.

Dan had been a Navy Hospital Corpsman attached to a Marine Special Operations Forces team, losing his life somewhere in Afghanistan. All we were told was that he died when his team went in on a routine training mission. Dan's chopper went down in a dust storm. Because of the classified nature of the mission, there wasn't much publicity. Just a solemn service in Arlington attended by a few of his closest buddies and the families of the fallen.

Our family seemed destined to experience tragedy. My father died in the line of duty. Then Dan died just three months after we were married. Mom was a total mess, and spent her days medicated, lost in an OxyContin haze with her new husband up in New Hampshire.

It was just me and Gramps left who were somewhat functional. Gramps was retired from the NYPD and living in Queens, running *The Harp and Keg*, the bar I worked at during the school year. He complained ever so softly about my year-long absence while I spent time living with Dan's family in Topsail Beach, North Carolina, trying to start my life again as a young widow. Trying to find out what happened and why Dan died. It proved futile so Dan's father Scott and mother Jeanne gave up and accepted that it was the usual mayhem that was Afghanistan.

One day, I hoped to understand what made people into killers. If I couldn't save my father or my beloved Dan, then maybe someone else.

The man standing in the doorway with the biker helmet had

that same *ready for action* sense about him that Dan had, with that same assessing gaze, his eyes narrowed as if he was constantly looking for threats.

He walked straight to the bar with an expression that made me panic. Like the day the sedan drove up the driveway to the house, two uniformed military men walking to the front door to tell us the news, their hats in their hands.

"Holy crap," Leah said when she saw him. My best friend from college, Leah had been my support for the past year while I recovered and learned to live my life again after Dan's death. She'd come down from Manhattan to stay in Topsail Beach after Dan died, taking a job at the restaurant so we could support each other.

She gawked at the man, unabashed desire on her face.

"What?" I said, my throat dry, although I knew exactly what she meant. I glanced away, not wanting to appear like I was checking the man out.

"He's *gorgeous.*"

Steve, a friend of Dan's family who worked at the bar during the summer, turned to look at the man along with the rest of us.

"He looks like a hood," Steve said, making a face of disgust.

"Hey," Leah said, putting her empty tray down on the bar. "Don't judge a book by its cover. He might be a really nice guy."

"Huh," Steve said and raised his eyebrows at me. "Looks like scum to me."

I shrugged, and managed to finish pouring the drink order in front of me. Steve was the second bartender, and would be taking the last shift.

When the man approached the bar instead of taking a seat at one of the empty tables, I felt a sense of unease overtake me. For some reason I wanted to run, so I turned to Steve and wiped my hands on my apron.

"Take over for a minute, okay? I have to get something out back."

Steve raised his eyebrows but took my place and continued to pour the drinks on my current order.

I ducked under the bar hatch, and made a beeline for the kitchen and the walk-in refrigerator. I didn't know why I wanted to avoid the man, but I did, every ounce of my being screaming that no matter how gorgeous his face and how hot his body, he was dangerous. Once inside, I leaned against the door, my eyes closed. The cool air was a relief and soon, my heart rate decreased a few beats and my breathing returned to normal.

Wow. He really spooked me. I had this sense of impending doom when I saw him.

I went to one of the shelves and fished around in a box of lemons and limes, choosing a few and leaving the refrigerator for the prep area where I cut them up methodically, trying to calm down, slicing a few twists of lime, a few wedges and a few slices as garnish. I knew I'd have to go back to pouring drinks but at least I'd be prepared.

"What are you doing in here?" Leah said, having followed me inside the prep area.

"I needed some bar garnish," I said, my voice wavery.

"That's my job, and there's lots on the other side of the bar. Let me get that," she said and tried to push me out of the way. It was her job, and there was garnish at the other end of the bar, but I needed to get away from that man.

She peered at me. "What's wrong, Mira? Are you okay?"

I took in a deep breath. "Yeah, that customer who just came in spooked me."

Her eyes widened. "You mean Mr. Hunk with the fuck-me face and to-die-for body?"

I nodded. "The very one."

"He had that much of an effect on you?" A slow grin spread across her face. "Girl, I told you that you need to get some."

I laughed, and a bit of my anxiety faded. "He's a biker," I said and shook my head. "He's hot, but he's a bad boy. I don't need one of them on my books. The FBI checks all your associates when you apply, so not even going to think of it."

"He's no biker," she said with a snort. "He's wearing a huge Cartier on his wrist. Bikers don't wear Cartier."

"Now, how can you tell he's wearing a Cartier?"

She winked at me and took the tray of garnish from me. "I know quality."

I laughed, relaxing a bit. She dated day traders from Wall Street almost exclusively when we both lived in Manhattan so if anyone could identify a Cartier from a distance, it was Leah.

She took the tray and left, and I followed her slowly. Before I went back into the bar, I glanced through the tiny window in the swinging door and saw that the man had moved and was sitting at the bar directly beside my pour station.

Damn...

Steve was busy pouring a drink order when I returned. I tried to avoid the man's eyes, but I could feel his gaze fixed on me.

"I'll take over now," I said to Steve, who nodded and stepped aside with some reluctance. I glanced at the next drink order – a couple of pretty easy drinks – rum and coke and a screwdriver – and set to work filling it, hoping my hands didn't shake.

The man said nothing while I worked, but he watched my every move. When I went to the other end of the bar to get a new bottle of mixer, he watched me. When I came back to his end, he watched me. When I bent over to refill the ice hopper, he watched me.

He held a menu in his hands. Unable to avoid him any longer, I stopped directly in front of him, my arms spread, hands resting on the bar.

"See anything you like?" I said, finally meeting his eyes.

He inhaled audibly. "I think I do." Slowly, a grin that was far too sexy for my own good spread on his face.

"She's not on the menu," Steve said quietly, butting in. I turned to him, shocked at that he said that.

"How unfortunate," the man said. He had this low sexy voice, deep and melodious. The kind that made you melt into a helpless puddle of 'yes.'

I couldn't hold back my grin, so I quickly turned my back to him and busied myself by sorting through the bottles on the shelf, searching for the one needed for my order.

I gestured to Steve. "Why don't you help our guest with his order. I have things to do."

Steve frowned and stood in front of the stranger. "What can I get for you?"

"Bourbon. What do you have in stock?"

Steve ran down the list of bourbon brands we had on hand and the man pursed his lips.

"What would you suggest?" the man asked.

Steve shrugged. "It all tastes like kerosene to me."

"What?" the man said, his voice sounding seriously affronted in a joking kind of way. "You work at a bar and you don't like bourbon?"

I stepped beside Steve. "Woodford Reserve," I said, remembering a taste-test Gramps made me take when I started working at his bar.

"Ah, the lady is beautiful *and* knows her bourbon. Consider me smitten," the man said. "Woodford Reserve it is."

I smiled to myself while I attached a new canister of soda to the dispenser.

"What are you smiling about?" he said, his voice playful with just a touch of an accent – Cajun, from the sounds of it.

"You're not from around these parts," I said as I scooped ice into some glasses on the bar and then started pouring. "But you know your bourbon."

"I'm an aficionado. Come from a long line of bourbon drinkers. Actually, a long line of drunks, truth be told."

"Oh, yeah? Where are you from? You sound Cajun." I bent down to take a beer out of the fridge, liking him despite my initial impressions because of his playful sense of humor. Unfortunately, I knew that charm was one of the chief character traits of sociopaths, so that didn't win him any points with me.

"Cajun, born and raised," he said as I sorted through the beer. "I lived in Louisiana just outside New Orleans for part of my childhood, so you know your accents."

When I stood up, he stood as well and bowed, bending at the waist with a flourish of his arm.

"Beckett," he said, and then he laid the accent on thick. "At your service. "

I laughed and wiped the bar with a clean cloth. "Is that a first or last name?"

"Both. It's my grandfather's name and my mother didn't want our family to lose."

"No last name?"

"Call me Beckett. I have too many names so just Beckett will do."

"Okay, just Beckett," I said with a grin. "People usually introduce themselves using their full name where I come from."

He grinned back. "I find it creates an air of mystery."

"Or suspicion," Steve said, standing beside me, his brow furrowed.

"You have to forgive Steve," I said and poked Steve in the shoulder playfully. "He thinks he's my big brother." I frowned at Steve but he didn't budge. Finally, he sighed and went back to his side of the bar.

I turned to the man who called himself Beckett, barely able to suppress a smile. He glanced up at me.

"There's that smile again," he said, his eyes twinkling, his voice very sexy. "I'm glad I amuse you, because it's a very pretty smile. *Très belle.* Maybe when you get off work, you'll let me buy you a drink so I can see you smile some more."

I snorted at that. "Flattery will get you nowhere with me, Mr. Just Call Me Beckett mystery man…" I said. "Back home I work in a bar surrounded by cops. I've heard every pickup line you could imagine. I need something really innovative to pique my interest."

"I'll bet you do." He grinned and finished his drink. "Tell you what, *sha*," he said, the way they say the French word *cher* in the Bayou. "You pour me another one and I'll work on something really innovative."

"Don't bother." I grabbed the bottle of bourbon and poured another shot. Then, I put the bottle down on the bar. "I pulled a double shift today."

"You should relax after your double shift. Have a drink with me. "

"Sorry. When I get off, it's right straight home to sleep for me. I work all day again tomorrow."

"Shame," he said, his eyes roving over me. "I'm only in town for a night."

"Shame," I said and grinned back, deciding to play it a bit dangerously, seeing as nothing was going to happen between us.

I went to the other end of the bar where Leah stood.

"What did he say?" she said, practically drooling over him. I noticed Steve floated over to where we stood and bent down to fiddle with the ice bin.

"He asked me to have a drink with him after work," I said quietly, feeling a bit weird because Steve was listening in. "I told him no."

"You're crazy," Leah said, eyes wide. "He's a total babe."

"He's too rough for you," Steve said and stood up, nodding at me like he approved of my decision.

Leah made a face. "It's none of your business, Steve." She glanced over at Beckett and sighed. "He looks high end to me. I told you the watch he's wearing is a Cartier. Expensive. Like thousands of dollars. And those jeans? DKNY Men. He's no biker."

"He probably got the watch off the corpse of someone he murdered," Steve said with a snort.

"Oh, *you*," she said and made a face at Steve. "Not everyone's a criminal."

"Bikers are, mostly."

"You're crazy," she said again and took the drinks off the bar, putting them on her tray.

"Certifiably," I said with a laugh, giving Steve a grin. He seemed so serious all the time. I went back to the other end of the bar and wiped the top.

"So," I said, enjoying Beckett's attention in spite of my earlier hesitation. "A stranger comes into town and all the locals wonder why he's here in Topsail Beach, of all places." I hadn't planned on talking to him, but I'd been through a long dry spell since Dan died and Beckett was so pretty, I had a hard time not flirting with him. "You a biker?"

"I ride a Harley, yes," he said. "I love working on engines and have since I was a kid. Nothing makes me happier than when I'm up to my elbows in grease and listen to an engine I've just fixed purr. Other than riding, that is."

"You must have some business here."

"I'm staying at the Yacht Club, scouting out locations for a staff retreat I'm planning."

I frowned. "The Yacht Club?" I said in disbelief.

"Why do you find that hard to imagine?"

"Maybe because you're a biker?"

He laughed at that. "Nah, I just like to ride now and then. I'm planning a retreat for my staff and will be giving a talk on security to some Wall Street types at a convention in Wilmington in a few weeks."

Hmm. Leah was right. He was high end.

"How did you find your way to *Oceanside*? It's a bit out of the way."

"I'm here looking for someone," he said. "Doing a favor."

"Do they live on the island?"

He nodded. "Just tracking someone down."

"Do they have a name? I might know them."

"That's classified info." He smiled a wicked smile. "I could tell you, but then I'd have to kill you."

"Then don't tell me." I grinned back. "I don't really want to know anyway."

He said nothing for a moment while I poured drinks.

"What time are you off?" he said finally.

"Midnight, but the answer's still no."

"Can't blame a man for trying." He glanced at the thick watch on his wrist and when he pulled up the sleeve of his leather coat, I saw a tattoo on his arm just above his watch. I couldn't make out what it was, but it seemed to be a dark blue pattern.

A tattoo of some kind.

"Have one drink with me at least, *sha*," he said, his voice soft, with a bit more of a Cajun lilt than earlier. "It's such a shame when you meet someone special and then have to say goodbye far too soon."

"You just met me," I said and rolled my eyes. "How do you know I'm special? For all you know, I'm just another girl bartending at some out-of-the-way restaurant in Topsail Beach."

He narrowed his eyes. "I'm an excellent judge of character. It's one of my many superpowers."

"Oh yeah?" I said in amused disbelief. "What are your *other* superpowers? Although, let me stop you," I said and held out my palm. "I can already guess."

"You'll just have to have a drink with me and find out," he replied with a grin.

I sighed. He was so damn gorgeous, his voice so sexy, and I was really starting to regret that I was almost ready to pass out from exhaustion. Even if he was only in town for a night, I would still enjoy a little male attention.

"You never did tell me what you do for a living," I said, unwilling to stop the little game that was going on between us.

"Like I say, I could tell you, but then I'd have to kill you."

I laughed at that, but given my family and my current career hopes, alarm bells went off in my head.

"I can't just have a drink with a perfect stranger. Especially one who warns me about having to kill me."

"I was just joking," he said and took out a thin wallet, pulling out some ID. A driver's license and an ID tag. "If you insist."

I took them both and examined them. The driver's license was from the State of New York. Beckett Tate. The ID tag was for a tech firm in Manhattan – Brimstone Solutions, Inc. His name on that was Beckett Tate. CEO.

Just then, Steve took the ID out of my hands and examined it closely.

"CEO?" he said with a scoff as I took the ID back.

"Yes," Beckett said and took another sip of his drink. "My company develops technology for the military. We also provide security intelligence and technical support for high value assets who have investments or companies that will be operating in conflict zones."

"High value assets…" I said with a grin. "Like Wall Street bankers?"

"Exactly."

"Are you a vet?"

He nodded, but didn't elaborate.

"A lot of vets go into the private military after they return," I said, trying to encourage him to speak.

He nodded. "You have family in the military?"

"You come from a long line of drunks?" I said and smiled. "I come from a long line of soldiers and law enforcement types."

He nodded, his expression thoughtful. "I was glad to get back to the real world. My time in the service was short, intense and I'm glad it's over."

I wanted to know more, what branch of the military he had been in, but he seemed closed off once it was mentioned so I returned his IDs and went back to filling drinks.

Beckett was glad to be back to the real world? That wasn't what Dan said when he came back before being redeployed the last time. He couldn't adjust. Hated the quiet. Hated the calm. We argued about him going back to Afghanistan, given the increasing violence there and our wedding. A few days before his last mission started, he said that if he didn't have incoming screaming in over his head, he didn't feel alive. That was why he went back – he needed that adrenaline rush.

I never saw him again.

"So, what do you say about that drink?" Beckett said, his voice pulling me back to the present. "You should unwind a bit from your long day of work. A shot of bourbon would be good for what ails you."

I pulled up a fresh bottle of lime juice for the drink I was mixing. "A shower and then a bed would be best for what ails me."

He grinned mischievously. "I could arrange that."

I laughed out loud. He was persistent if nothing else. "You are so charmingly direct."

"I know what I want when I see it."

"Oh, yeah?" I said, trying but failing to keep the smile off my face as I worked. "And what exactly is it that you want, Monsieur Tate?"

"What I see."

"And why, may I ask? A girl is curious..." I said, making a Game of Thrones reference.

I stopped pouring and turned to him, facing him squarely. I was enjoying his attempt to pick me up. He wasn't trying to hide it. He was going for broke. I had to admire that.

"Because what a man sees is just about the most delicious thing he's seen for a long time."

"Only just about?"

"Let me rephrase that," he said and leaned forward, licking his bottom lip. "What a man sees is the most delicious thing he's seen for just about ever."

Our eyes burned into each other's and heat rose in my face. Damn. He was the hottest man I'd ever met – next to Dan. He totally knew my Game of Thrones reference. Sadly for me, and given my career aspirations, I wasn't into one-night stands with strangers even if they knew about faceless men. That would make me a security threat.

"It's that *just about* that keeps getting me, Beckett." I leaned forward, our faces just a few inches away from each other. "I really don't appreciate feeling like second best."

"You can't tell where something ranks until you try," he replied. "Besides, life is short. You should just live dangerously for once, *sha*. Come on. Have a drink with me ..."

I sighed, wishing I could. "You're very tempting, Monsieur Tate with the Cajun accent. I'm hoping to get into the FBI when I finish my degree. Living dangerously is not on the agenda until after that. I have to watch my associates if I hope to get in."

"Well, in that case, I'm one of the safest men you could talk to."

"So you say."

"I'm scouting out locations for a staff retreat I'm planning. I spent some time at Camp Lejeune when I was with Special Operations Forces and I like the area. Besides, there's a convention in Wilmington coming up and so I thought I'd find a nice place for my staff retreat. Kill two birds with one stone."

That sounded like a good story, but I was still hesitant.

"You can see I'm a nice guy," he said, his voice coaxing. "I'm a business man. I'm a veteran. Have a drink with me when you get off work. Live dangerously."

"I'm not that kind of girl," I said with a sigh.

He sighed in return. "My loss."

I turned back to the stack of drink orders in front of my station and continued pouring while he watched me. I had a feeling it would be both our loss, because he looked like a man who would be exceptionally intense in bed. Demanding, accomplished, skilled, unrelenting. Most of all, Alpha. Just the way I liked it. The way Dan had been. My body responded to the thought of living dangerously for once, my heart racing, butter-flies in my stomach.

Damn…

I couldn't do it. Not only because I wasn't quite a year out from Dan's death but his memorial was coming up and the whole family would be traveling to Arlington for the ceremony. Besides, I had this sense that Beckett was dangerous in a way I couldn't explain.

He said nothing more for a while, occupying himself with his bourbon and watching me pour drink order after drink order. He seemed determined to wait me out, probably hoping to hit on me once more after I got off shift.

On my part, I watched the clock. I appreciated persistence, but wouldn't cave, no matter how gorgeous he was.

In about fifteen minutes, I asked Steve to take over while I went outside for a break. Leah popped out with me and lit up a smoke. I never smoked, but I still liked to stand out back and listen to the surf crashing on the beach a few hundred yards away, breathing in the salt air.

"Mr. Hot Stuff seems to like you," she said as she puffed on her cigarette.

"He's not my type," I said, although I had to hold back a smile.

She laughed at that, knowing me well enough to see it for the lie it was.

"Bullcrap. If he was into me the way he seems into you, I'd go for it. It's been almost a year, Mira. You've done your mourning."

"Steve doesn't like him."

"Steve doesn't like any man you might look at twice. He's jeal-ous, Mira."

"He's not jealous," I said. "He's like a brother to me."

"Not in his mind," she said and raised her eyebrows. "Maybe a stepbrother."

I laughed at that, thinking of a book we both read.

"Whatever," I said with a shrug. "Dan deserves a year."

"You should just take a chance and live dangerously for once."

"That's what *he* said."

She smiled. "You see? We're both right. You deserve it, sweetie."

"Like I told him, living dangerously is not going to get me into the FBI."

She shrugged and took a drag on her cigarette, leaning against the wall. "Then you won't mind if I do? He's too hot to pass up."

"Go for it," I said, regretting that I wasn't more like her, unable to keep a frown off my face. Leah saw it and laughed.

"See? You care. I was just kidding. Besides, Mr. Hot Stuff hasn't taken his eyes off you all night."

I smiled in spite of myself. My body warmed at the thought of taking Mr. Beckett Tate home with me, except of course, I lived with Dan's parents. Instead, I imagined going to his hotel room and seeing what was hidden beneath that white turtleneck and low-slung jeans. From the glances I snuck between pouring drinks, I imagined he'd be sporting a hard body with a nice six-pack. My body ached for a man's touch…

"Well, that's it for me," I said and opened the back door. "Gotta get back."

"I'll be right behind you," she said and held up her cigarette. "As soon as I'm finished."

"You know you have to quit that if we're going to start the fitness and rock climbing routine you have planned."

"One of these days," she said and smiled guiltily.

BECKETT

WHILE MIRA DUCKED out the back, I faced the male bartender, Steve, who I could tell didn't like the moves I was making on Mira.

"You should move on," he said to me, frowning. "She's not for you."

"I think that's up to her to decide," I said softly, trying hard not to take too much offense.

He stood eyeing me, polishing a glass with a towel. I sighed and turned away, then I decided to go to the back and see if the manager was in so I could ask about Dan's parents. They might have a local phone directory if he wouldn't give me the parent's address.

I went to the back of the restaurant, through a door that led to the kitchen on one side and the offices on the other. Down a long hallway was what looked like the main office, so I cracked the door open and checked inside. A light was on, but the room appeared empty. I looked on the desk for a phone directory, but saw nothing immediately resembling a phone book and I didn't want to go inside and check around. That would be going a step too far, even for me, a DEA rat.

I went down the hallway to the door leading back into the restaurant. Before I reached the door, Mira emerged from the other end of the hallway, adjusting her apron. She must have been in the staff washroom.

"What are you doing here?" she said in a disapproving tone.

"Looking for the manager." I needed to placate her, so I went up close to her and stared down into her pretty hazel-green eyes, which were very untrusting at the moment. "I need to speak to him."

"You better leave," she said, her voice wavering a bit with emotion. "Didn't you see the sign on the door? Staff only."

"I really need to see the manager."

I hoped she didn't press me. I didn't have the wherewithal to think up a story to cover for my being in the back. It wasn't as if I could just say to her *Hey, sweetheart, can you tell me where your ex-parents-in-law live so I can return the letters you wrote to your fallen-hero husband who died because of me? Thanks!'*

"He's not working tonight," she said pointed to the exit.

I wanted to dispel the bad feeling between us, so I laid on some charm. "Ladies first."

She turned to go back but I could tell she was still angry with me, and as a result, any chance I had of convincing her to have a drink with me after work would be dead.

"Look, I'm sorry if I insulted you," I said, keeping my voice soft. "It's just that you're very pretty and seem really smart and funny. I'd really like if we could just have one drink, talk a bit."

"I don't think so."

When she tried to leave once more, I put my arm on the wall, stopping her from leaving. It was done playfully. Of course, I would never force a woman. I didn't have to force them.

To my surprise, she leaned against the wall beside me and looked up in my eyes, the quirk of a smile on her lips. Pretty soft-pink lips, nice and full and which I knew would feel very nice on my lips – or elsewhere for that matter.

"All right, cowboy," she said, her arms crossed, smiling more widely now. "I'll have a drink with you when I'm off shift. You're just about the best thing a girl has seen in a long while, too."

I smiled, trying to hide my surprise. I really didn't think she'd agree to it after finding me in the back checking out the joint.

"Thank you, *sha*," I said and leaned down a bit closer. "I'll try to make it worth your while."

"Just try?" She had this playful expression in her eyes that sent a jolt of desire right to my dick, which was starting to perk up.

I laughed. "You give me a chance and I promise to make it worth your while."

She looked me over, like she was assessing whether I could deliver. "You talk big. I hope you live up to it."

Then, to my even bigger surprise, she leaned forward on her toes and... *kissed* me.

I was too shocked to even appreciate the feel of her lips on mine for the first time. My mind was too busy trying to figure out what her game was. She went from cold to hot in sixty seconds...

Soon, though, my mind forgot all about her game, and instead, focused on her soft mouth on mine. Real soon. Like, in three seconds.

I cupped her cheek and kissed her more passionately, wanting to see how deep she would let me go. Then, she slipped her arm around my waist and I tensed, even though I appreciated any sign of her interest, for her hand was close to my sidearm.

I pulled back a bit and our kiss broke.

"Oh, *sha*, you are delicious, but hold that thought until later," I said, wishing we could continue. Hell, wishing I could push her up against the wall and take her then and there. I was definitely ready, my cock already semi-hard. "I won't be able to walk back to the bar without a big limp if you keep that up."

"Shut up and kiss me," she said, and pulled me back down to her mouth. I was glad to oblige and kissed her now more passionately, putting my entire mind to it.

Then I felt her grab my gun.

At that point, instinct took over. I turned her around so that her back was facing me and I had her hands confined in one of mine. My other arm was around her waist, pulling her against my body.

Damn, woman...

"Sweetheart," I said, my lips beside her face. "Did you really think you were going to disarm me? I'm a foot taller and at least seventy-five pounds heavier."

She tried to wrestle loose, but she was far smaller and I was able to restrain her easily, enjoying the feel of her soft curves against me.

"I saw your weapon under your jacket," she said, her voice breathy. "You're armed."

"Yes, I'm armed. Licensed to carry a concealed weapon. I can show you if you want."

She wasn't placated. "Even if you have a permit, you're not legally able to carry a concealed weapon into this bar," she said matter of fact. "You saw the permit on the door. You are not legally permitted to drink alcohol while carrying a concealed weapon in this establishment so you're breaking the law."

"I'm DEA," I said, my face in her hair, smelling it – a mixture of some kind of fruity shampoo and clean sweat. Frankly, I could have stayed in that position all night, her butt pressed against my groin, my arm around her waist, my face variously in her neck or beside her cheek. "We can carry a concealed weapon in a bar and drink if need be."

It was the truth.

Finally, I released her when I felt her relax just a bit. I adjusted myself, straightening my jacket. I hoped she didn't notice my semi, currently straining against my jeans. Not that I was embarrassed about it. It was a fine specimen. No, I didn't want to make her embarrassed.

"I thought you're the CEO of a security firm," she said, standing in front of me, her arms crossed.

"Can't I be both?" I asked lightly.

She was quiet for a moment while I ran a hand through my hair.

"You understand that when I'm head bartender, I'm also acting manager. Let me see your badge," she said, holding out her hand.

I complied, reaching into my pocket for my other ID, which I held out for her to see.

"OK," she said and took my ID, looking it over. "That's the only exemption." She frowned at me. "Why didn't you tell me you were DEA? Are you really CEO of a security firm or is that cover?"

"Like I said, why can't I be both?" I took back my ID. "I'm impressed that you know your gun laws."

"I work at a bar," she said, sounding irritated. "As much as I'd love to carry on where we left off, I have to get back to work."

She turned and went to the door back into the restaurant. I caught up with her and stood beside the door before she could leave. "I hope this hasn't put a damper on our drink after your shift is finished."

She stopped and narrowed her eyes. "I like a man with a big… gun," she said and smiled.

"Oh, sweetheart," I said, a surge of adrenaline going through me that I hadn't blown it completely. "Then I'm just your type. Beretta M9A1, 8.5 inches from tip to base."

She laughed out loud at that, then pushed through the door.

Man, did I like this woman… She could keep up. She could dish it out and take it.

I wanted her to take it. Every inch.

"Look," she said and stopped me, her hand on my chest. "You're really funny and all, but I really can't have a drink with you."

I sighed, disappointed at her abrupt change of mind. "You

know, you kissed me. A man might take that as a woman expressing a certain interest in him."

"That was just to see if I could touch your weapon."

"You can touch my weapon any time," I said, grinning, trying to hide my disappointment behind a façade of good humor. "I'll be really sad if you don't give me a chance."

"I can't," she said and shook her head. "Sorry. And I mean that."

"Is that Steve guy your boyfriend?"

"What?" She frowned and shook her head. "No. What gave you that idea? He's a family friend who works at the bar in the summer."

"What gave me that idea is that he definitely sees you as his property and did not like me flirting with you."

She shrugged. "He's just being protective. We're not dating."

"Well," I said and followed her back to the bar. "He wants to."

She harrumphed at that but said nothing more. On my part, I knew the Steve guy wanted her. That much was clear.

I sat at the bar and sighed, sad that she had agreed to have a drink with me just to check my weapon. I knew she'd be cautious about me now that she knew I was DEA, probably trying to figure out why I had two jobs. I didn't want to explain my job with the DEA. I wasn't just an informer who met with a contact now and then to provide any intel. I was an undercover DEA agent. I took the training. I went for periodic exercises on how to do a recovery or takeout of a suspect. I kept my credentials up to date, with weapons training on the range and in the field.

But my main job was to provide intel on my family's contacts with the Irish-American mafia.

I could tell her none of that. Hell, I barely told Graham, except I had to come up with some excuse for the weeks I was away in field training. All I told him was that I was undercover DEA and that now and then, I'd have to take a week off for exercises.

So while she worked pouring drinks and restocking the bar, I put my earphones on and tried to work out what I'd tell her. I decided that it was best to tell her, well, whatever minimum I had to in order to appease her.

I listened to some music, watching her while she worked. When she saw that I had my earphones in, she came over.

"Our music not good enough for you?" she asked.

"I'm not much into Billboard." I shrugged, not wanting to insult the music, but it wasn't my favorite.

"Let me listen," she said, and reached for one of my earphones.

I was currently playing some Dylan and was curious how she'd respond.

"Who is it?" she asked, frowning. Then her eyes brightened. "It's Dylan. 'Knockin' on Heaven's Door.'"

That surprised me. Genuinely surprised me. Dylan was retro stuff. "The lady has knowledge about bourbon *and* music," I said and held a hand over my heart. "Goner."

She smiled but avoided meeting my eyes. "My father used to play it." She listened for a time and then nodded. "It's good."

Finally, I decided to ask her for the phonebook, since I hadn't been lucky enough to meet the manager or find one in the office.

"Do you have a phonebook?"

She nodded and bent down to sort through some things on the shelf under the bar. Then she placed the thin volume on the bar top in front of me.

"Thank you. I'm looking up someone." I paged through the directory, looking for the section with Scott Lewis's phone number and address. "Their address wasn't in the white pages on the internet. I hoped it would be in the local phone book."

While she continued to pour drinks, I flipped through the pages of the directory and found what I was looking for. Sure enough, there was an entry for a Scott Lewis, giving an address on Ocean Drive. I entered the address on my phone and then closed up the directory.

Then I drank down my bourbon.

"So you're really not going to have a drink with me?" I asked, making a pouty expression.

She shook her head softly. "I was just playing you, Mr. Tate. I wanted to check to see if you were really carrying."

"That's too bad," I said, a well of regret opening up inside me. *Damn...*

"I practically need toothpicks to keep my eyes open as it is," she said and held a hand up in front of a yawn. "I'm going straight home to bed and to sleep. I have a morning shift and will be bartending all day tomorrow."

"My loss," I said, wracking my brain to think of some way to convince her. "What about tomorrow night?" I asked, since I could always stay an extra day.

She shook her head again, smiling. "Already have plans."

I finished my drink and stood up, leaning on the bar so that my face was a few inches from hers.

"Last chance to reconsider," I said. "You seemed to really enjoy that kiss."

"Like I said, I wanted to see if that was really a gun," she said with a guilty grin.

I sighed and gave in, smiling back at her. "Damn, woman. I had my hopes up so high..."

"Sorry," she said. "I do appreciate the attention."

"That's something," I said with a grin. "Well, I'm off, back to my very luxurious and very lonely hotel room. Alone..."

"Wish I could help you with that, but as I said, I'm not that girl."

"My loss."

I smiled one last time at her, wishing I could find some way of convincing her that I was not a threat. I was not dangerous. She was so pretty, so smart and funny...

I left *Oceanside*, but I decided that I'd go back when I held my staff retreat and I'd make sure I convinced her to have at least one drink with me. I was a tenacious bastard when I had a mind to be and I had a mind to get to know the lovely Mira Parker a bit more.

A lot more, if she were interested and I had a suspicion she was.

I went back to my bike and rode off into the dark night, feeling that although I hadn't succeeded in getting Mira to have a drink with me, we had a nice back and forth between us. A nice vibe. I knew that if I could get her to relax a bit, she and I would have fun together. We both liked to laugh and could take and give it.

Someone like her was exactly what I needed.

I went back to my hotel room dejected but not defeated. I took off my clothes and watched the late news. When it was over, I turned off the lights and thought about Miranda Parker. She was beautiful, with her long auburn hair, doe eyes, and those freckles... They gave her this slightly impish look that contrasted with her beauty in a very nice way.

She was smart. You didn't do a Master's degree in forensic science without having a lot of brains. She was funny and spunky. There was a quiet strength to her that suggested she was self-reliant and independent.

I really liked that in a woman.

I wanted her.

God, I wanted her. I hadn't wanted a woman like that since... since Sue.

I thought back to our kiss, which was exactly the wrong thing to do if I wanted to get up early in the morning, go for a run, and then head back home. I needed to get at least seven hours of solid rack time.

So instead of thinking of the beautiful and curvaceous Mira Parker, how good her lips felt on mine, her tongue touching mine during our very deep kiss earlier in the back hallway of *Oceanside*, I should have been blanking my mind.

I should have, but memories of her delicious body and mouth

would not be chased away by sheer willpower alone. My dick ached from the memory of her body pressed against mine.

At that moment, I wished that instead of being alone in the dark hotel room with my cock in my own hand, I was with Mira, the lights on so I could watch her.

Despite knowing down deep that I was making a huge mistake, I wouldn't give up on Mira Parker.

MIRANDA

OF COURSE, I didn't hear the end of it the next day when I met Leah for lunch after I finished daily cash. I dropped the bank deposit off and walked down the road to the small beach hut we both liked. They served great seafood so I ordered a crab cake and slaw, having not eaten anything since the previous night.

"You should have at least had a drink with him, Mira," she said, shaking her head as we took our drinks and meals and sat at a picnic table under an umbrella. The sun was hot and I couldn't wait to change into my bathing suit and go for a swim in the surf. "From what I could see, he really had the hots for you and was very chivalrous. Steve was so jealous I thought his head would explode."

I laughed and waved her off. "Steve isn't jealous. He's just being protective. He's never said or done anything that would give me any other idea. And Beckett *was* trying to seduce me. Men who want something from you are always very chivalrous."

"Don't try to tell me you didn't have the hots for him, too. I saw you smiling at him like a girl on her first date."

"He was very persistent."

She slurped her drink and forked a piece of crab cake. "What did you two talk about? You talked a lot."

I shrugged, remembering back to our conversation, trying not to sound too interested. "He's a veteran. He was in both Afghanistan *and* Iraq. He's now in technology. Has a business that develops high tech for the military. That kind of thing…"

She punched me on the shoulder playfully. "He's perfect for you! Why on Earth didn't you at least have a drink with him? God, girl… You're *nuts*." She took a huge bite of her bun and chewed thoughtfully. "I'd have been all over him like white on rice." She swallowed and slurped down more of her drink. "Why didn't you bite? Still feel guilty?"

I raised my shoulder, not wanting to get into it. "I live with Jeanne and Scott. What would they think if I came home with some man I met at the bar? They'd think I was a floozy."

"Floozy?" she said in mock-horror. "I'll have you know I met all my past boyfriends at bars. Am I a floozy? No, don't answer that," she said with a huge laugh.

I grinned but said nothing.

"Compared to you, we're all floozies. Two men, Mira? You've only been with two men in your life. You need to get out there and sample a few so you know what you like."

"I liked *Dan*," I said, defensively. "I loved Dan. Dan was amazing."

"Of course you did, and he was a beast-God of a man fit to be worshipped and all that," she replied, her eyes wide. "But now, you gotta move on. You have to start your life again."

"I am," I protested. "I'm moving back to Manhattan. I'm finishing my degree. I'm moving on."

"Life means love," she said. "My nana always said that life is nothing without love. You need to find someone else. Get married. Have a family. The only way you're going to do that is by taking a chance on someone you don't know." She raised her eyebrows. "Am I right?"

I sighed. "Of course you're right."

"I know," she said and eyed her crab cake, poking it with her fork. "I'm always right."

"Annoyingly right," I said with a face of pretend-anger.

"You love me anyway," she said and chewed, her smile huge.

"I do," I said and nodded. I did love Leah.

She'd kept me from utter despair after Dan was killed. She spent so many nights with me sitting in front of the television watching sad movies, letting me cry and talk about Dan without complaint. She kept me sane at work, talking to me about all the characters who came to the bar. It became a game for us, concocting fabulous tales about the regulars.

It kept me from losing myself in depression. I was so glad she was returning to Manhattan with me, to finish her degree. She'd been there for the months before I married Dan. She'd been my maid of honor. She was there for me when Dan died.

She'd be there rooting for me when I returned to Manhattan to John Jay.

THAT EVENING, after a day spent on the beach, Leah and I worked at the bar once more. I was pretty exhausted after pulling a couple of double-shifts that week. Pete, the head bartender, was on vacation before the summer season ended and I left for Manhattan.

Steve was my assistant for the night and as I fully expected, he started to rib me about Beckett.

"I hope you went right home last night and didn't hook up with that hood you were talking to."

I frowned and pushed him playfully. "What the heck are you talking about? I went right home. Besides," I said and knocked the bottle of tequila I was holding down on the top of the bar, "he's not a hood. He's the CEO of a company. And it's none of your business. You're not my big brother."

"You need one," he said. "You don't know what men are like, Mira. They're dogs looking for a bone."

I grinned to myself, thinking of a snappy retort like "Maybe I *want* a bone…" but I held back. Steve seemed so serious and protective. As one of Dan's old family friends, I knew he was just trying to protect me.

"Just sayin'," he said and shook his head, polishing a glass with a fresh cloth. "That guy was trying to hook up with you. I could see it as plain as day."

I shrugged and went back to my drink order.

"Of course he was trying to hook up with me. It happens sometimes," I said. "I happened to say no, so don't worry about me."

Just then, Jeanne and Scott came in for dinner, which they did occasionally, to check out the service and make sure the food was up to snuff. I joined them during my break and sat across from them in their booth. They were two lovebirds who always sat side by side, holding hands despite the fact they'd been together for over thirty-five years.

I sighed to myself as I sipped an ice tea, watching them gaze lovingly into each other's eyes. I always thought Dan and I would be together for thirty-five years. Instead, I had a couple of years when we dated and then three brief months of married life – such as they were with him deployed to Afghanistan.

"So, are you excited about going back to school?" Jeanne asked, her eyes bright. "We'll miss you but you have to start your life again. You and Steve both leaving us. What will we do?"

"I'll miss you both," I said and smiled. "It'll be hard to leave Topsail Beach. I've had some of my happiest days here." Then I frowned. "I didn't know Steve was leaving too. Where's he going? I thought he was still going to bartend on weekends during the school year."

"He's transferring to Columbia. Didn't he tell you? We thought the two of you were…" She raised her eyebrows.

"Steve? No!" I said a bit too forcefully, embarrassed that they thought Steve and I were a thing. "We're just friends. Co-workers. He's like my big brother."

"I know," Jeanne said and reached out to squeeze my hand with affection. "It's okay if you find someone new. Dan would want you to finish your degree and get a job. He'd want you to live your life, sweetie. Find someone new."

"I will," I said, almost cringing because of the awkwardness of the conversation.

Then, they talked about Dan's memorial coming up in a month. We'd all drive to Arlington and visit Dan's marker in the memorial, then they'd take me north to Manhattan. Leah and I would get settled into our respective dorms for the year.

My stomach was filled with butterflies thinking about it but there was a small part of me that felt reluctant to leave Topsail Beach behind, as if doing so meant Dan would be lost to me forever.

I had to stop thinking like that. I would always have Dan in my memories and in my heart, no matter what.

Maybe I'd meet someone who could be a substitute. No one could ever replace Dan, but someone might be good enough to stand in for him in my life. Steve was a friend, but I never thought of him like that. He was uptight and always seemed so in need of being right about everything. I was used to Dan's freewheeling ways.

Steve was moving to Manhattan and transferring to Columbia? Well, that was sure news to me. He was studying business at UNCW. Sure, he'd said he'd miss me when I went back to Manhattan to finish my degree, but I never thought...

"A few of the other families will be meeting at Arlington on the 19th, so we can visit," Scott said.

I nodded, drawn back into the conversation from my thoughts of Steve. I really didn't feel like socializing with the other families. It was such an emotional time when Dan died. All the other families were at the joint memorial and I felt as if I couldn't get a hold of my emotions. Maybe with a year having passed, I might be better able to handle meeting the other families who lost their loved ones that day in the accident.

A year is a lot of time.

I smiled at the two of them and drank my ice tea.

LATER, after my shift was finished, I sighed and glanced around the bar, wishing that Beckett had returned and was there to make me smile and engage in some friendly banter. I had fun with him, despite how obvious he was being about trying to pick me up. He was a good sport about it, and didn't get obnoxious even when I turned him down. He was more resigned and amused. I could tell he enjoyed just talking to me. I had the feeling I would enjoy doing much, much more with him if I'd had the chance.

It was too soon. Or rather, Dan's memorial was too soon and my mind was trying to get around my whole move back to Manhattan and my return to school. A hookup with a new man was the last thing on my mind, despite how long it had been since I'd been with Dan. I felt guilty even going there, although my body did of its own accord in sexy dreams with faceless men. I'd even let myself imagine what Beckett would be like as a lover. I had a feeling he'd be intense and alpha. I had a feeling he'd know what to do to make a woman thank her lucky stars.

"Wanna go out for a drink, maybe a slice of pizza?" Steve asked as I removed my bar apron. "I don't feel like going home right away. I'll only be fifteen minutes."

I shook my head and tucked my apron into a nook behind the bar. "No, I'm beat," I said and covered my mouth while I yawned. "Plus I have to do daily cash in the morning…"

"Maybe another night," Steve said with a smile.

"Sure," I said and shrugged, leaving the bar. He was closing so he had to do the re-stock and cleanup. It was one of the perks of being head bartender. It felt a bit strange since Steve was older than me, but he was newer at bartending so Scott and Jeanne put me in charge. Steve got the grunt jobs.

I had the sneaking suspicion that maybe Leah was right... Steve *might* be interested in more than just a drink and slice. I hadn't thought of him like that before. It wasn't that he was unattractive. He was nice enough looking. It was that he was one of the family's oldest friends and I always felt more like a kid sister to him than a potential girlfriend.

The fact he was transferring to Columbia was a shock. I almost asked him about it during shift, but I didn't want to get into a long discussion at that moment. I was exhausted and so I waved at him and left the bar.

I walked the mile or so to the house and let myself in. The house was quiet, the lights low in the entry. I checked my watch – just after midnight. Scott and Jeanne would be in bed and so I tiptoed around, not wanting to wake them up.

"You back home, Mira?" came Jeanne's sleepy voice when I went down the hallway to the bedrooms.

"Sorry if I woke you," I said and made a face, standing in the hallway outside their room, which was just down the hall from mine.

"No, that's all right," she said and I could hear her yawn. "We just went to bed. Goodnight."

"Goodnight," I said and went into my room, closing the door softly behind me.

Jeanne was a light sleeper and always seemed to wake up when I got home, like she was waiting for me before she could go to sleep. Even if I wanted to, how could I possibly ever stay out really late with some new man for a hookup?

I MET Leah the next morning for a workout at the gym, and then went back home to have a shower before my afternoon shift.

When I arrived at the house, Scott was waiting for me, a package in his hand.

"What's that?" I asked, putting down my gym bag.

"It's addressed to you. I found it in our mailbox this morning."

I took the package and went to the island in the kitchen. It was a FedEx package that was addressed to me, but it hadn't been actually sent. There was no return address. I opened it up and inside was a manila envelope with Dan's name written on the outside.

"It's addressed to Dan." I frowned and opened the flap. Inside were two dozen letters wrapped in a blue foil ribbon. I recognized them at once as the letters I'd sent to Dan while he was on deployment. I read the first few sentences of one letter, and then sorted through them – thirty letters, written on airmail paper, in my tiny scrawl. Love letters I wrote to him when he was over in Afghanistan after our wedding. Dated from a week after we were married, they detailed my life while he was away, my plans for returning to class at John Jay in Manhattan, my hopes and dreams for our marriage and new lives together now that we had tied the knot.

There was a smear of blood on the ribbon and on several letters.

I held the letters away from me, for it had to be Dan's blood.

"What is it, dear?" Scott said, frowning when he saw me with the blood-tinged letters.

"They're letters I wrote to Dan…"

He took them and saw the blood. His eyes met mine. "Where did these come from? Why is there blood on them?"

I sat on the stool and took the letters back, reading them over, trying to figure out why these weren't sent back with Dan's personal effects.

"They must have been lost when they sent his kit back. Someone must have found them."

"But why the blood?"

I looked at him, my vision blurring. "He said he always carried them inside his uniform when he went on a mission."

Scott nodded and when tears filled my eyes, he came over and put his arms around me, held me to his chest.

"They must have been misplaced," I managed to say despite the choke in my throat. "Maybe someone found them and sent them back."

"I have no idea, sweetheart," he replied. "I would have thought someone would tell us if they did."

Jeanne joined us from outside, where she had been gardening, her straw hat still on, her cheeks rosy from the noon-day heat.

"What's the matter?" She put down her gardening gloves and a bouquet of wild flowers.

Scott spoke, his voice emotional. "Some letters that Miranda wrote to Dan were returned this morning. Someone dropped them off in the mail."

Jeanne took the letters and the FedEx envelope. "There's no return address. This wasn't mailed."

I nodded.

Then she saw the blood on the letters. "Oh, God…"

She put them down on the island and stepped back, her eyes widening when she realized what they were

"I'll call his CO and see what he knows," Scott said. "This is strange…"

I took the package and letters and went to my room, closing the door behind me.

"Are you all right, sweetheart?" Jeanne asked from the other side of the door.

"Yes," I said, my voice breaking. I wasn't all right. I felt numb. I felt on the verge of crying my eyes out.

I looked inside the FedEx envelope and found a thin slip of paper adhering to the inside wall. I removed it and saw that it had an image of an old schooner on it. It was from The Yacht Club, the hotel where Beckett was staying.

Beneath the logo was a handwritten message.

I'm so sorry I had to be the one to bring this to you. I know you'll have questions about how these came to be in my possession. Just know that your husband saved my life and that's why he died. I wanted to give these to you in person, but perhaps it's better to just leave them with you. Your husband was a true American hero. I can't really tell you any other details because it's classified, but I wanted you to have them. I wish you a truly happy and fulfilling life. You deserve it.

That was it.

Beckett brought these. He must have dropped them off at the house in the morning while I was at the gym. It looked like he was going to send them to me via FedEx, but changed his mind. Maybe he decided to give them to me in person but he didn't do that either.

I sat at the kitchen island and held the letters in my hand, sorting through them, tears springing to my eyes as I read my own words.

It all came back at that moment – the love we felt for each other, the hope we had for our lives together.

I took the letters and went to my bedroom – to Dan's bedroom with his trophies, with his ribbons, with all the tokens of his life that his mother had saved, and cried my eyes out.

THE FIRST FEW days after Beckett left were hell.

I managed to make it through the day after Scott gave me the package of letters and I realized who left them.

Beckett…

He had the letters all along. He knew who I was from the first moment he walked into the bar.

Why did he pretend to not know?

He said Dan saved his life and that's why Dan died…

Was it Beckett Dan's unit went to save the day his chopper crashed?

After Dan's death, I felt like a big hole opened up in my chest and nothing could fill it. I thought I was starting to get over him. Re-reading the letters I wrote seemed to break my heart all over again.

I worked the next evening, glad that it was a pretty slow night, but Steve wasn't helping things, and kept asking about my 'new boyfriend' and where he was.

"Stop," I finally said, holding my hand up to him, palm out. "He's gone back to Manhattan. He's not my boyfriend, okay?"

Even saying it made me tear up. Steve held his hands up and backed away, shaking his head.

"Sorry. My bad. I was just teasing."

I closed my eyes and exhaled, trying to get control over my emotions.

"I'm sorry," I said and wiped my hands on my apron. "It's just that Dan's memorial is coming up and I'm a bit down, I guess."

"Of course you are," Steve said and moved closer, his hands on my shoulders. He bent down and looked in my eyes. "If you need a shoulder to cry on, feel free. I'm here for you, Mira. Anytime."

I forced a smile I didn't feel and nodded. "Thanks." Then I pulled away, not wanting to feel his touch at that moment. I didn't know what I wanted – hell, that was a lie. I wanted *Beckett*. He was a good man. He was honorable. He'd risked his life in Iraq and Afghanistan. He was funny and sexy and so easy to be with. He seemed attracted to me.

But he was the reason Dan died?

What did that even mean?

I sat in my bedroom after my shift, and sorted through my letters, reading each one over, touching the blood stains on the paper. These were the letters I wrote to Dan after we were married and he was deployed with his Special Operations Forces team in Afghanistan. I had poured out my heart in these, wanting to keep our connection alive, even if he couldn't always write back. He never knew where he'd be sent or what temporary base he'd be billeted in. It depended on what mission his team was working on.

My Dearest Dan,

It's been two months since you left and my arms ache to hold you. I can't imagine going another month before I see you again. I can't imagine another three years of this separation. I know this is what I signed up for, but it's so hard! My only consolation is that you're doing important work over there. We all have to make sacrifices. I guess missing you is mine.

I'm really enjoying the house in Topsail Beach and staying with your parents. Bartending at a beach joint, as your dad calls it, is much, much different from the bar gramps runs in Queens. Tourists are a different crowd than cops and firefighters. I miss my gramps, but he understands that your dad needed a bartender and I was there so... I've become fast friends with Leah, so that's nice. She keeps me busy and laughing and we spend our off time cooking at her apartment and gossiping.

Enough small talk. Our three weeks together, before the wedding and on our honeymoon was so good. My brain was on pleasure overload after being separated from you for six months. Now I'm going cold turkey! No Dan inside me every day twice a day is not a good feeling. I feel empty without you in me and in my bed and in my house. Staying with your parents makes it somewhat more tolerable, because I get to sleep in your old bedroom (love the Star Wars sheets, BTW...I made your mom keep them on your bed LOL She wanted to put something frilly she bought, but I said, no. I was as big a SW freak as you! My only complaint is that I prefer Chewy over 3PO) but when I go back to Manhattan for classes in September, I don't know how I'll cope. Maybe I'll have to steal your old Star Wars sheets. Seeing you in August will be some consolation.

Stay safe. I love you more than anything.

Love, me.

I SORTED through the rest but they were all the same. Beckett read all these letters. He read the intimate details of my mind. He knew my husband had died in Afghanistan when he walked into the bar.

Beckett Tate.

I wanted him to tell me why he left without a word.

I googled his name, and came up with a Beckett Tate, CEO of Brimstone Solutions, Inc. There was a website, a pretty fancy one, for Brimstone Solutions, Inc. It was very military-themed, with images of soldiers on a battlefield, with planes in the sky, drones, and heavy artillery. They provided security and threat assessment services, security training, and of all things, guided tours of 'conflict zones' for the more adventurous traveler.

At least I knew that his story about Brimstone was the truth, for there were testimonials on one of the pages promoting the security training. There was also a monthly newsletter about the security situation around the world, of interest to investors. On the *About Us* page were images of Beckett and two other men – one was a Graham McKenny, Operations. There was an obituary for McKenny, who had been killed during a mission in East Asia, the text read.

Beckett Tate *did* exist. His image was at the top of the page, his handsome face making my heart squeeze in regret, his blue eyes so intelligent, neatly trimmed dark blond beard, slightly longish hair, square, square jaw. His eyes appeared kind. He had a pleasant smile on his face. He looked like the type of man you could trust.

I fell asleep with my letters surrounding me on the bed, an old photo of Dan in my hand.

BECKETT

Going to North Carolina was a *big* mistake.

I knew it somewhere in the back of my mind, but since Graham's death, I hadn't really been thinking straight.

I went with the best of intentions, but as the saying goes, that road leads to hell. My personal hell started the moment I walked into *Oceanside* and saw her standing at the bar pouring drinks. When I recognized her, I should have handed over the letters and told her everything. At the least, I should have backed out, taken my bike and rode straight back to Manhattan, but there was no explanation for my behavior except I needed to get to know her.

Mira with the pretty hair and freckles on her nose.

Mira of the love letters to her new husband telling him how much she missed him – in her life, in her arms, in her bed.

I found out where the Lewis's lived, left the letters and went back home, dropping them off in the mailbox and ringing the doorbell before I left. Then, I rode back to Manhattan. It was the hardest thing I'd done in a long time. Every mile marker I passed, I fought with myself not to turn back and go to her, try to explain my deception. Could she forgive me for not telling her the truth from the start?

I couldn't hurt her so I left, deciding that my own feelings were less important than hers. Finding the letters allowed me to return them to her, so she'd have something to remember him by.

All I left was a note:

I'm so sorry I had to be the one to bring this to you. I know you'll have questions about how these came to be in my possession. Just know that your husband saved my life and that's why he died. I wanted to give these to you in person, but perhaps it's better to just leave them with you. Your husband was a true American hero. I can't really tell you any other details because it's classified, but I wanted you to have them. I wish you a truly happy and fulfilling life. You deserve it.

I kept driving, regret growing inside of me that I hadn't told her who I was right away and handed the letters over in person. At least I could have waited at the door and handed them over to the Mr. and Mrs. Lewis, thanked them for their son's service and sacrifice.

I arrived back in town much later that night, hot and dusty from a long day on the road. After showering and eating something I heated up from the freezer, I sat on my couch and stared at the blank face of my flatscreen TV.

I thought I'd get settled back into the routine of my life, but I was wrong.

Try as I might, I couldn't stop thinking about Miranda. For the first few days after I returned, I was busy enough, but my mind kept turning to her when I had a moment of distraction. I remembered her pretty eyes, her lush curves, her smile. I remembered her kiss and the cheeky look in her eyes when she joked with me.

I had to forget her. Nothing helped you forget like alcohol and new people.

So, later that week, I stood at a bar somewhere in Hell's Kitchen and tried to remember the name of the pretty young woman I was supposedly talking to. The truth was every woman I met faded into nothing in my mind when compared to Miranda. While the young woman spoke to me, my mind was occupied thinking about Miranda and wishing she was with me instead of what's her name with the bottle-blonde hair and push-up bra.

My evening with Brandon spent with the intention of blotting it all out in a booze-filled night of dancing and drinking was not going nearly as well as planned.

Blanc was not my usual choice of after-work clubs. Brandon was my best friend from Stanford, who joined the Marines with me, and was one of my business partners. He dragged me to *Blanc* after a day from hell. I would rather have gone home and straight to bed, but Brandon was looking for a second wife and so he guilted me into going out.

Unlike Brandon, I didn't make long-term plans when it came to women. I learned my lesson a few years earlier when Sue was taken from me.

Don't plan on love. If it happens, great, but don't go looking for it. Don't expect it.

Life had a way of fucking up those plans so it was better to assume you'd be alone than plan on marriage and family and end up broken-hearted. I didn't plan on getting married but if I did, I would never set out to *find* a wife. You fell in love or you didn't. Being so mercenary about it was wrong, to my way of thinking. But since I wasn't ever going to get married, it really didn't matter. I never promised women anything I couldn't deliver. No strings and no demands.

Brandon, on the other hand, was desperate to look for his second wife. He wanted to create a business empire and an empire needs an heir.

As to the girl who was leaning in close to me, squeezing her tits together for me to admire, I wasn't usually bad with names, but I was so damn preoccupied that I didn't really listen when we were introduced earlier in the evening. The talk was loud and the music, too. My mind was elsewhere. I'd downed a glass or three of bourbon and was working on a serious drunk.

I wanted to forget everything.

So when she asked me to dance about an hour into the evening, I couldn't remember her name, despite spending the previous fifteen minutes bending down to pretend I was listening raptly to everything she said.

"Let's dance, Beckett," she said and grabbed my hand. I smiled and allowed myself to be pulled away from the bar.

"What's your name," I asked when we arrived in middle of the dance floor.

She stopped dead in her tracks. "You don't remember my name?"

I shrugged and tapped my head with a fist. "Sorry," I said and shouted into her ear over the noise. "It was a hard day. I'm pulling a blank."

"You've been talking to me for an hour and you don't know my name?"

She gave me a look of disgust and then went back to the bar, leaving me standing all alone, surrounded by writhing people. I didn't really care, because I hadn't planned on picking up a woman that night, but I could get into dancing. I needed something physical to work out the stress.

So I did what any drunk red-blooded American male would do when stood up by his dance partner. I started to dance by myself, slowly integrating into the mass of thronging bodies. No one cared that I was alone. In fact, everyone was happy to dance with me, male and female alike. Soon, I lost myself in the music, dancing song after song until I was so hot that I had to remove my suit jacket and throw it on a table at the edge of the dance floor.

I seriously needed to work out a mega-dose of business-related stress.

When I finally left the dance floor, I saw that the young woman whose name I most un-chivalrously forgot now leaning in close to Brandon. They looked hot and heavy and so I smiled to myself and went to get a beer at the other end of the bar. I'd let them romance each other while I cooled off.

I met up with another staff member and we stood at the bar and talked about the day at work, drowning our mutual sorrows. I switched to tonic water about then because I could feel I'd almost reached my limit.

About an hour or so later, I left the bar and went to the men's room for a leak. I stood at a urinal in the washroom and thought back to my day. I was a lot drunk, dealing as I was with a death of a best friend and potential death of the company he and I had founded and nurtured after we returned from the war.

I closed my eyes as I stood at the urinal and tried to blank out everything but no matter how hard I tried, I couldn't help reconsider my life.

Something nagged me. I couldn't say what it was, exactly. It was this nameless, faceless darkness that filled me. Maybe due to a dead war buddy and a business in jeopardy. And something else, but I decided to save the existential angst for some other time.

Whatever it was, it was enough to take the edge off my enjoyment of the night. I glanced around the tiny bathroom, the walls of which were covered in crude graffiti. Oversized dicks competed with hairy and hairless pussies, boobs and the names of women with numbers beneath them along with ratings. There was water on the floor from a toilet that overflowed, and cigarette butts had been ground into the tiles.

The grout was black from filth.

I washed my hands and stared at myself in the mirror.

Longish unruly dirty blond hair falling in my eyes and below my collar, my grey tie and the first few buttons of my white shirt undone, a neatly-trimmed beard on my jaw, some liquid spilled on my suit. Bloodshot blue eyes. A very bad taste in my mouth and the start of a headache brewing somewhere in my cranium.

Fuuuuck...

What the hell was I doing with my life?

I SPENT the next morning with Casey, one of my oldest and best female friends from Stanford who enlisted in the Army the same year Graham and I enlisted in the Marines – and no, we never fucked. The butchest lesbian I knew with biceps that rivaled mine when I first started lifting, she was my go-to girl when I needed a shoulder to cry on, which was almost never, of course. But after firing half my team and most of all, after losing my oldest friend, I needed a sounding board. Other than a few moments last night at *Blanc*, I hadn't seen her in weeks since she'd been out of country on some consulting job.

I needed my Casey time.

"How are things?" she said as I helped her with the barbell. I spotted for her in the weight room at the club we both belonged to.

"The shits," I said, and stood back, watching as she did her reps.

"Still upset about Graham?"

I nodded without speaking.

"That's tough, man. Sorry I missed the memorial. How're you doing?"

I shrugged. "How could I be doing?"

She eyed me. She'd been trying to get me to come to VA group grief counseling sessions for the past month but I didn't need that shit – airing my personal problems in front of complete strangers.

"What were you doing at a dive like *Blanc*?" she asked.

"You were there, too."

"Only because you invited me."

I laughed. "It was Brandon's pick, not mine."

"What happened with the girl you were with?" she asked, this hopeful look in her eyes. "You two looked pretty hot and heavy when I saw you at *Blanc*. Did you go home with her?"

"Umm…" Although I didn't always volunteer the truth, I couldn't lie to Casey so I shrugged and said nothing, biting my bottom lip to keep from grinning. "Nope."

"What happened? You're usually pretty smooth with women."

"I forgot her name."

"You forgot her *name*?" she said with disgust in her voice. "You manwhore." She gave me a glare and pushed the bar up, concentrating while it lowered. Finally, she relented and the glare turned into a grin. She liked pussy as much as I did.

"You need a real girlfriend," she said, staring at me over the barbell. "None of those chicks you bring home for a fuck and suck and never see again."

"I don't need a girlfriend," I said, frowning. "I need a partner with ten million to invest in my company so I can keep the wolves – I mean *bankers* – from the proverbial door."

"The proverbial door or an *actual* door?"

"Grammar Nazi," I said, not quite under my breath.

"Go to your uncle. It's your money, Beckett."

I frowned at the mention of my uncle. "You know better than to suggest that."

A mid-level tough guy in what remained of Hell's Kitchen's Irish Mafia, he was my father's oldest brother, who inherited my father's technology business when he died. Not my mother. Not me. My uncle had no experience or interest in superconductors except how he could use the corporation to launder money.

We contested the will, but when the other side has a judge in his pocket, it was hard to win. Since then, my uncle had perverted my father's business. The money was tainted, dirty, and the respect the corporation garnered over the years was being slowly eroded.

One day, I'd get the business back from him, but not until he croaked off – hopefully at the hands of one of his little Mafia friends.

After I left the service, I'd been recruited and worked undercover for the DEA, reporting on what I overheard at family dinners about their mafia ties and business dealings, listening when sitting around with my uncle and his boys shooting the shit over Guinness. I'd reinserted myself into my uncle's life with the intent of finding some way to kick him out of the family business, get something incriminating on him so I could take over and clean it up.

At least, that was my long-range plan. In the meantime, I started my own company with Graham and now that was on the rocks. Casey didn't know I worked for the DEA, and so I could tell her none of this. Instead I let her think I was refusing to take his money on principle.

I let the barbell rest in her hands a bit longer than I should, to pay her back for being such a hardass. Soon, Casey's arms shook and she grimaced from the strain. "Beckett, you bastard... Help me!"

I grinned and lifted the barbell into place. She shook her head and sat up, adjusting her gloves. A serious bodybuilder, she worked out every day and was far more serious than me. I did it just to get visible abs and biceps because the ladies were all about abs and biceps. Casey – she almost – *almost* – had a better clean and jerk than me.

She won competitions.

"Beckett, I know you like to think of yourself as a lothario, but men like you cannot live on nameless pussy alone. You need the love and companionship of a good woman."

I laughed out loud at that and smiled at her. "Yeah, *right.*"

"I'm serious. I know more about you than anyone alive. You'll find someone new if you let yourself. Things will be good again if you give it a chance to develop with the right person. I know it's hard for you to hear, but there are other women out there besides Sue."

I was going to say something smartass, but she was right. I was almost married to Sue three years earlier – until Sue died while we were on vacation in the Andaman and Nicobar Islands off the coast of India.

Stung by *Synanceia horrida,* the dreaded Stonefish. Her death was one of those freak of nature accidents that you would never believe could happen. A rogue wave threw Sue onto a bed of corals on which the stonefish was lurking, camouflaged from view. It stung her on the chest, which is about the worst place to be stung if you hope to survive long enough to get anti-venom. Stonefish are the most poisonous creatures on earth. Sue died in the local hospital within a few hours and there was nothing I could do. None of my training in special operations forces helped. The medical training – the survival skills – evasion and resistance skills – they were worthless.

Casey was constantly bugging me to find someone new and make something real like I had with Sue, but I couldn't. Nothing felt real after her death.

No one could replace her.

I couldn't connect with women any longer. Really connect. They all seemed petty and boring, more interested in my money or fashion than in anything real. Sue, on the other hand, was as real as they got – a nurse I met in the war and pursued once we both got out of the service.

Instead of trying to meet anyone new, I poured all my energy into building up my corporation. I was a bona fide entrepreneur, with a multi-million-dollar business developing innovative technology to assist the military. After several tours of duty in a Marine Recon unit, then Marine Special Operations Forces, I had a pretty good idea of what was needed, what was lacking, and had watched my fellow Marines die in too high a number due to inadequate communications. My goal was to provide superior communications tech for reconnaissance to better protect soldiers on the battlefield.

Except you can't completely protect yourself against random acts of violence done in the name of some extremist religious sect, as Graham found out in Malaysia. Or from poisonous fish that looked like innocent stones. All you could do was wear lots of body armor and stay the fuck out of Dodge.

"I have lots of girl *friends*," I said as we moved to some machines for cardio. "They give me what I want and I give them what they want. Fair exchange. Besides, I don't have time for a real relationship."

"You don't have time to waste, Beckett." Casey tilted her head and gave me the evil eye. "You of all people should know how short life is and how unpredictable Fate can be. I mean a real relationship with someone who's your equal."

"You're a lesbian," I said and grinned widely.

She laughed at that, but I meant it. She was a software engineer and the smartest woman I ever met. Luckily, the subject was soon forgotten as we both ran for twenty minutes on the treadmills that lined the weight room. I needed to build up a good sweat, get some of the toxins out of me. As I ran, I remembered the blonde from the previous night, the stinky restroom at the bar, the grimy floor and graffiti-scrawled stall.

Such a difference from meeting Miranda...

Maybe Casey was right. It had been so long since I met a *real* woman, as Casey described it, that I frankly didn't know where to start.

Miranda lived in North Carolina. I had no idea where I could ever find someone else like her. I worked with men all day at the corporation – former military types who acted as consultants, fellow software engineers who worked on prototypes. Besides lifting, and ratting on my thug of an uncle, I really didn't do anything else but work. Running the business took up all my time.

"So, how am I supposed to meet these *real* women?" I said when we finished our workout. "Should I sign up for classes at the community college? Take a singles cooking class?" I asked sarcastically.

I wiped my face with a towel and watched her response to my half-serious suggestions.

She eyed me for a moment. "Hun, if you don't know how to meet girls at your age, I'm afraid there's no hope for you."

I made a face. "I can meet women fine, *sha*. But the ones I meet aren't really the *bring her home to momma* types. And you're not really the best source of new material…"

She punched my arm, not so lightly. "I know a *lot* of straight people. You, for instance. You should stop going to bars to meet women or at least don't fuck them on the first date. Get real with a woman and you'll find someone."

"I could find someone any night of the week," I replied sourly. "besides, I met a very pretty lady at a bar only the other night."

"And why wasn't she with you at *Blanc* last night?" She wagged her eyebrows.

I didn't say more. I didn't want her to know the whole back-story about Miranda.

"You need to meet someone real," she replied and punched me on the shoulder again. I punched her back lightly, and we sparred briefly, ducking each other's punches before separating to our appropriate changing rooms. Before I entered the Men's, Casey stopped at the door to the Women's and looked at me, a serious expression on her pretty face, her eyes bright.

"I'm serious, Beckett. You need to find something real with someone real. Both men and women are only truly happy when they have someone to love."

For once, I bit back the snide retort and nodded.

Somewhere in the back of my mind, I knew she was right, but I fought acknowledging it, like to do so would be the end of the new Beckett. The one who emerged after Sue died. The Beckett that all the single ladies knew and loved but none of them could have.

Sure, I'd struck out with perhaps the prettiest woman I'd met in a long time – Miranda Parker. But that was because I hadn't really turned on the charm.

I'd rectify that lapse if I had the chance and I aimed to make sure I did.

LATER THAT NIGHT after I'd had a warm bath and was lying on my bed, watching late night news, I picked up the copies of Miranda's letters I made before I went to North Carolina. I felt bad copying them, but I wanted something to remember her by. It was a betrayal of trust to do so. Maybe even illegal, but when I read her letters, I felt such longing for someone like Miranda to feel that way for me.

I lay back on my bed, propped up with several pillows, and opened the envelope with the copies once more.

I sorted through the letters, organizing them by date to see what Miranda had written, laying out the photos that went along with the letters. I felt incredible guilt that I was reading them, but something made me keep them. I wanted to do it right. I wanted to meet Mr. and Mrs. Lewis, thank them for their son's sacrifice, and return the letters properly. I wanted to take Miranda out for dinner or a drink and talk to her about her life, see how far I could take it with her.

She was the kind of woman Casey would approve of. I had no doubt about it.

I fell asleep with the photocopied letters and pictures of Miranda on the bed beside me, the television still on, talking heads on the news network droning on and lulling me to sleep.

I SPENT the next week trying to get up to speed with Graham's work, sitting in his chair, working on his computer, and it didn't make me feel nostalgic. It made me angry. As soon as I could find another partner or some interim funding to tide Brimstone over, I'd be shutting down the war tourism part of the business.

It got Graham and a civilian killed so as lucrative as it was, I intended to close that part of the business down permanently.

My week was full of meetings with various clients, providing them with my hastily written proposals – work that Graham started but never got the chance to finish. He was the expert in war tourism, not me. He had all the contacts with people in war-torn areas of the globe where business men who had too much time on their hands and not enough adrenaline wanted to go for their 'vacation'.

Rich boys who wanted to play at being a warrior, or at least see a few dead bodies while they rode from Western hotel to Western hotel in HUMVEES, drank their hundred-dollar bottles of wine and talked about the stock market. It wasn't my idea of a noble pursuit, so as soon as I could, I'd wrap up that side of the business and send Graham's contacts to one of our competitors. It wasn't as if I could just find another partner like Graham. Men like him were few and far between.

No, I decided to find someone who was not into the war tourism business. I wanted someone who could augment my own field of military communications tech, or maybe someone with both military experiences – preferably in special operations forces – and a Masters or PhD in economics or political science who could advise clients on the political situation in various parts of the world where they wanted to locate their off-shore factories.

I had to start over again now that Graham was gone.

I MET with Casey later that night for a drink and then dinner. I needed a sounding board and wanted to talk to her about my company.

"So, what's up with your finances?" she asked as we sat at the bar in her neighborhood. "You gonna be able to make things work?"

I nodded. "I think so. I'm going to sell the old brownstone I own near here. It needs a lot of work, but it should bring me a nice sum that should tide the business over."

"Good," she said and held up her glass of bourbon. "That'll take some of the stress off. You look terrible, by the way."

"Thanks," I said with a sardonic laugh. "Always nice to hear. I haven't been sleeping well for the past couple of weeks."

"You need to get laid," Casey said.

"Tell me about it," I said, although I didn't mean it. Some men lost themselves in pussy. Others, me included, focused on business instead. "I have an interesting little intrigue going on."

She raised her eyebrows. "Oh? Do tell…"

I told her about the letters that I found when I went to the brownstone.

Casey nodded. "You think your stuff got mixed up?"

I shrugged. "My legal name is Daniel. The letters were addressed to Dan and there was no name on the letters from the woman. All she had as a signature was *Love, me*. They probably thought they were my letters."

Casey downed her drink. "That's quite a coincidence."

"Yes," I said and nodded. "He was killed when his chopper went down in a storm."

"That sucks," she said, nodding her head in understanding. "It's hard to lose people. Something you never really get used to."

We sat in somber silence for a few moments, and I examined the glass of bourbon in front of me. I'd lost too many people. Some were fellow Marines who were out on missions with me when I was in the service. Others, like Graham and Sue, were close friends or lovers. The man who stood side by side with me in battle. The woman I thought I would marry.

I exhaled heavily, my breath ragged. I was more tired than I realized.

"You really should come to group grief counseling with me, Beckett. You sound like you need it."

I shook my head. "I need to sell the brownstone and get a new partner. Then, I'll be fine."

"Stubborn bastard," she muttered.

I nodded. Stubbornness was a fault of mine. I drank down the rest of my bourbon and knocked the glass down on the bar. The bartender came right over and poured me another one. Tonight felt like a night to get drunk.

"Get drunk with me?" I turned to Casey, whose large brown eyes were all sympathetic.

"That's why you pay me the big bucks."

The bartender poured her another shot of bourbon and the two of us clinked glasses and proceeded to get drunk.

THE NEXT DAY, I spent the morning recovering from my night with Casey. I took a steam bath, then ate a heavy breakfast with Brandon. Finally, I sat in my office and reviewed the article on the death of Hospital Corpsman 1st Class Daniel Lewis.

It was almost a year since the accident and his death. I wanted to write to his parents to explain how Miranda's letters came to me, and so I spent the morning composing a letter that I hoped would express my gratitude for Lewis's service, his sacrifice for his country.

I felt incredible guilt as I wrote. What a cruel fate. At times, I felt like going back and getting revenge for the deaths of the Marines who lost their lives trying to rescue us in my accident. Instead, I hoped to make things better for Marines who had to risk their lives for the rest of us.

I remembered Miranda's letters and how she wrote about her work at the restaurant and how she enjoyed bartending to a different crowd than she was used to. She usually worked at her grandfather's pub in Queens while she put herself through John Jay College of Criminal Justice. The bar catered to police and fire-fighters, and she was used to hearing their talk about their work. She said it made her feel closer to her father and grandfather to work at the bar, for she had a better understanding of the men who risked their lives each day for our safety.

She wanted to do something with law enforcement as well, but didn't see herself as a cop. Instead, she wanted to work in forensic psychology, to understand what made criminals and terrorists tick. Fight them using her mind. She was too small to get into the police force, not making the height grade so policing was out of the question. She had to be a civilian member of the FBI if she were going to follow in her father's footsteps.

I admired her. Here she was, hoping to join the FBI, her husband a bona fide war hero, giving up his own life to save others. A member of a hyper-specialized special operations team.

She was the kind of woman I would want to date. Casey would approve of her – of that there was no doubt. I struggled to write a letter to her, trying to put in words a few thoughts about her loss but it all felt inadequate. Here was a young woman just starting her life with her husband and he was taken from her less than three months after their marriage.

Ella, my admin assistant, poked her head in my office at about noon. "John's on the line. He wants to let you know he's coming to the retreat."

I pulled my mind away from the Lewis family and considered a location for the retreat I had planned for my staff. We had booked a floor of rooms at a hotel in Wilmington, but now I reconsidered. The retreat was hastily organized and intended to boost my remaining staff's morale after Graham's death. Before Graham's death, I had promised to host a retreat where we could do a planning session for the next year. We'd have to transition out of war tourism now that Graham was gone so there was no better time than the present to hold the retreat. I thought of Topsail Beach and wondered whether it had adequate facilities for my dozen staff.

A convention of Wall Street investors in the defense industries was being held in Wilmington and I was going to attend a few meet and greets, so holding my staff retreat during that weekend would kill two birds with one stone.

"Check out Topsail Beach and see if there are any appropriate accommodations for the retreat. The Yacht Club's pretty nice," I said, thinking I could invite some of the investors from the convention to our brainstorming session. "It's pretty close to Wilmington, and a defense contract convention with some investors I know."

"Will do."

If I timed it right, we could run the retreat and I could finally meet Lewis's parents and thank them for his service and sacrifice. As to Miranda, I'd confess who I was and how I got the letters and let her take it from there. Not telling her who I was the first time I was in Topsail Beach was wrong. I wouldn't make that mistake again.

THREE WEEKS LATER, I drove down to Wilmington on my bike. It was still the summer season and there were quite a few tourists around, in the shops and on the beaches. The next morning, I went into the town to the Yacht Club and checked into my room, unloaded my gear, and sent my two suits, ties and shirts to the dry cleaning service so they'd be freshly pressed for the next day. Then I drove down the street to the fitness club and checked it out. A young guy with a man-bun and horned-rimmed glasses greeted me.

"How can I help you?" he asked, eyeing me up and down.

"I'm staying at the Yacht Club and wanted to see your facilities for my staff, who will be here for four days."

The attendant widened his eyes as if he was surprised I was staying at the club. I laughed to myself. I supposed my motorcycle jacket, helmet and boots made me look somewhat questionable, but that was his mistake. He showed me around the club, including the fitness room with row upon row of treadmills, exercise bikes, and universal gym, a classroom for fitness classes, and a larger gym with a climbing wall. There was a steam and sauna room with separate facilities for women and men.

As I was leaving the locker room, I ran into a mountain of a man whom I recognized immediately from my time at Camp Lejeune. Master Sergeant Brent Fillmore. A huge man with a boxer's build, he was the toughest Marine drill sergeant I knew. Stationed at Lejeune, he must have retired to live in Topsail Beach.

"Master Sergeant Fillmore," I said when I reached his side.

He turned to regard me, a frown on his face. "That's my name. Don't wear it out," came his reply. As usual, gruff to the end.

I held out my hand. "McNeil," I said, using the name he knew me by. "I was at Lejeune a few years back."

Then he looked at me more closely. "Well, I'll be…" He shook his head. "If it isn't Daniel McNeil, the Cajun Viking…" He eyed me up and down as if assessing me.

"I go by Beckett now," I said. "Daniel McNeil is my legal name, but for business, I use Beckett Tate. It's my mother's name and, well…" I shrugged. "It's a long complicated story that has to do with divorce, the Irish American mafia and other family bullshit you really don't want to know."

He glanced at me like I was some kind of flake but then nodded. "All right, Beckett Tate. I thought you got out and went to Manhattan. What the *hell* are you doing in Topsail Beach?"

"I'm based in Manhattan," I said. "As to why I'm here, I could ask the same of you." We shook hands and then fist bumped. "I'm here checking out the facilities for a retreat for my staff this weekend."

"Your staff?" he asked and we stopped in the hallway. "You an employer now?"

"I have a company that develops comms tech for the military."

"No shit. I thought you went Special Operations Forces."

I nodded. "I did. Did a tour of duty in Afghanistan before I got out and started my company."

"I'll bet the money's better," Fillmore said with a laugh.

"What are you doing, Master Sergeant?" I asked as we stopped outside a classroom "Teaching fitness?"

He pointed to a sign on the door beside us. *MCMAP Fitness Class.* "I'm retired but I try to keep in shape and do personal training on the side. Wife runs a touristy clothing shop on the strip."

I nodded. "We'll be staying at the Yacht Club for a few days. I'll make sure to bring my staff to one of your fitness classes. You can whip their asses into shape."

He grinned. "Hell, you can help me run the class. See if you remember your stuff. Didn't you used to do yoga or some other such Buddhist shit?"

I laughed and he walked me out of the club to my bike in the parking lot. It was good to see him again and I was surprised and a little chuffed that he remembered me.

"Make sure you come by Saturday," he said as I got on my bike. "I got a whole new crew of recruits starting."

"I will," and we fist bumped once more.

"*Semper fi,*" he said in Marine Corps tradition.

"*Oorah,*" I replied.

I WENT BACK to my hotel and worked on the presentation I'd be giving to a group of investors I was hoping to woo during the weekend, spending time describing Brimstone, its origins, its mandate and the work we had already undertaken.

Brimstone started as an idea Graham and I had during our time in Afghanistan. We were with Bravo Company, a Special Ops team and part of the Joint Special Operations Command. We'd spent time in the worst hell-holes in Iraq and Afghanistan, and undertook missions that put us in the most dangerous parts of the country. We worked with Special Operations Forces from other coalition nations, including the British Special Operations Forces teams and called in their artillery to enemy targets. Laser guided, the Brimstone missile the Brits used was effective against enemy armor. In addition to other duties, our recon unit went into enemy territory to find and eliminate armored vehicles so our own forces could move in.

We called ourselves the Brimstone team, not only because of the missile, but because we lived through hell while in Iraq. I got the idea of using the name when we came back from Afghanistan and left the Marines, intent on starting my company.

For the rest of the night I spent my time working on the presentation, eating in my hotel room. I hit the rack at midnight, feeling as ready as I'd ever be. I planned on driving into Wilmington in the morning to meet with a few of the Wall Street types and wanted to be fresh.

THE STRESS of everything must have gotten to me. I woke in the middle of the night in a cold sweat, my heart pounding, a nightmare of the explosion and aftermath of the accident in my mind's eye. I bolted upright in bed and once I realized where I was, I did some deep breathing to try to calm myself. The clock radio at the bedside table read 4:45 a.m. – the usual time I woke up when I had my nightmares.

Casey had urged me to go to the VA for PTSD counseling, but it just didn't feel right. I came out of the whole business with the least damage. I was alive. Sure, I had a very visible scar to show for it, but I was alive…

I had to buck up and take it like a Marine.

Maybe shaking Lewis's father's hand and offering my condolences to his mother, would help heal those wounds I did still have.

The kind of wounds you can't see.

I GOT up and went to the bathroom for a piss, then drank a glass of water and stood at the window. I cracked the drapes and looked out from the hotel towards the marina and ocean beyond.

A wind had picked up during the night, and the metallic sign outside the hotel swung back and forth, its rusty bearing screeching in a rhythmic fashion that I knew would grate on my nerves and prevent me from falling back asleep. Dawn was still an hour away, but I could see a faint crack of brightness on the far horizon.

Might as well get up.

I threw on my sweats and t-shirt, put on my running shoes and went for a run along the beach. Twenty minutes of running would wake me up, and if that failed, I'd run into the surf and that would be sure to do the trick.

When I returned to the hotel, the sky was visibly brightening on the horizon and so I went inside and decided to sit on the deck and have my breakfast while watching the sunrise. Luckily, the hotel restaurant was open at 6:30 and so by 6:45, after a quick shower and after I dressed in my casual clothes, I was seated at a table on the faded wood deck, a cup of coffee in hand, reading the Wall Street Journal on my iPad. A breakfast of fruit and eggs finished the early morning off.

While I waited for my suits to come back from the dry cleaner, I went over my first and second quarter financial numbers, wanting to show investors how much we brought in – what Graham and I brought in – to the company. Besides my DARPA contract, I had a number of clients I advised on security when they were over in Afghanistan and Iraq, or other countries in the Middle East or Pacific Rim states. Graham had the war tourism part of the business, and I'd been able to find a few old SOF guys to take a couple of his contracts, but they were only in the business part time and I wanted to get out of it completely.

After my suits were delivered to my hotel room, I dressed in my grey suit and arranged for a local car service to come pick me up and drive me into Wilmington for my afternoon meeting. I opened my laptop and read over the brochures I brought along with me for the meetings while the driver took me into the city.

THE MEETINGS WENT WELL. I knew a few former Marines who went into finance after they did their time in Iraq and it was those contacts that helped me get Brimstone Solutions Inc. off the ground when Graham and I started it three years earlier. The guys agreed to come out and spend an evening in Topsail Beach. I thought about going to *Oceanside* for dinner and seeing what it had to offer, but wasn't sure whether my presence would be appreciated.

To tell the truth, I'd become a bit obsessed with the Lewis family since I discovered how Lewis died over in Afghanistan and since I'd met Miranda and read her love letters. Her words kept coming back to me now and then unbidden – how she missed his touch, his kiss, and his presence in her bed. How she missed waking up with him on a Sunday morning in their place in Wilmington where they spent the summers while she was off from school and he was in between missions.

I thought about them making love in the warm sunlight and felt a stab of grief in my chest. Immediately, I thought of Sue and remembered our time together, and the last time I saw her.

I couldn't wait to see Miranda again, and learn if the way I felt when I met her before remained. Maybe this time, I could coax her into having dinner with me or a drink.

I aimed to find out. I couldn't tell her everything about the day her husband died. Parts of it were classified. Hell, I probably couldn't tell her the date he saved my life. But I could tell her that he did and tell her what a hero he was and that I owed him my life.

DESPITE BEING EXHAUSTED from a bad night of sleep, I knew my stuff and felt comfortable talking to them about Brimstone. Former SOF, they appreciated the work Brimstone did and were interested in helping with funding. I hoped it would mean I could continue on and not declare bankruptcy and so I left the meeting feeling better than I had for several weeks.

One of the investors, Dane O'Hara, was interested in helping out with some advising work. He was the kind of man I was looking for to step in for Graham – dual degree in Political Science and law and topped off by an MBA, Dane was smart, capable and was independently wealthy from an inheritance. He thought it would be great fun to get in on the ground floor with Brimstone during its resurrection.

As I left the boardroom, we shook hands and agreed that he'd meet me in Manhattan and sit down for a longer conversation about what role he could play in the business. He was sick of the Wall Street crowd, and wanted to get back involved in the military in a more operational fashion. Advising businesses about locating factories in war-torn areas of the world would allow him to get his very clean banker's hands dirty again.

If things worked out with Dane, that would be well worth the trip right there, let alone anything else we accomplished this weekend.

I went back to Topsail Beach with a promise to meet up with the guys on Saturday night at one of the local hangouts. We'd share a few drinks and rehash old times over in Afghanistan.

THE NEXT MORNING, I got up early to go to the fitness club and so I dressed and had breakfast, intending to go there for an early workout before returning to the hotel to plan my day. I would meet my staff as they arrived one by one, and make sure they were set up for the day in the hotel. We had a meeting scheduled after lunch, and people were arriving and staying in the hospitality suite I had booked until their rooms were ready. We'd meet in the boardroom at 1:00 and spend the afternoon reviewing numbers for the first two quarters of the year.

The next day would be in brainstorming how to replace the business Graham brought in, transitioning out of the war tourism business into more threat assessment.

So, after a quick shower and after a light breakfast, I drove my bike down the strip to the fitness club and showed my pass to the attendant at the front desk. He remembered me and gave me a lock so I could use a day locker in the locker room. I went out to the main fitness rooms and popped in to see Fillmore.

After a round of hellos, I got down to business.

"We got a lot of students?" I asked and he handed me the clip-board with a print out of a list of students for the class. Twenty-three, including – of all people – *Mira Parker*.

I had to check twice, because it was too hard to believe, but I remembered her saying something about getting back into shape. Her being in the class was a fortuitous coincidence – one that I intended to fully exploit.

"Don't be late, Tate," he said in that raspy voice I remembered from boot camp.

"I won't, Master Sergeant."

Then, I walked down a hallway and saw a larger gym, so I peered inside. There, I saw Mira and the cocktail waitress who worked with her the night I met her at the restaurant. They were standing at a small climbing wall and Mira was already in her climbing harness, a helmet on her head and climbing shoes on. She looked really cute in her little t-shirt and sweat pants, but her expression suggested she wasn't quite sure about climbing.

I wondered how she felt when she found the letters in the mailbox. Did they break her heart all over again? Or was she happy to have them as mementos of their time together?

Did she realize it was me?

I stood back for a moment, trying to decide whether I should just turn around and leave rather than try to entangle myself in her life. It would be the more honorable thing to do, rather than pretend or keep pursuing her in hopes that something more would result.

But she was just so damn cute...

In for a penny, in for a pound, my grandma used to say.

I was in way over my head and even though I knew it, I dove back in anyway.

MIRANDA

"You know you want to do it," Leah said.

We stood at the bottom of the climbing wall and looked up. Leah had a doubtful expression on her face.

"I want to," I said, "but I also value my life."

We both laughed. I looked up the wall to the ceiling and reconsidered my plan to live life more fully. I'd always been the safe one – the responsible one. The one who did my chores, who came home on time, who did my homework, who sent thank you cards on my birthday.

I always asked for permission instead of forgiveness.

Dan made me brave. I did things with him that I would never have done on my own, but now that he was gone, I had to find the courage in myself. My old life was over. Living safely hadn't turned out well for me, so from that day onward, I was going to live on the edge. Like Dan did.

"You haven't lifted a finger since last year," Leah said doubtfully. "Are you up to it?"

Since last year. No one ever said *since Dan died* as if not mentioning his name made it somehow less personal and therefore easier to bear. Even now, people were trying to shield me from thoughts of him, but I thought of him every single day.

That had to change. I had to start over.

I hadn't had regular exercise for most of the past year. Today I was going to start a new routine.

"I need this," I said, forcing my voice to be all positive and coachy. "Let's seize the day. *Carpe diem*, babe."

Seize the day.

It's what I wanted, but why is starting something new so damn hard?

As we were standing there, fiddling with the harness, Mr. Beckett Tate, CEO and DEA officer, walked up.

A shock went through me. What was he doing back in Topsail Beach? I'd often thought of him, regretting that I didn't have that drink with him, being cautious as usual. But now, here he was and I was suspicious. Since he'd left, I'd been so tempted to track him down in Manhattan to ask about the letters and how he came to possess them, and most importantly, why he hadn't told me right away about them when he walked into the bar.

But I'd chickened out.

I even thought about checking into Dan's missions to see how any men he'd rescued so I could find Beckett Tate, but I didn't.

"Hello again," he said when he came to my side. I stared at him in silence, a bit unnerved and at a loss for what to say.

"Are you stalking me?" I said finally.

"No, of course not," he said, frowning. "I told you I was looking for a place to hold my staff retreat. I liked Topsail Beach and so we're here for the weekend. This is the only decent place to work out on the island. All guests at the Yacht Club have day passes."

I didn't know what to say for a moment as I adjusted the straps snaking between my thighs. I wore a helmet and gloves, kneepads and elbow pads, my hair pulled back into a ponytail, which poked through the hole in the helmet.

Leah stood beside me. "Are you going to introduce me to your friend?" She wagged her eyebrows.

I frowned and turned to Beckett. "Beckett Tate, this is Leah Grant. Beckett left the package of letters I wrote to Dan."

"Oh, yeah…" Leah said. She frowned at him.

"Pleased to meet you," he said to Leah, bowing low.

She glanced at me, and I knew she was trying to gauge how I felt about him returning to Topsail Beach. I gave a tiny shrug. Part of me was shocked to see him, but another part was excited, a thrill in my gut. Perhaps he'd explain how he got the letters and why he didn't say anything when he first met me. He had to know they were my letters. If Dan saved his life, he should know I'd want to talk to him about Dan.

"Do you know how to do this?" Leah asked finally, breaking the silence. She pointed to the climbing wall. "We had a lesson but I have a feeling that one lesson isn't enough."

As usual, Leah was totally cool about the fact that a stranger from out of town who I met weeks earlier returned and apparently, was now at our health club. She went with the flow.

"I just so happen to be an expert climber," Beckett said with a grin. "One of my many superpowers." He winked at me and as much as I wanted to smile at him, appreciate our private joke, I couldn't.

Leah turned to me. I was still unsure of what to say. I was ambivalent about the fact that Beckett had come back to Topsail Beach, and I wasn't sure how to think about him coming to the fitness club. It felt a bit like stalking. A lot like stalking.

"Hey, Grumpy Cat," Leah said, one eyebrow raised. "Are you going to climb or are you going to stand there like a deer caught in the headlights?"

"I hate when you call me that," I said with a frown. "Do you want to go first?"

She bit her bottom lip, trying not to laugh. "Go ahead and climb. Remember what Craig said. I'll watch you the first time."

"Suit yourself," I said and shrugged.

"You promised to take risks," she chided.

"I'm here, aren't I?" I said a bit crossly. "Doing anything's a risk with you."

"That's because I'm so damn *fuunn*."

"Let me help you with that," Beckett said. He checked my harness. Once everything was fastened, he turned to me. "Ready?" he said, looking deep into my eyes. "Remember to use your feet and keep your center of gravity over them. Don't be afraid. I'll catch you if you fall."

"I'm not afraid," I said, a little too tartly and in total denial of the way my knees were weak but I wasn't going to let him know that. I shook the ropes. "I'm as ready as I'll ever be."

I turned to the wall and looked up to the top.

I'd made a pact with myself that from now on, I was going to do everything I was afraid of – *everything*. In no particular order, that meant:

Climb a mountain.

Fly an airplane.

Go on a roller coaster.

Eat sashimi.

Bungee jump.

Visit the top of the Empire State Building.

Skydive.

Take self-defense classes.

Have a one-night stand with a gorgeous man just to see what it was like…

Okay, that last one was made up on the spot after seeing Beckett again, dressed in his low-slung faded jeans and white mock-turtleneck t-shirt. If fate was going to come barreling out of nowhere and kill me like it killed Dan, I wanted to have lived a little – make that a *lot* – first.

Beckett checked my harness one last time and then held up his fist, so we could fist-bump. I almost missed his I was shaking so badly.

He grinned at me. "You'll do fine. It's a kid's apparatus."

"Thanks," I said with a laugh, starting to relax a bit. Maybe he had a valid reason for being back in Topsail Beach. Leah didn't seem the least bit concerned. Maybe I didn't have to be so freaked out.

I looked up the wall and tried to replicate what I learned when our instructor demonstrated earlier. Why make it any harder than it already was?

"Here goes nothing."

It was hard and it was easy.

Hard because I used muscles I didn't even know existed. Easy because it was only fifteen feet high and it was the beginner wall, designed for children or people who had never climbed before. I climbed one knobby outcropping at a time, sliding my fingers over rocks and between crevices, testing my footing, pulling myself up slowly, carefully. When I got to the top, I exhaled in relief, not realizing I'd been holding my breath, and glanced down. It wasn't so bad after all. In fact, I freaking *loved* it.

Elated that I got to the top of the wall rather quickly, I smiled down on Leah and Beckett and waved, as if I'd just won the Academy Award for best Actress.

"Take it slow," Beckett called up to me when I started down. It didn't appear so hard from where I stood but I did what he'd told me and pushed off while he let the rope release slowly, a few feet at a time. The rappel down was actually fun once I got the rhythm of it.

I could actually *do* this.

When I reached the bottom, Leah and I high-fived then Beckett fist bumped me again, and this time I didn't miss.

"See," I said, laughing. "Nothing to it."

I wanted to feel fearless like that all the time. About everything. I wanted to think there was nothing to whatever it was that I faced in life. I knew it would feel spectacular.

You'd think the daughter of a career FBI Special Agent would be fearless, but you'd be wrong. If anything, I was even more obsessed with safety than average, aware of bad guys and criminals and threats to life and limb. You'd also think that someone with a fear of violent death would avoid going into the criminal justice profession but you'd be wrong about that, too. Surrounding myself with all things law enforcement was the only way I felt truly safe.

I had to break out of that mold if I ever hoped to move on with my life.

"Your turn," I said to Leah as Beckett helped me unhook the harness. As I took it off, I looked at Leah. "Nothing to it."

Then Leah took a turn, and Beckett and I watched while she climbed the wall. She was a bit more hesitant than I had been, but she seemed just as happy when she reached the top.

"Are you going to climb?" I asked while Leah descended.

"Nah," Beckett said. "I climbed the highest mountain in Afghanistan. This is really so..." he said, hesitating as if he were struggling to find a non-insulting way to phrase his words.

"So... childish?" I said for him.

"Something like that," he said with a soft laugh, his blue eyes playful.

"So tell me," I said, getting up the nerve to ask about the letters. "Why didn't you tell me right away that you had letters for me? Why the subterfuge?"

"Subterfuge?" he said and gave a small laugh. "More like not wanting to give you something that would remind you about your loss face to face. I didn't know how you'd respond and so I thought it would be best to leave them in the mailbox."

"You chickened out, in other words," I said, arching my brow.

"Exactly," he said and turned to me, an impish smile on his face. "I'm sorry. It's not every day I have to deliver something that might make a person's heart break. You were working. I didn't want you to have to deal with it at that moment."

"Fair enough," I said, and nodded in understanding. "So tell me, how did you get my letters?"

He shrugged. "It was just one of those mix-ups that the military never seems to be able to explain. But I did want to return them to you since Dan saved my life."

I smiled. "I'm glad he did. That was what motivated him — rescuing the brave soldiers, sailors and marines who were willing to put themselves in harm's way for our country."

He shook his head, his cheeks actually flushed like he was embarrassed.

"Anyway, I was in the military for long enough to ever expect a straight answer for these mixups. Instead, I just accept that the bureaucracy screwed things up and move on from there. SNAFU, in other words."

I laughed. "That's what Dan used to say. FUBAR and SNAFU were two words that were absolutely necessary in any soldier's vocabulary."

"That is totally true," Beckett said and smiled back at me.

I wanted to push more, but he was right. He got the letters by mistake, and returned them. I would have liked more of an explanation, but I decided to just accept that fate put them in his hands, and now, he'd returned them to me.

When Leah got to the bottom, we high-fived, the three of us.

"So?" she said, grinning widely. "What's next?"

"Martial arts," I said and turned to Beckett. "We signed up for a class."

"Have a great time," he said with a mischievous grin. Then he walked off and although I had been worried about him being there, I felt a pang of regret in case I never saw him again.

Part of me was relieved. I did *not* want Beckett to watch me do a martial arts fitness class. My legs were already wobbly from a combination of adrenaline and weakness from too many hours sitting on my ass for the past year.

"I'm not sure I'm up to it," I said, wondering if I should leave then.

Leah laughed. "You said you wanted to do it all."

"I did." I smiled ruefully.

Leah followed me to one of the rooms where a dozen people, male and female, had gathered to take the class.

A sign on the door caught my attention.

MCMAP. Beginners. All Fitness Levels.

That was hopeful. MCMAP. I knew what *that* was.

I turned to Leah in disbelief. "Did you know what this was when you signed us up?" I asked.

"No, but it said all fitness levels, and that includes couch potato, right?" Leah said hopefully.

I shrugged and took a place beside her, glancing at the chalk-board at the front of the room.

"I'm not sure I can do this."

"Hey, you," Leah said and pushed me playfully. "*Carpe diem.* Those were your exact words."

I sighed. "All right… But you may regret it once you know what it is."

"Why? What does MCMAP stand for?" Leah asked while she craned her neck to look around.

I smiled. "You're the one who signed us up," I said and turned away, scoping out the other students. "Believe me, you don't want to know."

"Seriously," she said and stood in front of me, noting my failed attempt not to smile. "Tell me what it means."

I took in a deep breath and held it for a few seconds. "Marine Corps Martial Arts Program." Then I burst out laughing.

Her mouth fell open. "What?"

I smiled at the look on her face. "Yeah, Dan used to do it back before…"

Then I stopped myself. I was going to say "back before he died," but I didn't.

"*Crap...*" she said. "I had no idea. Sorry..."

"No, it's okay. Dan used to do it. I know all about MCMAP but just so you know, I'm probably going to die since I've been a sloth for a year..."

"You said you wanted to take a huge bite out of life and live on the edge. I guess this is living on the edge."

On the blackboard at the front of the classroom was the following:

Please warm up for 5 minutes before class starts.

I watched as the other participants shook out their arms and legs as if they knew what 'warm up' meant. I tried to follow their movements, bending over to touch my... my knees and then arching my arm over my head.

"Be prepared to puke the first class. Look." I pointed to the wall. A tin bucket like a janitor would use stood by the door, a mop beside it. "There's a bucket."

She checked it out, making a face of alarm.

"Oh, and there's a portable defibrillator, just in case..." I pointed to it and she laughed out loud.

"Oh, my *God*. Why did I sign us up for this? I should have chosen Zumba."

"I honestly have no idea. We're in for it now, sister," I said, swallowing hard when the instructor entered the room, almost puking at the sight of him. He looked like the Marine Corps bulldog crest on his t-shirt, his head covered by a thin brush cut, the sides sheared right down to his skin. He had a neck as thick as a tree trunk and he wore grey sweats and a loose black t-shirt with a snarling bulldog dog on the front. I could practically see his muscles rippling beneath his clothing.

United States Marine Corps Devil Dog the t-shirt read.

It brought back so many memories...

"Sorry about the military thing," Leah said. "I just saw fitness class and since it was at the right time, I signed us up..."

I shook my head "Don't worry. I have to move on, right?"

She nodded and we turned to face the instructor who was speaking with a student. I glanced around at a few of the others, and they looked just as shocked and in awe as Leah and I were.

Then, I saw Beckett in the doorway, glancing around as if checking to see if he was in the right place.

Damn. He was going to join the class?

Despite my reluctance, he was everything I could want. Tall. Handsome, hell—*gorgeous.* Smart. Hard working. Sexy. Funny.

Leah went to the drinking fountain, which was right beside Beckett in the small workout room, scoping him out behind his back. She raised her eyebrows at me when she returned.

"He's sooo hot," Leah said, tilting her head in Beckett's direction. "He really likes you, Mira. Why don't you be nice and have some fun? *Carpe diem*, right?"

The instructor turned to Beckett. "You're late," he said, his voice gruff.

"Sorry, Master Sergeant," Beckett said, taking off his boots, stripping off his jeans to reveal a pair of black basketball shorts.

"You better get warmed up. *Fast*." The instructor stood with his hands on his hips watching Beckett get ready, looking like he was ready to bark out an order at any moment.

Beckett took a place at the side of the class, shaking his arms and legs as if trying to warm up. He was absolutely gorgeous. He glanced around and his eyes came to rest squarely on me. Another shiver that made my skin all goose-bumpy went down my spine when our eyes met, and it wasn't the air conditioning.

I glanced away quickly.

He definitely looked like he belonged in a Bond movie or a catwalk in Milan, and so as I stretched and tried to warm up, I tried to imagine what he really was. DEA agent? Maybe undercover? Or CEO of a tech company? Could he really be both?

I watched him while I bent over, trying to touch my toes on one side.

"Good day, recruits," the bulldog said when he was finally ready to start the class, his blue eyes piercing. Then he frowned. "That's a joke."

We laughed nervously.

"I'll be your instructor for today. My assistant will be a former Marine you can call Beckett, who knows his way around the MCMAP. I usually run this class alone, but since he's in town, I decided to give him the privilege of helping. Some of you will be new to the MCMAP. Do what I say and you won't get hurt – too much."

Finally, Bulldog smiled, but it was hard to tell the difference between his angry face and his happy face.

Beckett took his place at Bulldog's side at the front of the class and surveyed us.

"Beckett will start with a warm-up," Bulldog said and motioned to Beckett.

Beckett nodded and turned to us. "All right, class. We're going to start with some yoga poses to limber you up. When we start the self-defense portion of the class, we don't want you pulling muscles or tearing ligaments."

"Yoga?" Leah whispered beside me. "Some bad boy…"

I kept my mouth shut and tried to follow Beckett as he moved through a few poses. I recognized some of them from a beginner's yoga video I'd watched on YouTube. Mountain Pose. Sun Salutation. Downward Dog. Warrior Pose. Tree Pose. Child's Pose. Cobra.

Triangle Pose.

Beckett and Bulldog walked around the room, correcting people's posture. Beckett stopped beside me while I was struggling to keep in Triangle Pose and helped position my body so that I was balanced properly.

"There you go," he said, his voice soft, his strong hands on my hips to steady me.

"Um, thanks," I said, feeling like a total spaz, hyper-aware of his touch, his hands warm. When I wobbled, he held me more tightly, his big hand splayed over my left hip, the other curving around my waist. A thrill went through me when his hand touched my bare midriff and I flushed, my cheeks hot.

"That's better," he said once I stabilized.

After he walked away, Leah glanced at me and wagged her eyebrows. "He *likes* you," she whispered.

"Get a *life*," I replied, rolling my eyes, but inside, I knew she was right.

After about ten minutes of yoga poses, we moved right into the self-defense portion of the class, and learned how to punch, how to defend against a punch, and how to fall.

I didn't puke after all.

I did, however, hurt my ass during break fall training. Leah and I worked together, but I kept my eye on Beckett Tate the Viking CEO, DEA Agent and ex-Marine, who spent time with several duos, showing them how to perform each move. When he came to Leah and me, he used me for the demonstration, putting me in proper position while explaining everything to Leah.

"I told you he likes you," Leah whispered when he moved on to another pair. "He had his hands—his nice strong hands—all over your body."

"Shh," I said and smiled to myself. "Down, girl."

After class was over, I felt elated, the endorphins from the workout stronger than the pain signals from my aching body. Not to mention a little buzz from all the attention Beckett paid to me.

Leah and I high-fived and went to the drinking fountain. Beckett stopped by, waiting after me for a drink.

"Good class," he said and smiled at me.

I have to admit that my heart skipped a beat when I looked in his eyes.

"If you like to break your bones," I replied.

"You did well for someone new to this. If you stick with it, you'll learn how to prevent broken bones. It's a great workout."

I smiled. "I was a bit surprised at the yoga part. You don't look like a yoga man."

"I'm a man of many talents," he said suggestively and then grinned. "Capable of moving my body into many positions, whether for warfare or other pursuits." He winked at me. "Just another superpower…"

I laughed with him.

"So what are you really doing back in Topsail Beach?"

"Are you interested?" he asked with a grin. "I'm available if you are and can offer you a variety of personal services…" He had this wicked expression in his eyes – an expression that sent a jolt of desire through me despite how hesitant I had been when I first saw him.

"Just curious."

He shrugged. "It's nice here. And as I said before, I had to arrange a retreat for my staff and thought this would be more private than somewhere in Wilmington. There's a convention in Wilmington I needed to attend and so I thought I'd kill two birds with one stone. Maybe we could get together for a drink?"

"Maybe," I said, not wanting to turn him down directly.

"That's better than no," he said and smiled.

I nodded but didn't say anything else, not knowing what else to say. He took a long drink, grabbed his things and left.

I wished at that moment that I had the gumption to invite him out for a drink. But I didn't and kicked myself mentally. He did offer his services…

I went to Leah's side.

"God, he's *hot*," Leah said, making a face of awe as we watched him walk to the men's locker room. "He looks great coming *and* going. That ass… I wish he would have taken off his turtleneck, though, so we could see his abs. What did he say to you?"

"Something about it being a good class and that I did well. Suggested we might have a drink…"

"I told you he has his sights set on you," she said, elbowing me. "What did you say?"

"I said maybe." I frowned. "He was just being friendly."

"You should encourage him. Have that drink. A nice summer fling is just what you need."

"I'm leaving in a few weeks," I protested.

"That's more than enough time, babe," Leah said and wagged her eyebrows. "One night would fix what ails you."

I rolled my eyes again but she was right. He seemed to single me out from everyone else for a little extra attention, but I doubted I would see him again and part of me was disappointed. Hell, part of me wished I could go to his hotel room and spend the entire weekend with him, but what would I tell Dan's parents?

"Now what?" I asked, hungry and wanting some food.

She laughed and wiped sweat from her brow. "Now we shower, dress and then work our shift and finally, we go out for a well-deserved drink."

I smiled. "I have to be at work early tomorrow and work all weekend so I can't be too late. I need some sleep."

"You can sleep when you're eighty," Leah said and grabbed my arm, pulling me down the hall. "You have to live now. We're going to the club tonight. It's Marla's birthday and she wants us all there. Besides, there's a bunch of Wall Street types in Wilmington for some convention. Don't worry, Cinderella. I'll get you home before your carriage turns into a pumpkin. Maybe I'll meet the future Mr. Grant."

"They're all psychopaths in suits."

"Hey!" she said and stuck her tongue out. "I'll have you know I almost dated a stockbroker by the name of Blake. I was *this* close," she said and held up two fingers, measuring about an inch. She wanted a rich stockbroker as a boyfriend or husband. She made a plan and it included moving back to Manhattan with me when I returned to finish my degree and going to clubs frequented by business students.

"Close only counts in horseshoes," I said as we walked down the hallway. "I married someone, and look where it got me."

She made a face, and I knew she felt bad once more for reminding me of my short experience with married life.

I was already starting to cramp up badly. Instead of a night at a fancy club with a hot stranger, I probably should have stayed at home with a hot water bottle and Advil but this was the start of my new life and I was going to live it to the max.

"I probably should stay at home," I said.

"You're coming out with me if I have to tie a leash on you and drag you out."

"I'm not that kinky," I said and grinned widely, dodging her when she tried to grab me.

"You're probably very kinky," she said with a laugh. "All the quiet ones are."

THAT AFTERNOON, once I'd finished daily cash, Dan's mother brought the mail to the restaurant before she left for the city. I stood at the bar and examined a letter addressed to me for clues. Thin, the letter was from the FBI and I was reluctant to open it. I'd applied for the Student Internship with the FBI, hoping to get some experience in the Bureau as a way to cement my application when I graduated. The envelope was far too thin to be anything but a rejection letter. Letters of acceptance most likely included information on when I'd start and probably forms to sign.

Leah had come and peered over my shoulder at the letter.

I went ahead and opened it.

It was from the Director, the Federal Bureau's Special Research Unit, Psychopathology.

Dear Miranda Parker,

I am pleased to inform you that you have been selected for the position of unpaid intern, and will be responsible for a variety of administrative and research duties in the Special Research Unit, the Federal Bureau of Investigation, Manhattan Division. Your term will begin on Monday, January 15 and will end on July 15...

"Oh my God," I said, totally excited, a sense of euphoria welling up inside of me. "I got it!" I checked the letter again. "I got the internship."

"No freakin' way," Leah said, grabbing the letter from my hand. "You go girl. Congrats!"

We hugged and danced around the kitchen.

"What did you get?" Steve asked, frowning.

"I got an internship with the FBI after Christmas!" I said and smiled, holding out the letter for him to see. He took it and read it over, his brow furrowed.

"This demands a celebration," Leah said. "Milano's tonight or bust!"

I flopped down on a barstool and took the letter back from Steve. "I'm broke. Milano's is expensive..."

Leah stood with her hands on her hips. "We're going. You said that either way, acceptance or rejection, we'd go. I got a hair appointment for later this afternoon," she said and fluffed her blonde tresses, "and I bought a new dress..."

She had such a mournful expression on her face that I knew I couldn't say no.

"I really can't afford to go out..." I protested, opening my wallet and counting up my change. "I have a shift tonight."

"Early shift. You'll be off by nine and can come right home, shower and you'll be ready for the fun to start You have to come out and celebrate!"

"I can only afford a beer," I said and shrugged. "We'll have to walk because I can't afford a taxi. Room and board at The New Yorker is twenty-two grand..."

"Never you worry," she said and pulled out her own wallet, retrieving a credit card – a VISA – and flashing it in my face. Probably from Daddykins, who was a rich investor.

"Okay," I said, feeling like a mooch, but a girl had to celebrate, right?

"Maybe we'll meet someone really hot," she said, leaning forward, her voice low. She wagged her eyebrows. "That will make up for it."

"Leah," I said, wearily. "Seriously, I'm not looking for a man."

"You are seriously in *need* of a man," she whispered, and wagged a finger at me. Steve was behind the bar, moving around, placing bottles back on shelves. He could overhear us and I frowned at Leah but she wasn't getting my hint to be quiet. "You are now re-virginized after a year with no sex – more, since Dan was gone for three months before…"

"Leah!"

She stopped short of saying the rest. Before Dan died.

"Anyway, you need to get out there and lose it fast. Get back in the saddle. Maybe Beckett will show up…"

"You are crazy," I said, making a face.

"We're going to Milano's," she said, her voice firm. "There's a convention of Wall Street money managers and brokers at the Yacht Club for a retreat. You might meet a millionaire who likes his women with a bit of flesh on her bones and all your problems will be solved."

Steve turned and watched us. "More likely to meet some hustler if they're from Wall Street," he said, disgust in his voice.

Leah shot him a look that could kill. Then she turned back to me and waved Steve off. She seemed so hopeful, as if Lady Luck was going to shine down on her any time.

On the other hand, I wasn't so sure that something more in line with Murphy's Law was more likely to be my fate. Besides, I couldn't imagine meeting anyone more attractive and desirable than Beckett Tate. He said he was staying at the Yacht Club and was going to give a talk to a group of investors. Maybe he'd be at the club.

I thought of a little black number that hugged my curves and displayed my boobage, and decided to suck it up. I doubted I'd meet a millionaire that night, but I might have a dance or two and a drink on Leah's credit card.

Beckett might even be there, but I didn't say anything about him. Leah seemed to forget him and so I needed to as well.

Leah grabbed my arm and pulled me out of the bar. When we were out of earshot of Steve, she squeezed me.

"Seriously, Mira, you should just hook up with Beckett. He was seriously into you and would probably be really hot in bed."

"I don't know..."

"Oh, you!" She crossed her arms and stood her ground. "Honestly, Mira. The longer you wait to have sex with someone, the harder it'll be."

"I want it nice and hard," I said and snorted at the look on her face.

She laughed with me for a moment but then turned serious. "Find someone. Get rid of your new virginity. Free yourself and move on. You know you have to do this eventually. If you pick up someone you'll never see again and have really hot but meaningless sex, it won't be such a huge deal when you do meet someone you like."

I took in a deep breath. There were days when I craved feeling a man inside of me, but it was so hard to imagine being with anyone. I fantasized about faceless men in my bed, making me come, and frequently woke up in the middle of the night, my body convulsing from the dream alone.

I needed a man. *Bad*.

Leah was right.

But Beckett? I wasn't so sure he was the right one. Despite being hot as hell, he was far too close to what I was used to.

He was too much like Dan.

WE ARRIVED at Milano's late, and the party was already in progress, the laser lights flashing, the dubstep blaring. People danced in clusters on the dance floor and the tables were packed with well-dressed and well-heeled men and women in their mid-twenties to late thirties. Waitresses in black miniskirts and white tops threaded their way through the tables to deliver drinks, and the VJ danced to his music on the far wall.

The music got to me right away and I wanted to dance and celebrate but we had to get a drink first and the only thing I drank at these places was beer or vodka coolers. I'd heard too many stories about women getting roofied to drink anything else.

I stood by the bar while Leah ordered and paid for our drinks. I ordered a local craft beer and she had a Bud Light. While I waited for her, I glanced around the bar and was startled when I saw Beckett. I recognized the dirty blond hair but instead of being unruly as it had been earlier, it was combed back and looked stylish instead of wild. Instead of wearing faded jeans and a leather bomber jacket, he wore an impeccable black suit, crisp white shirt and silky black tie. He looked like a million bucks and was deep in conversation with two other well-dressed men. When he turned and glanced over in my direction, *Holy Mother of God...*

He looked stunning, his blond hair tucked behind his ears and touching his collar, dark blond scruff on his very square chin and jaw, and those blue-grey eyes... I almost drooled, but succeeded in holding it in and when he smiled at me, I managed to smile back without giggling.

But it took a great deal of effort.

If he was going to be there, and if he was going to be even half as determined as before, I didn't know if I could resist.

At the same time, I glanced over and saw that Steve was there as well. He must have called in and got Kent to work at the last minute, because I could swear he had been on the schedule for the late shift.

He saw me and came right over, leaning in close.

"You look really nice tonight," he said and glanced over me. "I don't get to see you all dressed up very often."

"Why are you here?" I said in confusion. "I thought you closed tonight."

He shrugged. "I asked Kent to take my shift. He needs the money, so…"

I nodded. "Since I got accepted into the Intern program with the FBI," I said, grinning, "Leah and I are out celebrating."

"That's right. I didn't get a chance to congratulate you," he said and leaned in, kissing me on the cheek, his lips lingering a bit too long. He pulled back and held onto my shoulder. "That's amazing. Will you be in Manhattan or will you go to Virginia?"

"Manhattan," I said and forced a smile. I pulled away, uncomfortable that he was still holding onto me. Luckily, the bartender returned with our drinks. I glanced over and saw that Beckett reached for his own beer from the table. We each picked up a bottle of the same brand of artisanal beer and when he noticed, he smiled and came right over, nodding to me and Steve.

Steve visibly bristled like he was angry that Beckett came over.

"Excellent taste in beer as well as bourbon," he said to me in a very warm, sexy voice with just a hint of that Cajun accent. A grin cracked one side of his mouth and I wondered how it would feel on my various body parts, one in particular, which was currently perking up.

I held my beer up and we clinked the necks together. Leah was busy leaning over to speak to the cute Tall Dark and Handsome next to her.

"We meet again," he said, looking at me and then at Steve.

"You're back in town?" Steve said, his voice low.

"Yeah," Beckett said and stood up a little straighter. Not only was Beckett taller than Steve, he was also bulkier. "I'm holding a retreat for my staff and Topsail Beach is a very nice place to be." Beckett looked into my eyes and raised his eyebrows.

Steve said nothing. On my part, I felt a little thrill in my gut because of the way Beckett was looking at me. We stood smiling at each other, and I wished Steve would get a clue and leave us alone.

"It's like Fate is pushing us together," Beckett said. "Who am I to argue with Fate?"

Steve harrumphed at that and finally turned away.

"What are you doing here?" I said, glancing over him, noting his impeccable suit and tie. "I thought you were at a retreat…"

"Like I said," he said and smiled. "I'd tell you but I'd have to kill you."

I laughed and took a sip. "Okay, then," I said. "I'll give up on the interrogation."

"Just kidding," he said, as if thinking better of his Mr. Mysterious ploy. "Our session for the day was over and we have the evening off. I'm here with a few of my staff," he said. "But I'm glad to see you here. They want to talk shop and I'm fed up to my craw with work. I need a pleasant distraction. So tell me," he said and leaned his elbow against the bar. "What are you doing in Topsail Beach?" He leaned a bit closer to me, his gaze moving over me.

"It's a long story," I said, not really wanting to explain.

"I have all night." He tilted his head. "Want to go somewhere quiet? We could…talk."

I couldn't help but snort at that. "Talk…" I said in disbelief while my mind went through all the delicious possibilities.

"I'm serious," he said, putting on an innocent expression. "Why would you doubt me? There's a coffee shop down the street where we could sit and talk. And of course, it's incredibly convenient because the Yacht Club is just a half block away and my room is upstairs…"

"I just got here," I said in protest, although leaving with him right then and there sounded fantastic. "I came to dance and have fun. Besides, I'm here with Leah."

At that, he frowned. "She can't look after herself?"

When I didn't respond, he stepped closer. "Do you have a boyfriend?"

"No," I said.

"Whew," he said and wiped his brow dramatically. He grinned. "For a moment there I thought it would be sabers at dawn."

I laughed out loud at that. One thing was certain – Beckett was not shy about indicating his interest in me.

He was definitely interested.

"So, *Miranda*," he said and leaned closer. "Since you're here to dance and have fun, care to dance?"

I held up my beer. "Just got this," I said. "Don't like to leave a drink around just in case. You know," I said, then grimaced internally at my scintillating conversation, which hinted at anything but being fun.

He nodded. "Tell you what," he said and took the beer out of my hand. "You dance with me now, and I promise I'll buy you a fresh one."

I glanced over at Leah, who was busy flirting with her man.

Steve was standing beside us, staring at the bar like he was interested, but I was sure he was listening in.

"Sure," I said and Beckett took my hand. He led me to the center of the dance floor and when we arrived, I saw that Steve was watching us, leaning against the bar, his brow furrowed.

We danced, the music blaring, the laser lights bouncing around like crazy.

"I won't ask you if you come here often," Beckett said, leaning down to speak into my ear. "I have to come up with better conversation than that."

"I don't come here often," I answered back. "Leah does."

"Are you from this area?" he said, staying close, leaning in. His eyes roved down my face to my cleavage. "North Carolina, I mean."

"No," I said. "I'm from Queens, New York."

"Queens?" he said and made a face. "How did you end up here?"

"With Dan," I said and he nodded.

"I understand. The base is close by."

"His family's here. I just stayed behind after he passed."

He nodded and touched my arm sympathetically. "I understand. So, how about I ask you your future plans."

"Just got accepted as an intern for the FBI starting in January," I said, unable to keep a huge smile off my face. "When I finish my degree, I hope to join the FBI if they'll take me."

"Wow. A woman of substance as well as looks. No one new on the horizon?"

I shook my head. "I've been recovering for the past year."

He nodded. "I'm sorry. This must be hard for you. So, you're going to finish your degree?" He smiled. "Beauty and brains. My favorite combination. What are you studying?"

"Forensic Psychology."

He nodded but said nothing more and I was out of small talk – thank God. My small talk needed work big time. I'd been out of the dating scene for... well, since I met Dan during my first year at CUNY when he was on leave and on a trip to visit his uncle in Manhattan. We were together from then on, with Dan spending every weekend he could with me or I'd travel down to his parent's place in North Carolina. Before Dan, I'd been with my high school sweetheart who I met in my freshman year and dated until I started at CUNY.

Dating was not something I looked forward to.

I focused back on Beckett. What a gorgeous man... He was obviously interested in me and I felt a thrill of excitement go through me. I started classes in a few weeks, but I was going to have fun tonight. Serious research would commence then so until then, I was free.

We danced with nothing else being said for the music was really blaring now and I thought *fuck it*. When he put his hands on my hips and danced really close and sexy, swaying his own hips in time with mine, I put my hands on his shoulders and didn't complain. I was definitely feeling it, my mind moving to where I'd like those hands to go next.

We danced for at least five songs and I was starting to get really heated, not only from the dancing, but by the incredibly sexy way he moved in closer, leaning down so his face was beside mine, his lips at my ear, his breath warm on my skin.

Then, out of the blue, Steve appeared at our side and leaned over to me.

"Care if I cut in?" he said to Beckett.

Beckett glanced at my face, but when I said nothing, he stepped back and bowed.

"Be my guest." He shot me a meaningful glance and then turned back to the bar.

On my part, I turned to Steve and was frustrated. You didn't cut in on people anymore. That was so antiquated. You waited until the person finished dancing and then you asked them to dance the next song. You didn't cut in.

Unless you thought you had rights…

Did Steve somehow think he had rights to me?

Steve and I danced in silence for a few moments, and I wondered what the heck he was up to.

"Was there a reason you interrupted us when we were dancing? Some kind of important message or something?" I said, trying to keep the acid out of my voice.

"I don't like him," Steve said, leaning closer to me. "You know nothing about him."

"I'm not marrying him," I said. "I'm dancing with him. Besides, I know enough about him. He's a former Marine. He's a successful businessman. Dan saved his life over in Afghanistan. Or maybe Iraq. I'm not sure which. I know more than enough."

He sighed. "I care about you, Mira. I don't want you to be hurt. That's all."

"I'm a big girl," I said and glanced away. When the music shifted to another song, I was happy to stop dancing. I turned and went back to the bar, unsure if Steve was even following me.

Beckett was standing by himself at the bar, a fresh beer in his hand for me. I joined him and took the beer and we tapped bottles together lightly. He smiled while we each took a sip.

"Is he keeping watch over you?" Beckett said lightly.

"He thinks he's my big brother," I said and rolled my eyes.

Then, I forgot about Steve and stepped closer to Beckett. He also moved closer as well, his face just a few inches from mine.

"You're a good dancer," he said.

"You're not too bad yourself."

We smiled into each other's eyes.

Damn... There was nothing about this man I didn't like.

"Why not leave with me tonight?" he said, his elbow on the bar. "I promise to take you away from all this and make sure you don't regret it." Then he reached out and ran the backs of his fingers over my bottom lip, bending down and then kissing me, his mouth warm on mine.

We kissed for a long moment and my knees were weak with the prospect of finding out what he meant. When he pulled back, ending the kiss, I looked around for Leah, but she was on the dance floor with her tall dark and handsome stranger. Steve was standing a few people down at the bar. I caught him watching us, and he quickly glanced away.

When I turned back to Leah, she caught my eye as the song ended and came back before I could respond, laughing, her man trailing behind her, hand in hand.

"Hey, Mira!" She pulled him over. "This is Brandon. Brandon, this is my best friend Mira."

I smiled at Brandon "Nice to meet you." I turned to Beckett, who was watching me from over the top of his beer. "This is Beckett," I said and pointed to him.

"Mr. McNeil and I are old friends," Brandon said.

I glanced at Brandon and then at Beckett. *McNeil?* I said, frowning. My back stiffened. "Strange how I thought you were Cajun, not Irish..."

Had he *lied* to me? I saw his ID...

"I'm American. First Generation," Beckett said. "Father was born in Northern Ireland, and I was born in Hell's Kitchen. My parents separated when I was ten and I used my mother's maiden name, which is Tate," he said to Brandon, who nodded. "I use it for my business even though my legal name is McNeil."

"Of course," Brandon said and hit his forehead. "I forgot. Beckett Tate." He turned to me almost pointedly. "We knew each other in the Marines."

After a round of hellos, we stood there in silence. I didn't know what to say. Had he lied? Or was it a case of using his mother's name the way he said? He did say he had too many names...

Brandon took Leah's hand and pulled her back towards the dance floor. "You said you wanted to dance your head off. Let's go."

She winked at me and the two left Beckett and me alone.

I didn't know what to think but at that moment, I felt a sense of hesitation about any plans to go back to Beckett's hotel to 'talk.'

As if he sensed this, Beckett leaned in and whispered in my ear. "The music's too loud. Want to get out of here and go someplace quieter? More ... intimate?"

Steve's warning came back to me. "I don't know what to believe about you. CEO? DEA? McNeil? Who are you – really?"

"I told you I have too many names," Beckett said. "I use Tate now, for my business, but back when I was in the Marines, I went by my legal name, which is McNeil. I didn't mean to deceive you. It's just complicated..."

He smiled and he looked so damn desirable and so hot in that expensive suit.

I'd been scoping him out when he wasn't looking and admired once more his nice broad shoulders and how they pulled at the fabric of his jacket. I also noticed his nice narrow hips when he slipped a hand in his pocket and his jacket fell open. He smelled great. He was all man.

There was nothing about him that wasn't appealing but still I hesitated. I had no idea who he really was, and I was planning to work with the FBI... They expected discretion from their employees. When I'd applied to do a paid internship with them in the spring, I had taken a polygraph test and answered a series of questions, which seemed to focus on whether I engaged in risky behavior in my personal life. I had answered no, truthfully. So here I was, contemplating hooking up with Beckett.

"So, come have a coffee with me? Talk?" he said softly.

"I don't even know anything about you," I said. "For all I know, you could be a psychokiller, who'd tie me up and beat me black and blue."

He laughed at that. "I might tie you up, if you wanted me to," he said and leaned closer, smiling broadly, "but I'm not into pain. Besides, I don't know anything about you either. You could be a crazy bitch who wants me only for my money and that would make me so sad..." He pouted and then grinned widely, his smile brilliant, his eyes twinkling.

"Look," he said and stepped even closer, touching my chin with a finger. "We're both young and good looking and attracted to each other. Let's go to my hotel. It's very nice. We can have a drink and you can decide if you want anything to happen." He brushed a lock of my hair back. "You have nothing to fear from me."

"I'll think about it," I said.

"If you don't want to go to my hotel room just yet, why not go out for something to eat? There's a great bakery that stays open late. We could get a coffee and a pastry. They do a great Napoleon slice."

I inhaled and made a decision I hoped I wouldn't regret. "Sure," I said. "Coffee sounds great." I took out my cell and sent Leah a text.

I'm leaving with Beckett for coffee. I trust you're a big enough girl to get home on your own...

Then I turned and followed Beckett, my hand in his. Before I got outside, I turned back and saw Steve following us with his eyes. I wished he would just get a life and quit being my big brother. Then I put Steve out of my mind and I let Beckett lead me outside and into the warm summer night.

BECKETT

I TOOK her hand and pulled her out of the club. The vehicle that I had hired to ferry my guests around the island waited at the curb. The driver threw down his smoke and opened the rear passenger door when we walked up.

"Sir."

I shook my head. "We're walking down the street to the bakery. Follow us and wait outside."

The driver nodded and got inside the car, starting the engine.

"You have a driver?" Miranda said, surprise evident in her voice.

I shrugged. "Just for the weekend. I don't drink and drive."

I took her hand and we strolled down the street. I enjoyed the warm night air and the prospect that if all went well, Miranda might actually come to my hotel room with me.

As we walked along the boardwalk, we talked about ourselves. She told me about her degree and classes and I told her about mine. I already knew most of what she told me and felt like a complete fraud when I pretended to be surprised, but I was in so deep at that point, I had no idea how to extricate myself even if I wanted to.

"You went to business school?" she asked, her eyes bright.

"Stanford, after I came back from Afghanistan."

"Stanford? Beauty and brains," she said and smiled, mirroring my own words. "My favorite combination."

I laughed. "You see?" I said and squeezed her hand. "You should just come to my hotel room and fuck me now."

That got her attention and she gave me a laugh, shaking her head at me. I was blunt, but I didn't like to lead women on. If I wanted one, I let her know. I let her know what I wanted and what she could have from me beforehand so there'd be no miscommunication. No regrets.

"Don't look at me like that," I said, smiling. "It's true. We'd be almost at my hotel if you agreed and in no time at all, we'd be getting off on each other's bodies."

She looked away. "If all I wanted was an orgasm, I could get one myself easy enough with my magic wand."

Oh, man… That got me right in the dick. I loved that she could dish it out as much as take it.

"Sure, so could I," I said, grinning widely. "It's always much more fun to have someone help you with that."

"I like to know what I'm getting before I buy," she said, a smug look on her face. "You know – kick the tires, look under the hood so I don't end up with a lemon."

I laughed out loud. "You can look under my hood any time." I glanced her way only to see her trying her best not to smile. "But I'm not for sale or rent. I'm all about giving it away. Helping those in need. Philanthropy, you know."

She grinned at that. "I'm sure there's always someone in need that you can help."

I smiled as we arrived at the coffee shop and I held the door for her. "Beautiful ladies first."

We went inside and stood in front of the display of pastries. The staff person came over to the counter.

"We'll take a couple of coffees and a Napoleon slice, two forks," I said.

Mira turned to me, a look of amusement on her pretty face. "Do you always order for your date?"

"Always," I said and leaned closer to her, trapping her against the counter, my arms almost around her. "I like to take control. When I dance, I lead."

That was the truth. I did like to lead – in all things in business and mostly in pleasure, although I loved it when a woman felt secure enough to take charge during sex.

I led her to a small table by the window and pulled out her chair. We sat and watched the traffic on the street while we waited for the server to bring our food.

"So, tell me more about yourself," Mira asked, her eyes on me, an inquisitive expression on her face. "First, how did Dan save your life? I searched the Military Times for mention of your name, but didn't find anything about any accident you were involved in."

I glanced down, realizing I had to tell her something. It was only fair.

"It was an operation that's classified. I can't tell you anything else, but he saved my life. That's really all I can say. He was a very brave man."

That seemed to satisfy her, at least for now.

"How is it you have a DEA badge and run a business?"

I had to tell her something, but I didn't want to get into the whole business of my DEA career. Or my family, for that matter.

"I showed you my badge so you wouldn't worry about the gun. You should just forget you ever saw that badge." I raised my eyebrows suggestively.

Mira nodded and appeared satisfied a second time. Her life growing up as the child of an FBI Special Agent must have prepared her for dealing with clandestine business. Plus, if she intended to get into the FBI, she understood discretion.

After our food arrived, we talked about ourselves for a while, and she asked me question after question about who I was and why I signed up.

"I was too young on 9/11 or I would have signed up right away," I said, remembering how I felt after the attacks. "When I was old enough, I'd already started at Stanford. When we started getting reports about how bad it was in Fallujah, I decided it was now or never."

She looked at me like she respected my answer. "How long were you in?"

"Only five years. When I came back home, I finished my degree at Stanford and started my own business. The rest is history."

That was just about enough info on me. I decided to turn the tables and focus on her. I didn't want to talk about myself anymore, especially my father's side of the family, and I was genuinely interested in her. I knew a lot about her fallen husband, but very little about her.

"So tell me about you. You want to work for the FBI…"

She told me about her father, and how he was killed in the line of duty.

"Some guy wanted for racketeering. I guess the man didn't want to go back to jail and there was a shootout."

"Did the bad guy die?"

She shook her head. "No," she said, her eyes distant like she was remembering. "He went to jail."

I nodded, but something about her story rang a bell with me. I remembered hearing about a shootout in Hell's Kitchen and an FBI Agent being killed. There was a lot of talk about it among my uncle's thugs. "That must have been hard. When did he die?"

"Five years ago. It was hard," she said, and I could see she was still affected by the memory. "My mother fell apart. She hasn't been the same since."

"So you have law enforcement in your blood," I said, trying to change the subject to something less painful.

"Born and bred. Gramps was in Korea and then NYPD until he retired to run a bar in Queens."

"See?" I said and held out my hand. "You and I have so much in common, besides mutual attraction."

She smiled at that and I was pleased that in addition to us being physically attracted to each other, we actually could admire each other. Casey would love her.

"What bar does he run in Queens?"

"It's called *The Harp and Keg* and is frequented by the cops from the local precinct. What about your biological father?" she asked, sipping her coffee.

We'd veered back into my life and I didn't want to have to explain any of the connections we had with the Irish underworld in Hell's Kitchen.

"He died, left the business to his gangster brother after I moved away with my mother and her new husband. That's pretty much all you need to know about that side of the family."

I tried to get the topic back onto her life and so I asked her about Dan. She wasn't going to talk about him. I wondered if she felt guilty, considering the anniversary of his death was fast approaching.

"Don't want to talk about it?"

She shook her head. "It's a sad story in the past. That's all you need to know about it."

"Fair enough." I knew I couldn't push her for more after that.

Her cell buzzed and she checked it. I got a text almost at the same time. I read it and smiled.

"Brandon and Leah," I said softly, wondering what her response would be to the fact her friend and my friend were going to the hotel.

"Yes. I just got a text from her saying I'd have to find my own way home."

She looked a bit uncomfortable and yawned, checking her watch like she wanted to go home.

"Bored with my company already?" I asked, almost resigned to the fact she wouldn't come back to my hotel room.

"I have to work in the morning," she replied and smiled, shrugging like there was nothing she could do about it.

"At the bar?"

She nodded. "I do the daily cash in the mornings."

"I can make sure the hotel gives us a wake-up call…" I said, ever hopeful but not really believing it would happen.

She shook her head and smiled almost apologetically. "I have to go home."

I sighed and finally, she leaned forward.

"Beckett," she said, not meeting my eyes. "I really like you, but I can't…"

"Why? If you like me and I like you, what's wrong?"

"There are reasons," she replied.

"Are you dating someone?" I asked, even though I knew the answer but I wanted to be sure she wasn't dating someone and my intel was wrong.

She shook her head.

"Engaged?" I asked, feeling a bit like a fraud, since I knew she wasn't.

"No," she said simply. "If I was, I wouldn't even be going out for coffee with anyone."

"Are you a lesbian?" I asked, grinning, hoping to make her smile.

"No!" she said and looked up at me, but then she smiled back. "Not that there's anything wrong with that."

I laughed. "I don't see that there's anything keeping you from enjoying my manly assets, which are at your disposal."

I knew she was probably going to say no, but I wanted to give her every chance. I hoped she would take it, but given her history, I had my doubts.

She looked like she wanted to say yes, but couldn't.

"I really should go home now," she said and checked her watch again.

"Let's walk a bit first." I offered her my hand, wanting to postpone our parting. "It's such a beautiful warm night."

I took her hand and led her out of the café. Then we talked about nothing in particular but everything at the same time – her classes, Brimstone, everything except what was hanging between us – whether she would come with me to my hotel room.

After about fifteen minutes, I stopped and waved to the driver of the limo. "Let's drive the rest of the way."

The driver got out and opened the door. I helped Mira in, trying to be as much of a respectful gentleman as I could muster.

"Where to, Sir?"

"The hotel."

Mira glanced at me. I was going to try to convince her, but only very gently. When we drove off, I put my arm around her shoulders and helped her with her seatbelt. She was nervous – I could tell by the way she smiled, her mouth quivering a bit. She was so beautiful, her long auburn hair falling softly on her shoulders, her cheeks flushed from the walk. Her dress hugged her delicious curves and yet wasn't over the top sexy.

"You have a delicious mouth," I said. "I want to kiss it again. I've wanted to kiss it again ever since you kissed me."

Then I did kiss her, and she let me. In fact, more than let me – she kissed me back and that gave me hope.

I wanted her so much. My reasons were just as venal as any other hot red-blooded American male. She was beautiful and desirable, but also, I wanted to do more than just fuck her. I wanted her to want me. I wanted her to be helpless to refuse her own desire for me.

I slipped my hand from her shoulder to her waist, and then around her nicely curved hip. I broke the kiss and looked in her eyes.

"Your body is so lush." I kissed her again and continued to explore her body, my hand roving over her silky dress, down her thigh to her knee, and then up between her legs.

Of course, the car stopped in front of the Yacht Club at that precise moment. I pulled away. "The driver will take you home from here."

Then I brushed hair from her cheek, and kissed her once more, this time, more deeply, needing to impart some of my desire for her so she knew that if she wanted me, I was hers.

When I pulled away, her eyes were closed like she was swept up with desire.

"Come up with me," I whispered.

"I'm not…" she whispered, and I could hear regret in her voice.

"I know you're not," I said and put a finger to her lips. "It's just so rare to meet someone who is so perfect for me in every way. I can't stand the thought of you just walking out of my life."

I stepped out of the car before turning back to her.

"Come upstairs with me, Miranda," I said and took her hand, pulling her out with me, gently. "Don't leave me out here counting stars…"

MIRANDA

BECKETT STOOD AT ARMS-LENGTH, a slight tug on my hand. I took him in—tall, blond, well-built, narrow hips, his hair now a bit wild, his blue eyes heated. He looked like a million dollars in his suit and crisp white shirt, black silk tie.

He was the most gorgeous man I had ever seen, let alone imagined being with.

I let him pull me, giving in – to him and to my own desires.

WE WALKED in silence into the hotel, a high-end three-story building attached to the private marina. Inside was all dark wood and brocade wallpaper with thick Persian carpets and mirrors everywhere. We passed the concierge and took the elevator and I was glad it came right away, because I didn't know what to say to him, now that I'd decided to go to his room. This was the part of a date I had little experience with and felt awkward, but Beckett seemed as if he knew what he was doing so I let him lead.

Once inside the elevator, and as the lone occupants, he continued the kiss, pulling me against him as he leaned on the elevator wall. My body warmed in response to the touch of his

tongue, his hands gliding over my back and lower, not quite grabbing my ass, just resting above it but low enough to remind me
how close he was. I kissed him back, hungry for him, my eyes
closed tightly, just giving myself over to the sensations he elicited
in my body with his touch. It had been so long since I was in a
man's arms and felt his hard body against mine that I couldn't
stop, and shoved my guilt down deep.

He took my hand when the elevator door opened and pulled
me down the hallway to a room on the third floor, past gilded
mirrors and deep gold brocade wallpaper, the furniture dark
wood with ornate carving and paintings of old ships. After he slid
the keycard into the door lock, he opened the door and pulled me
inside as if he feared I'd change my mind at the last minute. He
didn't have to worry for if I was on the fence before about what
was going to happen, I wasn't any longer. I wanted this.

I wanted *him*.

He led me in deeper into the dark interior of his luxurious
suite, equipped with a full living room and bar and kitchenette. I
barely noticed the décor as he took my hand and led me through
the suite, except that it was dark grey and white and burnished
silver – very masculine. We went into a separate bedroom with a
huge king bed and stood beside it, kissing once more, our hands
on each other, now more intimate since we were alone and in his
bedroom. He pulled me more tightly against his body, pressing his
erection against me, sending a jolt of lust to my core, my breath
hitching. His hands roved over my body, down to cup my buttocks
and then up to squeeze my breasts through the fabric of my dress.

"Let me get this off," he said as he reached down to the hem of
my dress and pulled it up and over my head. I struggled a bit to
get it over my head, but soon it was off and I stood before him in
nothing but my heels, lace bra and thong. He took me in despite
the dimness of the room, letting out a low whistle.

"You are so lush…"

I started to remove my heels, but he stopped me.

"Keep them on."

I nodded, a shaky smile on my lips. Then he almost devoured me, his mouth moved down from my lips to my chin. He sat on the side of the bed and pulled me into his arms, his lips sliding down the skin of my neck to one breast, pushing aside the fabric to reveal my nipple. He sucked it into his mouth, sending stabs of desire through my body right to my clit. I squirmed helplessly, almost panting with desire.

"I have to see you," he said and left me to turn on a bedside light, the lamp casting a warm glow over the room.

When he returned to me, I reached up and pulled off his jacket. "My turn," I said, my voice wavering from desire. He helped me, throwing his jacket onto a chair against the wall, then we both attacked his tie and cuffs, until I was able to unbutton his white shirt, opening it to reveal hard washboard abs, just as I expected. He removed his shirt and finally, he was bare from the waist up.

I ran my hands over his chest and down to his abs, my eyes lingered on his pants, which revealed a lovely bulge from his more-than-ample erection, but before I started to unfasten his belt, I ran my tongue over his chest to one nipple and he let out a low moan when I circled it with my tongue.

It was then I saw a thick scar on his neck, running ragged from a few inches beneath one ear to the middle of his neck.

As if someone had tried to slash his throat or behead him.

The edges still had a sewn-up look, faint dots beside the seam where the knots of each stitch had been. Whoever sewed him up did it really quickly.

It wasn't a surgical scar -- that was for sure. It was an injury, the stitches looked like they saved his life but only just.

"Oh, my *God*," I said, unable to help myself, stepping back. "How..."

He sighed and covered his eyes with a hand, then pounded his temple with a fist. "I'm so sorry, Miranda. I didn't think…"

"What is that?" I said, my throat tight. "What happened? Is that what Dan did to save your life?"

He sighed heavily. "I'm so sorry you had to see it."

"Was that in Iraq or Afghanistan?" I said, undeterred, every ounce of desire seeping out of me. "Were you attacked?"

He nodded. "Shrapnel from an IED."

The scar brought everything back to me – learning of Dan's death in Afghanistan during a routine training mission. Two uniformed men driving up to the house, getting out, their hats in hands. Jeanne crumpling onto the floor as she realized what their presence meant. Me running to the back of the house, not wanting to hear the truth, covering my ears as if that could prevent it from being true.

Dan was dead…

"I…" I swallowed hard, my desire drowned in a wave of emotion that still felt like grief even almost a year from the day I got the news. "I don't know…"

"Don't," he said and reached out for me. "Don't pull away." He tried to embrace me again, but I couldn't respond, my mind returning again and again to the war and to Dan. "Let it go."

"It's just that," I said, my voice cracking. "Dan…"

He touched my face, his fingers caressing my cheek, tracing my lips. "Tell me."

"You know that Dan was killed in Afghanistan a year ago…" I didn't want to say another word, because it was still raw – the emotion connected to his memory. "I wrote those letters to him while he was there."

He nodded. "I know. I'm sorry," he said and took my hands in his, kissing them tenderly. "I read about the accident. That's how I found you to return your letters. I understand." Then he pulled me into his arms and we stood together and I let him hold me.

I relaxed a bit, but the desire that had built up in me from his kiss and touch, from the feel of his body against my hands, his scent, all died when I thought about Dan.

Dammit!

"I'm sorry," I said and looked up at his face, forcing a smile. "It made me think of the war and…"

He nodded but kept me in his arms. "I understand."

We stood like that for a while, his arms wrapped around me, my head against his bare shoulder.

"Do you want me to take you home or will you stay?"

I sighed. "I should go home."

He sighed heavily in turn. "Will you have dinner with me tomorrow night?" He tilted up my face and looked in my eyes. "We can sit out on the deck at Louis's Backyard and enjoy the sunset. Talk. Take up where we left off – whatever you want."

"I work tomorrow from five until ten."

"A late supper? They serve food until midnight."

I smiled at his persistence. "I'd like that."

"Whew," he said and wiped his brow dramatically. "I don't want to leave without seeing you again."

He bent down and kissed me and it was tender rather than passionate and I felt a stab of regret that this happened.

"You have to understand," I said, my voice soft. "I've been with two men in my life. My childhood sweetheart and Dan. It's not easy for me…"

"I do understand," he said and frowned. "I'm sorry that I didn't warn you about my scar. It really creeps out some women…"

"It doesn't creep me out at all," I said and shook my head, surprised that anything about Beckett could creep any woman out. He was just way too gorgeous. "Is that why you wear a turtle-neck even in the summer?"

He nodded. "I don't like to have to answer questions about how I got it. Most people aren't ready for the truth."

I understood completely. I didn't really want to know what happened to him, for it brought back too many memories of the time just after Dan was killed, when we tried so hard to find out what happened, but only got a few reports about the crash in the storm. It was a terrible time in my life and in the life of Dan's parents and family.

The thought Dan saved his life made everything so much more complicated. It was like something that bound us together even though we were strangers.

I slid out of his arms and picked up my dress, pulling it over my head and smoothing my hair, while he put his shirt back on. He left the top buttons of his shirt undone and then pulled on his jacket.

"Let's go. I'll take you home."

I stopped him, my hand on his arm.

"I'm really sorry."

"No apologies," he said and touched my chin with his thumb. "When you're ready – hopefully before I leave – we can try again if you want. I know I want it."

"I do," I said, kicking myself mentally for my reaction. "I really do. It was just a shock. I didn't know it would bring me back like that."

He smiled softly. "Next time, you won't be shocked. I'll make sure to wear a plain old t-shirt and you'll look at it all during our date. By the end of the night, it'll be old hat."

He grinned, a mischievous expression in his blue-grey eyes, and I couldn't help but smile back.

"I look forward to it."

"Good."

Then the driver took us to Dan's house. Beckett sat close beside me, talking along the way about Brimstone, the company he created when he returned from the Middle East. When we arrived at Dan's house, he kissed me once more, long and deep before I left the car. I stood on the front porch and watched the limo drive away.

How amazing to meet someone so much like Dan…

THE NEXT DAY, I met Leah at the restaurant for breakfast and sat on the deck, talking about the night before.

"So," she said, wagging her eyebrows. "Was your night as hot as mine? Brandon's a god. Beckett looks pretty damn hot, too."

"We didn't," I said and couldn't meet her eyes. I braced myself, for I knew what was coming.

To my surprise, she said nothing. I glanced at her and she was staring out at the ocean, which was calm and relatively quiet.

"You're not going to say anything?" I said with shock. "You're not going to tell me that I had to lose my re-virginity? That I needed to move on?"

She shrugged and then turned to face me with a sneaky smile. "I don't have to. You said it all yourself."

We smiled and I took a sip of my coffee, twirling Dan's wedding ring on my middle finger. I wanted to talk about what happened. I waited for her to ask me.

"Tell me," she said. "You know you want to…"

"He was so hot," I said immediately. "We made it to his bed. He took off my dress, and I took off his shirt, and then, BAM. End of story."

"Why? Was he deformed or something?"

I shook my head. "He has this scar," I said and motioned to my neck to show her where on Beckett the scar was located. "He got it in Afghanistan. Dan saved his life. Seeing it brought back too many memories and put a stop to things."

"Oh, I'm so sorry, sweets," she said and reached out to touch my arm. "I never saw any scar on him so I bet it came as a shock."

"It did," I said and nodded. "It looked like someone tried to behead him and that made me think of Dan and how he died."

"Did you ask Beckett what happened?"

I shook my head. "He didn't want to talk about it," I said. "I didn't really want to talk about it either. I felt so awkward and embarrassed but he said it was shrapnel from an IED explosion."

"What was he like? I mean, was he upset that you guys stopped?"

"He felt really bad but he was super nice and understanding. We're having dinner tonight when I get off work. Maybe try again."

"Oh, good," she said and smiled. "You need it, hun, more than anyone I know."

"I do," I said with a laugh. "I'm in serious need of a babe like Beckett. Someone like him is a great sendoff to my old life and the start of my new one."

She and I clinked our coffee cups together and sat watching the surf for the next fifteen minutes, until I needed to start the daily cash out from the night before. Dan's mom, Jeanne, taught me to do the daily cash as a way for me to earn money and stay in Topsail Beach with them for the whole year so I didn't have to go back and face real life. They understood that Dan was everything to me, besides my grandfather in Queens and my studies. Without Dan, I felt lost, without anything to ground me. Staying with them for the year I took off from my studies had been healing. They were both so understanding and loving.

It made up for the loss of Dan and an absent mother and dead father.

Now, I'd be moving to Manhattan to finish my degree – finally – and then do my internship. I'd apply for the FBI when I was done with my Master's Degree, which was in another two years.

We cleared up our dishes and I went into the office while Leah went to the prep area to help get things ready for the lunch crowd.

DAILY CASH TOOK about three hours total, so it was after lunch when I was finished. I had lunch with Leah once she had cashed out, and we sat back on the deck, off to the side once the other patrons had gone. "You're working tonight?" she said, although she knew my shift as well as her own. "I'm off tonight and seeing Brandon for dinner and then we're going to Milano's again. He likes to dance as much as I do."

"Yes. I get off at ten and we're going to have a late dinner."

"Good," she said and squeezed my hand. "When you go back to Manhattan, you'll be a brand new un-virginized woman, ready to face the future."

"Un-virginized. Honestly," I said with a grin, "I don't know where you get your material."

She stood, and leaned down, pecking me on the cheek. "I'm here every Thursday through Saturday." She winked at me and then left me alone.

On my part, I went back home and had a shower, changing into my work clothes. I ran into Jeanne on my way out.

"How are you doing, sweetheart?" she said, stopping in the doorway to her home office. "I've barely spoken with you for a week, it seems."

"I'm fine," I said with a smile. "Been busy taking extra shifts. Went out dancing last night."

"Good for you," she said and came closer to me. She was in her fifties and was still attractive, with her salt and pepper hair in a bob, her makeup meticulous, and dressed in something business casual. "You know, it's time for you to get out and meet people again. Dan would want it."

I glanced away, not sure what Dan would want.

"I mean it," Jeanne said, turning me around and looking me straight in the eyes. "He wouldn't want you to become a spinster. He loved you and wanted you to be happy. So," she said and leaned closer. "Be happy."

We hugged and I didn't say anything but it made me feel so good to hear that from her lips. For the past few months, I'd become a bit stir crazy, spending all my time at the restaurant working in the bar or doing the cash in the morning. My only relief was Leah. She was a godsend. I was so lucky to have a friend who was willing to help me through the hard times in my life.

I PULLED the afternoon shift as a bartender and instead of Steve, Brent worked in his place. The usual crowd came in – local workers finishing their shifts, tourists looking for a drink and dinner in the restaurant, young people partying it up. I wondered if Beckett would show up and when, but by nine o'clock, he was still a no-show. I thought he might arrive early and sit at the bar so we could talk. Perhaps he'd changed his mind. Maybe I was more trouble than I was worth.

I was so attracted to him, and last night would have ended up in bed – on the bathroom counter, on the floor – wherever. If only it hadn't been for that scar of his…

When I thought about last night, I cringed inwardly. Why would any guy put up with someone like me – so hesitant to take the plunge? He was hot enough that he could have any woman he wanted. I was certain that he had no trouble getting some if and when he wanted.

So why keep after me? Sure, I was attractive enough. I ran a hand over my hair, which was long and thick and straight and a shade of red that was almost auburn. I was told I had nice eyes – Dan used to tell me I had bedroom eyes, whatever that meant. My figure was curvy – what Beckett called lush. I had decent enough fashion sense, when I had a need to use it.

But overall, there were more attractive women at the bar last night. Beckett could have gone home with anyone else. I saw other woman looking at him, checking him out, talking to each other about him.

He wanted *me*.

In other words, I wasn't an easy lay, which he could have with any number of women. I was complicated. I had issues. I would take time.

Why me? I just couldn't get that question out of my mind, and my confidence wasn't high enough to say why not?

I had to conclude that there was something special about him and about us. Our lives were linked because of Dan.

I sighed to myself and shut it off, deciding not to second guess myself any longer. Thing was, I was not used to one-night stands. In fact, I'd never had one. I had been with two men in my life and so I was used to meaningful relationships – not meaningless fucks.

Last night, I just wanted to feel Beckett inside of me. I wanted to feel like a desirable woman again – the way Dan made me feel.

About a quarter hour before my shift was scheduled to end, I was starting to think that Beckett stood me up, when he arrived, dressed the way he looked when he first walked into the bar – faded jeans, thick black belt, leather riding boots, a white t-shirt, and a black leather jacket, his helmet under his arm.

Damn, he was hot. Seriously a babe. His hair had been recently washed and was still a bit wet, but the ends were drying. He looked like he'd just stepped out of a shower. Or off the beach or swimming pool.

He gave that brilliant smile when our eyes met across the bar, and my cheeks heated in response. As long as I didn't do something really stupid tonight, I'd probably end up fucking him later and that knowledge sent a wave of desire through my body, ending with a pleasant throb.

"Hey, lovely lady," he said as he walked up to the bar and claimed a stool. He put his helmet on the stool next to him and sidled up to the bar, his hands folded. He leaned forward. "You look like a glass of water to a man dying of thirst."

I laughed and raised my eyebrows. "That's high praise," I said and grinned. "I'm wearing a black t-shirt, black jeans, Doc Martens and a green apron. I bet I look like a working stiff, not some glass of water..."

"You do to me." He smiled and we locked eyes for a moment.

"What can I get for you? Woodford Reserve or something different?"

He leaned back and eyed the bottles lining the shelves behind and on either side of me. "I'm thirsty. How about a nice glass of draft? Whatever's on tap."

I listed the various draft beer we had on tap and he chose a local craft beer as he had the night before. I pulled him a pint and placed it on the bar in front of him, along with a paper coaster.

"Busy day?" I asked, trying to make conversation.

"Lots of meetings and talks with potential clients," he replied. "And a nice long ride along the island."

"It's beautiful, isn't it?"

He nodded enthusiastically. "You're lucky to live here. My dream is to have a nice cottage on a cliff somewhere warm overlooking the ocean. You know, one of those cottages with nautical decorations," he said and glanced around the bar. "Like this place has. Shells, paintings of old ships. Everything beach and sand and surf."

"Sounds fantastic."

I poured a drink and then turned back to Beckett. "Tell me more about Brimstone," I said, wanting to give him the chance to talk about himself. "When did you start it, where did you get the idea?"

He took a sip of his beer and nodded. "I'm ultimately interested in how artificial intelligence can play a support role in the military. How it can improve communications and make for better outcomes. I was in a recon unit in Iraq and our biggest problem was communicating intel about potential threats when we found them. When I got back, it seemed logical for me to try to turn my computer skills to good instead of evil."

I laughed at that. "You mean instead of making a zillion dollars in computer games?"

"Exactly," he said. "Although we are creating computer games of a sort, but as a way to teach soldiers how to use our technology."

Then he spent the next fifteen minutes telling me about Brimstone while I cleaned up my pour station and restocked my end of the bar so I could get off shift. I finally finished and untied my apron, hanging it up and ducking under the bar hatch.

"I have to go and sign out and do my cash-out," I said, taking my cash tray out of the till. "I'll be about ten. Do you mind waiting?"

Beckett shook his head. "No prob. I'll finish my beer and watch the game." He turned around on his stool and faced the flat screen TV that was on the opposite wall.

On my part, I went to the back of the restaurant and did a quick cash out, signing my deposit and placing it in the safe in the office. Then I went to the bathroom and checked myself out in the mirror. I'd had a long day of work and felt like I needed a shower. In fact, I knew I needed one. I wondered what Beckett would think if I asked to have a shower at his place, because I didn't want to take him home to Dan's parent's place while I had a shower there. But I also wanted to be able to go back to his room, if the evening went that way.

I decided to get him to drop me off at home. I'd have a quick shower, change my clothes, and then I'd meet him for dinner.

Jeanne did say I needed to make a new life for myself...

Still, it made me cringe a bit inwardly that Scott and Jeanne would know I was seeing someone new – so close to the anniversary of Dan's death on top of it.

I left the office and went out to the bar, pulling up and sitting on the stool beside Beckett. He turned and smiled when he saw me and then leaned in, kissing me softly on the lips before I could even think.

"So, are you hungry?" he asked.

I looked in his eyes, wondering if he was serious or was hoping we'd go right back to his hotel.

"I'm starving. I haven't eaten anything but bar garnish since noon." I checked my watch. It was now ten fifteen.

"What do you feel like? I'd love some fish."

"Sounds good to me," I said with a smile. "You said Louis's Backyard? It's pretty decent seafood."

"Great," he said and finished his glass of beer. He stood and waved to the door, and then he offered me his arm. I took it and we walked out of the bar and into the warm late summer night.

"Before we eat, do you mind if I go home and have a quick shower and change?" I asked. "I feel pretty grimy after a long shift. You could drop me off and then I could meet you there."

He stood by his bike, where a helmet was attached to the rear seat. "Look at me," he said and pointed to his jeans and t-shirt. "I'm not all gussied up."

I laughed at that. "I need a shower. I need clean clothes."

He smiled. "Sure. I do, too. I'll go back to the hotel and change. I can go to Louis's and get a table. They have a nice patio overlooking the beach. Check out the stars."

"Do you mind? I feel a bit weird bringing a strange man to the house."

"Strange?" he said with a grin. "I'll have you know I'm a completely middle of the road kind of guy. Don't let this suave and debonair exterior fool you."

We both smiled and I took the spare helmet from him, pulling it on and fastening the strap. He did the same and then sat on the bike, starting it up and revving the engine. I sat behind him, my feet on the bars and my arms on his shoulders.

"Hold on tight," he said and we zoomed off. I had to slip my arms around him, and it felt so good, holding onto a man like that. We drove down the street to Scott and Jeanne's house and he stopped the bike and took off his helmet when I took off mine.

"Don't stand me up," he said, looking at me from the corner of his eye. "I'll be waiting for you at Louis's."

"I won't stand you up," I said, shaking my head. I handed him the helmet. "I'm hungry. They have great fresh fish and crab cakes."

"Sounds great." He smiled once more and leaned in, kissing me on the lips before I could pull back. Part of me wanted to stop him, push him away in case Scott or Jeanne were looking out the window. In fact, I was certain they were looking out the window, given the sound of Beckett's bike. The other part of me ached for his touch and didn't want to care who saw me with Beckett. I loved that he was so affectionate, kissing me when we met and parted, touching me, smiling. He seemed really attentive and that made me feel so desirable.

I hadn't felt that way for a long, long time...

"See you soon," I said and smiled.

"I'll be waiting."

Then, he put his helmet back on and revved the engine, driving off back the way we came.

I turned and went inside, closing the door softly behind me. I put my bag down and removed my shoes, then took the stairs to the second floor where my bedroom and ensuite bathroom were. I hoped I'd be able to quickly shower and change my clothes without having to face Scott or Jeanne, but my hopes were dashed when I heard someone closing the door to the living room.

"Mira?" Jeanne said. "You home to stay?"

I stopped on the stairs and turned to face her. "No," I said, my voice a bit wavery from nerves, a wave of guilt filling me that I was going out with a new man. "I'm meeting a friend at Louis's Backyard for a late supper."

"That's nice, dear," she said and smiled. "Don't let me keep you." Then, she went back into the living room and closed the door behind her.

I sighed in relief that she didn't press me on who I was meeting. I tried to quell the guilt that filled me, but it was hard, my throat a bit choked from emotion. I pushed it out of my mind and went to my room, quickly showering, changing into a more casual sundress, and sandals. I put on a touch of mascara and lip gloss and then finished drying my hair. Once I was done, I called a taxi and waited outside, hoping that neither Jeanne or Scott came out to check on me.

Then I went to him.

BECKETT

O<small>N THE WAY</small> back to the hotel, I considered what I should do. Did I really want to keep seeing Miranda?

Part of me, the hot blooded man part, said damn straight. We were attracted to each other. No doubt about it. Sex would be fantastic for us both. I'd make sure of that.

The drive back to the hotel was spent debating with myself. I knew that I was trying to rationalize my own desire for her. I couldn't deny that I wanted her. Maybe all it could be was a great erotic encounter between us. Nothing more. If that was good enough for her, why did she need to know anything else?

It wasn't like I planned on marrying her or anything…

I finished my shower and stood on the patio overlooking the water, staring across the expanse of sand to the surf below. The roar of the waves filled my ears, but all I could think of was Miranda and how much I wanted her. I wanted to be with her and was so torn. I glanced up at the sky but the stars offered no answers. I'd have to find them myself.

Leave her alone, my brain kept telling me, but there was this other part of me – a very selfish part, that said, *go to her. You want her. She wants you. Life is short.*

So I went to her.

I LEFT THE PATIO, dressed in my other suit and tie and then took the limo service to Louis's Backyard. I found a table near the edge of the deck overlooking the beach and waited for Mira to arrive. While I waited, I texted Casey, because I was having a bad case of ethics break out and needed her.

BECKETT: Help! I think I'm being an asshole and need your advice.

I waited for her response, which came a few moments later.

CASEY: Hun, if you think you're being an asshole, you are. Take my word for it.

I exhaled heavily.

BECKETT: At least you could have encouraged me a bit...

In a moment, she texted me back.

CASEY: You don't need encouragement. You already know the answer, Beckett.

Predictably, Casey spoke the unvarnished truth.

BECKETT: I'm waiting to have dinner with this wonderful intelligent beautiful woman and I know I should leave and never see her again because as soon as she knows the truth, she'll tell me to get lost.

I waited. She responded.

CASEY: Then leave. Discretion is the better part of valor. Don't break her heart. You can get laid any time you want. Don't hurt her if she really is as wonderful as you claim.

I was frustrated. I wanted Miranda. I wanted more to develop between us. She was more than just a fun bout of sex. An orgasm or ten. She was more and I knew it, but I couldn't give her what she deserved.

My cell dinged.

CASEY: Who is the lovely woman, may I ask? You haven't mentioned anyone special...

I hesitated. How much truth should I tell her?

BECKETT: *She's the woman who wrote those letters. She has no idea who I really am...*

There was no response for a few moments and I wondered if I hadn't finally driven Casey away.

CASEY: *You mean the widow? Seriously? You're seducing the wife of the man who died saving your life? You fucking dick...*

There was silence for a few moments and I thought that was it. She'd hung up on me.

CASEY: *Do the right thing, Beckett. I know you. With someone like her, it's either all in or all out. Nothing else will do. You know this. Do the right thing. Tell her the truth. Let her decide if she wants you even knowing what happened.*

I sighed. Of course, I already knew this. Casey was right – with someone like Miranda, I had to either commit fully or leave and never see her again.

I checked my watch. I could leave then and there, stand her up, and go back to my hotel. She'd be hurt, but so far, nothing but a few kisses and some serious flirting had happened between us. If I left now, I could get away before she arrived and she'd never know what a total selfish jerk I was...

Then she walked onto the deck in her sexy little sundress with thin straps that hugged her delicious curves, her long hair shining in the light from the lanterns, and I was a goner.

I was toast.

Every ounce of resistance drained out of me when she caught my eyes and smiled.

Her dimples did it. I was a sucker for dimples. And the fine spray of freckles on her nose...

I stood when she walked up and I pulled out her chair.

"Whew," I said and wiped my brow. "Glad you decided to join me after all. You look beautiful."

"Thank you," she said softly. "You don't look too bad yourself."

I sat beside her as close as possible. If I was going all in, I was going all in.

"You look like you just came out of a meeting," she said, eyeing me up and down.

"I didn't want to look too disreputable."

She laughed and I motioned to the waitress, who came over and took her drink order.

"You hungry?" I asked when the waitress left.

"Starving."

"Good," I said and laid my arm on the back of her chair.

For the next hour, I tried to draw her out about her life. We spoke about her family, about her plans to join the FBI – the usual 'getting to know you' material. Finally, I decided to prod her about Dan.

"Care to talk about Dan?" I asked, wanting to get her to talk about Dan. "I see you have a gold wedding band on your middle finger. Is that his?"

She held out her hand and looked at the ring. "Yes. I know I should take it off. It's been almost a year, but I think I'll wait until after the year's up."

She said nothing for a moment, and then shook her head thoughtfully. "Dan and I met when I started college and he was at a party with some old friends. He enlisted and we started dating when he came back from his first deployment. We decided to get married after he redeployed and was doing some pretty dangerous stuff with special operations forces."

"Just in case?"

She nodded, her face flushed. I could tell she had a hard time talking about Dan.

"He loved what he did, but I felt incredibly afraid he'd die and we'd have never had a chance at married life. So we made plans, had everything in place, and he came home on leave and we were married. Within three months, he was dead and I was a widow." She smiled a sad smile.

I reached out and took her hand. "What was he like?" I asked, trying to keep my tone respectful. "If you don't mind talking about him."

Then she told me about Dan. Stuff I'd gleaned from reading various comments and memories on his obituary.

"So what about you?" she asked. "Ever married?"

I sat up straighter. "Nope," I said, not wanting to get into my relationship with Sue. "I used to think I was the marrying type, but not anymore. You have your sad story? I have mine. Besides, I saw my parents get divorced and how nasty it was between them. Don't plan on getting married or divorced any time soon, if ever."

She frowned. "What about family? Don't you want kids?"

"My whole life is my business. I wouldn't want to have kids only to neglect them and never see them the way my father was. The only real father figure in my life was my uncle and he was great but not a real substitute."

"What did your father do exactly?"

I didn't answer right away. Instead, I took a sip of my beer. I told her as much as I wanted about my father and his business, but I wanted to turn the discussion away from me and back onto her.

The food came and we ate with gusto, all the while exchanging little tidbits about our families. I learned more about her father, who sounded like a real stand-up guy – the kind of man I would like as a father. Solid. Strong. Upstanding. Ethical. It was something we had in common – fathers who had died too soon. I felt a sympathy for her that I didn't feel for many people. She'd lost so much.

We both had.

When we finished our food, I turned to her. "Care for a walk along the beach?"

She hesitated but then smiled. "Sure."

I paid the bill, refusing to let her chip in. "No way, *sha*," I said laying on the Cajun charm. "This is my treat. Maybe you can cook me a meal some day when you're back in Manhattan."

"I make a mean *linguine agli scampi,*" she said.

I did want to see her again, back in New York. I wanted to see her every night. But I hadn't thought it through. I didn't want to think it through, because if I did, I knew it would end badly.

Then we walked along the boardwalk that followed the beach, and even took off our shoes and went into the water for a dip, laughing like we were two kids on vacation. It was great, I felt completely comfortable with her, no awkward moments.

I could get used to her.

I pulled her into my arms and we stood together, watching the surf, enjoying the moment. I kissed her, softly. Gently. Now was the moment. I had to make a decision.

I could drive her back to her place and say goodbye.

Or I could jump in with both feet.

The feel of her soft curves against me decided for me.

MIRANDA

WE WALKED along the boardwalk that skirted the beach road, and listened to the sound of the surf in the distance. He held my hand and we breathed in deeply the cool salty air. It was a relief after the heat of the day.

We stopped at a narrow walkway that led to the beach and he pulled me towards it.

"Want to go wet our feet?" he asked.

I laughed and kicked off my heels. "Sure," I said, wanting to have fun for a change. Usually, I'd be afraid to be out in the darkness with a strange man, but I felt safe with Beckett. Besides, the limo was trailing along beside us.

Beckett removed his jacket and tie, then unbuttoned his shirt before rolling up his sleeves. He removed his socks and rolled up his pant legs, and we ran down the beach towards the surf. There was a full moon out and so the foam was white and the lights along the beach road ensured we could see pretty clearly.

I reached the edge of the surf and squealed when the water surrounded my feet and went up to my ankles.

"Holy cow," I said with a laugh. "That's cold."

Beckett ran into the surf, laughing out loud when he was

soaked up to his knees. He whooped and ran around, then splashed me when I tried to get away. Finally, we held hands once more and he pulled me against him, his other arm around me. I nestled into his embrace and we stood and watched the ocean. Moonlight glittered on the waves and the surf roared.

Then he kissed me, one hand on my cheek. When he pulled back, I saw the scar from the corner of my eye and couldn't help but look at it. At first, it sent a jolt of adrenaline through me but then I looked up into his eyes, so blue and honest. I knew that I wanted him, no matter what. The scar just made him more real to me. Human. Vulnerable.

He could have died in Afghanistan. He was brave.

He was a hero. Like Dan.

"Come back to my hotel," he said, his voice warm and deep.

I said nothing in reply. Instead, I leaned up on my tiptoes and kissed him again. When he kissed me back, I heard his sharp intake of breath, as if he didn't think I'd agree and was surprised.

He kissed me deeply this time, hungrily, one hand sliding down my back to stroke and then squeeze one buttock through the thin fabric of my dress. It sent a thrill of desire through my body, and my flesh throbbed in response to the thought that soon, there'd be nothing between us. I couldn't wait to feel his hands on me, his mouth on me, and to taste him.

He grabbed my hand and pulled me up the beach to where we left our things and where the limo waited. The driver opened the door for us and I slid in with Beckett following me. I took my seat and struggled to fasten the seat belt, but he stopped me and did it for me, smiling at me when he noticed my hands shaking just a bit.

He buckled his own seat belt, and put one arm around me on the back of the seat, pulling my face towards him for another blistering kiss. I sank into the kiss, turning off everything else in the world except for his mouth, his tongue, his hand slipping down my cheek to my shoulder and then my breast. He squeezed it, pressing it up, then he broke the kiss and bent down to kiss the top of my breasts before running his tongue up from one curve to my throat and then he nipped at my earlobe.

All of this sent shocks of lust to my core, igniting my desire, which had lain dormant for so many months since Dan died and I was mourning him. But now, Beckett woke all that up once more and I felt alive again.

Fully alive, my senses awake, my body ready for him.

I barely noticed the drive to his hotel, absorbed by his mouth on me, his kisses along the curve of my bare shoulder after he'd pushed down the fabric and slid down my bra strap to reveal one breast, nipple and all. I didn't care if the driver saw Beckett suck my nipple. I was too focused on the warm wetness of his mouth and tongue as he sucked and ran his teeth softly over the hard bud. He slid one hand up my thigh, under my silky dress, until he found my panties and slipped his fingers underneath the fabric.

I wantonly spread my thighs ever so slightly, because at that moment, I wanted to feel his fingers on me, needed to feel his fingers touch me. He pushed me back and stroked me gently, and when he finally touched my clit, I groaned and that seemed to encourage him.

Of course, it was then that the car came to a stop and I came back to reality, my eyes flying open. Beckett pulled away and helped straighten my clothes, pulling up my bra strap and the shoulder of my dress. He looked in my eyes and smiled knowingly, then adjusted himself. I couldn't help but glance down and in the light coming in from the brightly lit hotel entrance, I saw his erection straining at his pants.

The knowledge that in only a few moments, I'd have him in my hand, in my mouth, in my body, made my heart race, a thrill of pure excitement in my belly.

As we struggled out of the limo, Beckett helping me, holding my hand, I imagined sitting on him, riding him while he leaned forward and sucked my nipples, one after the other.

Beckett said something to the driver and then pulled me into the hotel, past the concierge and the night desk clerk, who nodded at him.

We made our way down the hallways, the familiar decorations reminding me of the failed attempt to do this last night.

Tonight, I would not balk when he removed his shirt and I saw his scar again. Tonight, I couldn't wait to get into the room with him and take off his clothes so I could see what was underneath the crisp white shirt and sober grey suit.

We took the elevator, and as soon as the doors closed, he wasted no time and leaned against the wall, his hands on my hips, pulling me against him so that I felt his erection. We kissed as the elevator rose, and then separated when it opened to the top floor.

Beckett pulled me down the hallway and opened the door to his suite. He admitted me into the dimly lit interior, and before I could even put my bag down, he closed the door and pressed me against the wall beside it, taking my bag out of my hand and dropping it to the floor.

"I can't wait to see you naked," he practically growled against the skin of my neck. The sound of his need, of his desire, coupled with the press of his erection against my belly made my knees weak. I didn't hesitate to help him when he lifted the hem of my dress and pulled it over my head, revealing my lacy bra and thong. I stood before him in my undies and heels and he stepped back and admired me, his eyes roving down my body from my eyes to my feet and back. I couldn't hold back a smile. He seemed as if he hadn't seen a woman undressed for a while, but I couldn't believe that. He was far too hot and good looking to go very long without getting laid.

I let him look at me for as long as he wanted. He pulled me over to the bed and once more, he sat on the side of the bed and pulled me between his spread thighs.

"Let's continue what we started last night," he said in a husky voice. Then, he pulled down one strap of my bra and exposed my breast to the cool air. Immediately, my nipple hardened and puckered and he responded by covering it with his mouth, his tongue stroking it, sucking it between his lips while his hands stroked down my body.

I stood there with my eyes closed, my hands resting on his shoulders and enjoyed the delicious sensations while he sucked and licked my nipple. He moved to my other breast and repeated the treatment, and finally he undid the back of my bra so that it slid off me and fell to the floor.

Once more he pressed his face between my breasts and his hair tickled my skin while his tongue teased my nipples, his whiskers brushing me as he moved from one breast to the other. My clit throbbed in response and I felt my flesh swell. But I waited, wanting to see what he would do and what kind of lover he was.

He stood up, and turned me around, pushing me back onto the bed so that I lay back, my legs dangling off the side. He bent over me and kissed my knees, then moved up farther, kissing each thigh in turn before hovering over my lace thong. I leaned back on my elbows, watching him, my heart pounding. The light from the bedside lamp cast everything in a warm glow.

He licked me through my thong, his tongue running up from between my thighs to my mound, my clit aching for his touch. Then he hooked his thumbs in each side of my thong and pulled it down and off one leg and then the other. Before I could respond, he pressed my thighs open so that I was fully exposed. He stood with his hands on my thighs, keeping them open, and stared down at me, his eyes hungry to see my pussy spread like that.

I was not completely shaved – just a bikini wax that left a small strip of pubic hair on my mound. Finally, he seemed to have waited long enough and knelt down, pulling me down to the edge of the bed, slipping one of my legs over his shoulder.

"I've been wanting to taste you all night," he said with a gruff voice, filled with lust.

I swallowed hard, waiting for him to lick me, and finally, he bent down and ran his tongue between the lips of my sex, sliding up to stroke my entire slit and then my clit. I moaned out loud, and that spurred him on. He clamped his mouth over me, covering me completely, and began to lick and suck, his tongue sliding between my lips, then dipping inside of me, thrusting inside, before he took my clit between his lips and sucked.

I groaned and spread my thighs wider, my eyes closing, completely absorbed with the sensation of his warm wet tongue all over me, inside me, swirling around me. When he slipped a finger inside of me, then two, I shuddered, because I was already so close, I knew the added pressure would soon take me over the edge.

He pressed his fingers up and began to slowly stroke me while he sucked and licked my clit. I began to thrust my hips in time with his fingers, pressing my pussy against his mouth like a wanton woman. Then I came with a cry, my body shuddering around his fingers, my hips thrusting against his tongue.

I fell back, my eyes closed, breathing hard while my orgasm waned, my body still clenching around him. Finally, he stopped, but kept his mouth on me. My body pulsed as my orgasm faded, and he seemed to enjoy feeling my spasms under his mouth. When he licked me once more, I shuddered and it was almost too much, but not quite.

I glanced up at him when he stood. "Hold that thought," he said with a grin and began to strip off his clothes. I sat up and helped, wanting to see what was underneath the silk suit and starched white shirt. While he unbuttoned his cuffs, I unlatched his belt and unzipped, so that his pants fell down and off his narrow hips. He wore boxer briefs which captured his very thick and long erection. He stepped out of his pants and I helped him by removing each sock in turn.

When he had his shirt off, I stood up and pulled him down for a kiss. We stood together, arms around each other for a moment, and now it was my turn to taste him, to pleasure him. I pulled back and examined his scar, which ran from beneath one ear and around to the base of his throat. It didn't shock me this time. I was ready for it, and instead of taking me back to Dan and my own loss, I thought about how brave he must have been to volunteer and go over to Iraq. How he must have feared for his life when the terrorist – or whoever did this to him – slit his throat.

He hadn't wanted to talk about it and I understood, but I was so curious. If I got a chance, I planned on asking him about it when we weren't in such an intimate moment. Instead, I kissed it, and then trailed my lips down from it to his shoulder and chest, licking one of his nipples and smiling when he groaned softly in response. While I moved to the other nipple, one hand slid down his back to cup one of his nice hard buttocks, firm and round beneath my hand. He pressed his hips and his delicious erection against me in response.

I sat on the side of the bed and focused on his abdomen, which was rock hard and sculpted, running my tongue along one hip crest and down. I wanted to tease him as much as I could, wanting him to ache for me the way he made me ache for him. I pulled the boxer briefs down and his erection sprang out, almost hitting me in the cheek. I smiled and removed the briefs, and he stepped out of them eagerly. Then he stood before me, fully naked, waiting. Finally, I ran my tongue over his erection, from the base to the tip, and received a moan in response. I pressed my mouth over the head and ran my tongue over the head in slow circles.

"Oh, God," he said in a voice thick with lust.

I grabbed his hips and pulled him closer, then looked up, catching his eye while I leaned forward and licked the head of his cock, sampling the fluid that glistened in the tip.

"Oh, *fuck*," he said and inhaled deeply.

I took the head in my mouth and sucked, running my tongue over the head and around the rim lazily, before taking more of his length into my mouth. He gave a little *mmm* of approval when I took him as deeply inside my throat as I could without gagging, cupping his heavy balls in one hand while I pulled him closer with the other hand.

"Fuck, I need to be inside of you right now," he growled and pulled out of my mouth. He lifted me up and pushed me back onto the bed, then started once more to shower my body with kisses and licks, brining me back to full arousal.

When he got back down to my pussy, I was groaning with lust, my body aching to feel him inside of me.

"You want me to fuck you now?" he said in a smoky voice as he lay over top of me, his cock pressing against my clit, sliding against it.

I nodded and licked my lips, barely able to speak.

"Say it," he demanded. "Ask me."

I closed my eyes. "Fuck me now," I whispered.

"No," he said and took my face in his hand. "Look me in the eyes and ask me."

I opened my eyes and looked into his. "Beckett," I said, my voice throaty. "Fuck me now."

He bent down and kissed me hard and then reached inside the bedside table drawer for a condom, which he removed from the foil wrapper and then unrolled over his very hard and very thick erection. When he was done, he placed my feet on his shoulders and stroked the head of his cock against my clit, sliding it down to the entrance to my body and back again, several times. I groaned, thrusting my hips up to meet his every stroke. Finally, when I was almost blind with desire, he guided his cock inside of my body. When the tip slid inside, it felt so good I shuddered and I knew it wouldn't take long for me to come again once he began thrusting.

"Fuck me," I said softly.

He slid his entire length in me and he was so nice and thick and hard, I gasped.

"Oh, that feels so damn good," he said, his eyes closing. He remained still like that, his cock filling me up completely, and we both panted for a moment.

He bent down and took one nipple into his mouth, sucking hard and that made me squeeze around him, clenching around his cock.

He rose up, his hands pulling my hips against him with each thrust. He watched himself fucking me, his eyes moving up over my naked body to my face and then back down to where our bodies joined.

"You are so fucking beautiful," he whispered. Then he stroked his thumb over my clit slowly, deliberately, timing it with each thrust. My orgasm built, and I knew it would only take a few more thrusts like that to make me come.

I met his thrusts and soon my orgasm crashed through my body, from my core out, up my chest and down my legs it was so intense. It seemed to go on and on as Beckett thrust, keeping his thumb on my clit while I shuddered.

Then he finished, thrusting fast and deep, his face red from exertion and his expression strained.

"Oh, God," he said when his orgasm started. He grunted with each ejaculation, then fell on top of me, breathing hard. "Oh, God, that was so *good*," he said, his voice husky. "You are so fucking *good*..."

I smiled, my eyes closed. "Only good?" I said in a teasing voice.

"You are fucking *great*," he said and when I opened my eyes to see his response, he smiled back. He bent down and kissed my throat, then my nipple, tugging at it gently with his teeth. "I want to fuck you again right away."

I laughed and when he bent down to the other nipple, I ran my hands through his hair.

"You gotta give a girl a rest now and then."

"No rest for the wicked," he replied, his breath warm on my nipple. He sucked it once more and my body clenched in response.

I glanced at the clock radio on the bedside table. It was nearly one o'clock. I had to get home.

"I have to get home soon," I said, feeling sad I couldn't stay all night. "I have to work and… I don't know if I want to stay out the entire night. You know I live with Dan's parents…"

He leaned back up and kissed me. "Damn," he said and pouted. "I wanted to do that again and again. I could get addicted to watching you come while I fuck you and eat you."

That made my body clench in renewed desire. "I'd like that, but maybe some other night. Before you leave?"

"Count on it. We'll start earlier so we have more time. When are you off tomorrow?"

"All evening," I said.

He kissed me again and then slid out, removing the condom from his still semi-hard cock. He was deliciously thick and big and I knew I could have many orgasms with him if I let myself.

"Good," he said after dropping the condom in the trashcan beside the bed. "I'll pick you up from work, and then I'll eat you until you come, and then I'll fuck you until you come, and then we'll eat supper and then we'll do it again. How does that sound?"

I smiled. "You have it all planned out?"

"Eating you and fucking you so I can watch you come again and again?" he said with a huge grin. "Absolutely. Yes. Count on it. Promise."

I smiled when he pulled me up from the bed and kissed me again.

"I'll hold you to that promise."

"I am a man of my word." He winked at me and helped me get dressed, taking care to fasten my bra and help me with my thong, then pulling the dress over my head. He stroked my hair to smooth it and then kissed me once more.

"There you go, beautiful lady," he said softly. "I wish you could stay for round two, but we'll do it tomorrow."

I helped him with his shirt, and when I did, I saw a small tattoo in the middle of his strong back. I ran my fingers lightly over it, tracing the design. A stylized dragon's head in a circle. It was the same symbol on his ID for Brimstone.

"I like your tattoo," I said and pulled one sleeve over his shoulder.

"Thanks," he said and smiled at me as he fastened a few buttons. "Brandon, Graham and I all have one. We were in the same Special Operations Forces Team in Afghanistan. It's a dragon's head and symbolizes Brimstone."

I nodded and watched while he put on the rest of his clothes. Then, I went to the bathroom for a pee. When I returned, he was wearing his suit pants and white shirt, unbuttoned several buttons. He opened the door, handing me my bag.

"It's not too late to change your mind," he said with a smile. "If you stay, I promise to make you come twice more. And then again, when we wake up..."

I laughed and touched his cheek. "You sure know how to tempt a lady. I really have to go."

"I understand," he said with a sigh. "Can't blame a guy for trying..."

He walked me out to the waiting limo and kissed me once before I slid inside. As the limo drove off, I glanced back and waved at Beckett, wishing I could stay but not wanting any questions from Dan's parents when they noticed I stayed the night somewhere else. Especially not with a new man.

I was old enough to do what I wanted, but I hesitated because of Dan's parents. I wanted to wait until after the memorial and my return to Manhattan before I officially started seeing new men.

I thought it was the least I could do.

BECKETT

I SHOULD HAVE LET her go at that point, never to see her again. I should have sent her back to Dan's parent's home and said goodbye forever.

I couldn't.

I wanted her more than I had ever wanted a woman.

As the limo drove off, the reality of what I had done came back to me all at once. I'd fucked the widow of the man who died saving my life. There was nothing wrong with that, if she knew who I was and decided to fuck me anyway, but she had no idea. Instead, I was a total asshole. I should have just walked away and never seen her again. She might be momentarily hurt that I broke my promise, but she'd forget about me all too soon.

She was the kind of woman I would have wanted to become involved with seriously – if I did that sort of thing anymore.

But I didn't.

Instead, I went back to my room and after I stripped off my clothes, I flopped onto the bed and stared at the ceiling.

Fuck...

What the fuck was I going to do now?

I REACHED for my cell and dialed Casey. I could text her, and it was late, but I needed to hear her voice.

"What's up?" she said, her voice sleepy. "Are you okay?"

I bit my lip, feeling bad about calling her so late. "I fucked up."

"Let me guess…You fucked the widow?"

"Yep," I said, running my hand through my hair. "Miranda. Beautiful, intelligent, funny, sexy as hell, Miranda…"

"Sounds like you're hot for this woman. Confess to her now, before it's too late. You wait too long and she'll feel really betrayed. I'm telling you, Beckett. I speak the truth. You know I'm right. That's why you called me."

"I know, I *know*…" I sighed heavily and bit my bottom lip again. "She'll be pissed."

"Rightly so." Then, I heard the impatience in Casey's voice. "Tell her. Confess. Let her call you a sonofabitch. Say that she's right and you deserve it. Tell her how you feel. Why you did it."

"Because I'm a fucking horndog?"

"Because you *fell* for her," Casey said, her voice chiding. "You read her letters. You mooned over her for weeks. When you met her, you were a goner. Tell her the truth."

"What do you mean, I mooned over her for weeks?"

"You did, Beckett, you bastard," Casey said with a laugh. "You are such a dick. You're in love with this girl and you couldn't stop yourself."

"I'm not in love," I said, frowning. Love was a word I couldn't face. Being in love was that feeling of being swallowed up in a warm ocean, the water blissful, but you are unable to breathe…

Kind of the way I felt when thinking of Miranda. When talking with Miranda. When lying naked with Miranda. …

Fucking Christ…

I SPENT the next day busy with the retreat, doing all these team building exercises designed to bring us together after the trauma of losing one of the founders, and half the staff. I tried to focus, but found myself distracted by thoughts of Miranda and the turmoil in my mind over what I should do about her.

I knew what Casey said was right. I had to confess.

But really, truthfully, what good would that do? I couldn't tell her I was in the crash – my presence there was confidential. SAD ops were never publicized or admitted in public, nor were operatives permitted to reference any particular operation.

In truth, I had to deny I was even at the crash site by law. The only people who knew what I did in Afghanistan, outside of those directly involved, were Graham and Brandon and that was only because they were part owners of Brimstone.

I couldn't have a relationship with Miranda. For fuck's sake – her brand new husband died because of me. A brutal nasty death. It was because of my mission with SAD that we were in that part of Iran. Yes, Dan was always at risk when he was deployed, but this was purely to see if my tech worked in the field.

I should have just walked away. Not called her. Not seen her again.

She'd be pissed. She'd be hurt but she'd move on. Go back to Manhattan and her classes and then the FBI internship after Christmas. She'd meet some smart young FBI Special Agent and they'd fall in love...

Fuck.

I didn't want to think of losing a woman like her.

So I didn't.

MIRANDA

THE NEXT DAY went extremely slowly and it was all I could do to keep from squealing out loud with excitement that at the end of my afternoon shift, I'd be whisked away in Beckett's limo or on his bike to his hotel room where I'd be treated to a double orgasm. And then some more. He'd promised we'd spend the entire evening in pleasurable pursuits and frankly, it had been so long since I had sex, I couldn't wait.

Leah arrived for her afternoon shift as a cocktail waitress and she leaned against the bar and smiled at me.

"So, how did it go? I haven't really spoken to you since lunch yesterday."

"I've been busy," I said and tried not to smile. "Looks like you've been busy, too."

She grinned. "Brandon is an absolute doll," she said and sighed. "He's smart. And he's extremely fun in bed as well as out."

I laughed. "So is Beckett."

"Oh my *God*," she said and leaned against the bar, her arms reaching out to grab my apron. "Tell me you are no longer re-virginized!"

"De-re-virginized," I said quietly, glancing around to make sure no one could hear me. "Twice. Hoping for more tonight, as a matter of fact."

"Did you spend the night with him?" she asked, her face eager, eyes wide. "Tell me. Deets, please!"

"He's very well-endowed and knows how to use all his body parts, shall we say," I said, wagging my eyebrows, grinning like a fool.

"Oh, my God, Mira! I'm so happy for you. Finally," she said and wiped her brow in mock relief. "I was beginning to think you'd become an old cat lady."

"Not yet, at least. Can't make any promises. Beckett is definitely easy on the eyes and body. I have a feeling there aren't too many like him roaming around free..."

"He really likes you," she said with a sly smile. "Are you going to see him when you get back to Manhattan?"

I shrugged, trying not to get too excited about it. "He said something about me making him dinner when I get back to Manhattan..."

"Oh, he really *does* like you," she said.

"I like him, too," I said. "He's really smart, and hot, and nice. Plus, he understands all about loss."

"Did he lose someone? Friends in Iraq, I bet."

"I think so. But he seems to have lost a woman, too. He didn't give me any details, but it sounds like he had a broken heart."

She nodded. "Brandon and I made a plan to see each other again, too."

I smiled. It was so easy for Leah. She always had some man sniffing around her.

The rest of the afternoon went by quickly, and before I knew it, Beckett walked in the door to the bar, his motorcycle helmet under his arm and a wide brilliant smile on his handsome face. His blond hair was a bit messy, but he still looked like a hunky

Viking. I hoped that soon, he'd be conquering my body and my flesh swelled in anticipation, a pleasant throb in my core.

"Well, hello lovely lady," he said and plopped his helmet on the bar. "Your knight riding on a chrome bike is here to take you away from all this," he said with a laugh. "To mix a few metaphors."

"Mix away," I said with a grin. "I have to finish restocking, but then I'll be ready to be swept away by you."

Beckett sat at one of the stools and watched the game on the big screen television while I restocked the ice hopper and hauled a few cases of beer from the back, restocking the fridge for the evening shift. When Keith arrived, we high-fived each other and I ducked under the bar hatch.

I winked at Leah, who smiled knowingly at me. She spoke to Beckett while I was in the back cashing out, and when I arrived back, they were leaning in close to each other, and seemed deep in conversation. Their expressions were serious, but when they saw me, they both pasted on bright smiles.

"Hey, you two," I said and narrowed my eyes. "What are you two conniving about?"

"Nothing," Beckett said. "Just asking about the local cuisine."

Leah smiled and then winked at me, before leaving us alone so she could take a drink order.

Beckett held out his hand and I took it and followed him out of the bar.

"I really need a shower and a change of clothes," I said. "Maybe I should go home first…"

"I won't hear of it. You'll come to my hotel and have a nice shower and then, you're going to be naked for the rest of the night."

I laughed, a thrill going through me at the thought. "That's the plan?"

"That's the plan," he said and handed me a helmet. I smiled as I put it on. Then I climbed on the bike behind him and together, we drove off towards his hotel and what I knew would be a night of pleasure I wouldn't soon forget.

I WASN'T WRONG. As soon as we arrived back at the hotel and in Beckett's room, he pulled me to the bathroom, which was large and lined with granite tiles. There was a huge standup shower in addition to the Jacuzzi tub.

"I'm going to wash every inch of you and then I'm going to eat you and then fuck you," Beckett said as he began to strip off my clothes. "How does that sound?"

My heart raced at his words. "It sounds divine."

"Good," he said, as he removed my t-shirt and squeezed my breasts, his hands covering my lacy bra. "Then I'm going to do it again and again."

I closed my eyes when he pulled one bra cup down and sucked my nipple.

He did exactly what he said he would – he washed every inch of me once we were both naked and standing in a stream of hot steamy water under the rain showerhead. The walls of the glass enclosed shower steamed up and my body heated up, the way he touched me, his hands all soapy, slipping deliciously over my skin, into ever crevice, while he kissed me deeply. I returned the favor, lathering up my hands and washing his every inch, and there were a lot of them. I thought he must be almost nine inches and his girth was huge, thick, so that I could barely get my fingers around his shaft. I couldn't wait to feel him inside me once more, and to come around his cock while he fucked me.

Before he did, he ate me once more as he promised. When I was fully rinsed off, he turned off the shower and had me lean back against the wall. Then he knelt down on the floor and placed one of my legs over his shoulder while he licked me, holding my hips so I didn't fall over or slip on the wet surface.

His tongue worked wonders on my very hard and throbbing

clit. I soon came with his tongue thrusting inside of me while his thumb stroked my clit, my eyes practically rolling back in my head I felt so much pleasure.

"Mmm," he murmured against my pussy. He licked me slowly again and again, sending jolts of too-much pleasure through me. "I love your pussy," he said, meeting my eyes. "I love eating you."

I swallowed hard, and closed my eyes. "I love it when you eat me."

He finally stood up after licking me again and again, as if he were trying to keep me at a high level of arousal. "Now," he said and turned me around so that I faced the wall, my hands spread out, my thighs wide. "Stay right there," he said. "I'm going to get a condom, and then I'm going to fuck you and make you come again."

He left the shower and when he returned, I saw the condom on his very erect cock. He stood behind me and slipped his fingers down my body from one breast to my clit while he gripped my hip with the other. He slid his cock inside me and fucked me hard and fast, his fingers stroking my clit. I did come again, very quickly, my orgasm shattering. While I panted, my hands spread on the steamy shower wall, he thrust deeply, hard and fast until he too came, shuddering, his mouth on my shoulder while he ejaculated.

"Oh, fuck," he groaned as he thrust, his mouth next to my ear. "Oh, *God.*"

Yes, it was an *Oh, God* moment for me as well.

My legs started to shake from exertion and finally, he pulled me up and against him, his cock still deep inside of me, his knees bent. "I want to stay like this forever," he whispered in my ear.

I smiled and closed my eyes.

THE REST of the evening went pretty much the same, with a break in between bouts of sex for a lovely dinner that Beckett ordered in

– fresh catch of the day, salad and French bread, with a lovely white wine. We lounged on the bed naked, watching a game on the pay-per-view and talking about his corporation and my degree in forensic science.

Late that night, I lay on my stomach and watched as he peeled a banana from a fruit basket that was left for him when he checked in.

"So you were never close to being married?"

He smiled briefly and then took a bite of the banana before handing me a piece. "Close but no luck."

"So you *were* close to being married?"

"I was. It didn't work out."

"What happened?"

He shook his head. "Don't really want to talk about it. Let's just say that I wanted to get married but Fate had other ideas."

I frowned, wondering what that meant. I ate the piece of banana he handed me and tried to imagine. Did she cheat on him? Did she run off with his best friend? Did she leave him at the altar?

Any one of those things would be enough to put you off marriage. I knew better than to ask anything else so I rolled onto my back beside him and watched the television, hoping we could move past the sudden darkness that seemed to descend over Beckett at the mention of his being close to marriage.

"What about you?" he said, his voice soft. "Tell me more about Dan."

Now it was my turn to shake my head. "He was everything to me. As I told you, we had been married for only a few months when he died."

"I'm sorry," he said and squeezed my hand.

"The anniversary of his death is coming up in a few days," I said and sighed. "Our family's going to Arlington for a memorial. He was a Navy Hospital Corpsman with Special Operations

Forces. The guys who go in where others can't go. The guys who go in and rescue soldiers who are in danger."

"He was a hero," Beckett said softly.

I turned to him and smiled, amazed that Dan had saved his life. "He was."

I glanced away, watching television because I felt guilty being with Beckett and thinking of Dan. I had to stop that – I had to move on. I *was* moving on.

Beckett and I seemed to be really good together.

But there was still a part of me that felt incredibly guilty that I'd been with another man. That another man did to me what Dan used to do, had been inside of me, had made me come. Despite my guilt, a tiny part of me hoped that when I went back to Manhattan, we would see each other. He did mention me cooking a meal for him. I hoped it was more than just him being nice or trying to butter me up.

I could get used to being with Beckett. Everything about him was easy. His smile, his conversation, sex…

Sex with Beckett was fantastic.

We had sex again before midnight, this time on the bed, and it was hot and good and intense. I felt well-used by the time we were lying together, him on top of me, his face beside mine, breathing hard as he recovered from his orgasm and I my fourth one for the night.

"That was sooo good," he said and then grinned. "I mean, great!"

"You're going to wear me out," I said with a laugh. "I'll be sore in the morning."

"But it's a good kind of sore, I hope…"

"The very best kind."

We lay together for a while, his cock still deep inside of me, slowly deflating. When he pulled out and removed the condom, he lay back down on top of me and leaned on his elbows, stroking my face.

"I hope I can talk you into staying the night," he said, his voice soft. "Can't you text your family and say you're staying the night at Leah's or something?"

I shook my head. "I can't lie to them. After all they've done for me, it would be bad to start now. I'll go home. Besides," I said and slipped out from under his body. "I have to get up early and meet Leah at the gym for more rock climbing and the MCMAP."

He resisted letting me out from under him, pinning me beneath him then tickling me, making me squeal with laughter.

"Beckett!" I cried out, twisting in his arms. "I have to go…"

Finally, he rolled off me and sighed heavily. "I forgot about the MCMAP. Sadly, I have a business meeting so I have to bow out of it."

I stood up and nodded, not wanting to say anything about wishing he was going to be there like before. I had to remember the real reason he was here in Topsail Beach. He was attending a convention and holding a retreat for his staff. He wasn't here to get laid and spend time with a new woman.

I went to the bathroom and had a quick pee, then washed my hands and face. I was standing naked in front of the mirror when Beckett joined me and took a pee as well. It seemed far too domestic considering we were really strangers, but I guess since I had his cock in my mouth only moments earlier, I shouldn't feel shy with him.

It made me think of everything I missed with Dan. He was away deployed so often that we only spent a total of a few months living together so I missed out on a lot of the domestic moments that married couples – or even engaged couples – experienced. Being engaged and then married to a soldier during a war meant that you spent most of your time separated.

With Beckett, if anything did develop between us, I could have a real relationship and that small part of me that craved it felt sad that after the weekend, I would probably never see him again.

"Penny for your thoughts?" he said and stood behind me, his

arms around me, his chin resting on my shoulder. One hand moved to cup a breast and squeeze.

I smiled and met his eyes. "If you keep that up, I'll never get home."

"Mmm," he said. "Now that I know how easy you are to seduce, I'll keep you captive for the rest of the week."

I smiled when he squeezed me and kissed my cheek. He turned me around in his embrace and we kissed more deeply, and then enjoyed the embrace, our naked skin warm against each other. I could stay like that for hours, but I wanted to get home before it was too late. I didn't want to wake Dan's parents when I came in and then have to face any questions about where I was and what I was doing.

I dressed while Beckett called the limo service. Then, he pulled on his swimming trunks and a t-shirt and sat on the bed and watched me. When I was done, he walked me out of the hotel to the car that was waiting in the driveway.

"What are you doing tomorrow night?" he said lightly.

"I'm working the late shift, so I won't be off until two. I have to clean up and restock for the morning shift."

"Conventions over on Wednesday. I'll be heading back to Manhattan. I'd like to see you before I go. Give me your cell phone."

I handed him my phone and he quickly added his phone number and details.

"Call me when you have some time so I can see you before you go. Lunch. Dinner. Whatever time you have."

I smiled and we kissed once more before I slipped into the limo and closed the door. I felt a pang of sadness as the car drove off and I watched him standing under the bright lights of the hotel entrance.

He waved and stood watching me until we turned a corner and I couldn't see him any longer.

I DIDN'T WAKE anyone up, luckily. I had a quick shower, and then crawled into bed, nestling into the cool crisp sheets, wishing I was still with Beckett. I lay in the darkness, listening to the sounds of the surf in the distance. He was leaving on Wednesday. I worked all day at the restaurant.

When would we see each other again?

MIRANDA

THE NEXT DAY, I met Leah at the gym.

"So," Leah said, her eyes bright. "Is Mr. Viking God coming to do the MCMAP with us again?"

I shook my head, sad that he wasn't. "No," I said and looked at the front of the class where Devil Dog stood, speaking to a new student before class started. "He has a meeting this morning."

"Are you going to see him again before he leaves Topsail Beach?"

I shrugged. "He said we should get together for lunch or dinner but he's gone on Wednesday."

Leah pouted. "Brandon's already gone," she said. "He's leaving today. Why is Beckett staying another day? The convention's already over."

"Beckett said it was over tomorrow."

"Brandon said today. I think Mr. Viking wants to stay so he can see you again. You really should try to swap shifts tonight so you can be with him."

"Can't do it. Steve is off early tonight because he has a thing."

"Can't Mr. Lewis take over?"

I shook my head. "No," I said with a sigh. "He hurt his shoulder and doesn't bartend any longer. It's me or no one."

"Too bad. Are you going to do lunch with him? Afternoon delight? You have some time…"

I pursed my lips and considered. If Beckett was really going back tomorrow, I wasn't sure I wanted to see him again. If we weren't going to see each other when we both returned to Manhattan, it would be awkward saying goodbye. Even though the prospect of sex with Beckett was pretty enticing, I wasn't the type for an afternoon delight as Leah called it, especially if we were never going to see each other again. Better to cut ties completely.

"He put his contact info in my phone so if I want to connect with him, I can. We're leaving for Virginia for the memorial."

"Call him when you get back to Manhattan. You'd be crazy not to. He really likes you, hun. Don't let a man like him slip away."

I smiled and faced the front of the room when Devil Dog turned back to us, his hands on his hips.

"Okay, recruits! Time to work on your lazy asses!"

When I bent down to do the warm-up, I did ache in all the right places, and that ache made me think of Beckett.

I'd call him later, or text him and invite him for dinner at Joe's Bar and Grill. It was one of my favorite restaurants and served up great seafood. I had an hour and a half off between shifts and so it would be the only time we could connect.

The workout was grueling and I felt like I'd been through the wringer by the time it was done. Leah laughed and shook her arms out as we walked down the hallway to the locker rooms.

"God, my arms are weak. Gonna have to do this once we go back to school. There's probably some place that has the MCMAP."

"I can ask Devil Dog if he knows of anything in Manhattan," I said hopefully. I really liked the idea of being able to defend myself and getting in better shape. MCMAP was grueling but I knew that if we kept it up, both Leah and I would be toned and strong.

I showered and then went back home for a change of clothes for my afternoon shift.

THE NIGHT WENT FINE, and I was glad when the clock showed I had only a short while before I could start clean-up and then go home for a much-needed sleep. I was exhausted.

Of course, it was then that Beckett showed up looking like a zillion dollars in his slate grey suit, the one that made his eyes look grey and mysterious, maybe a little dangerous. My heart did a little flip-flop when I saw him arrive just before last call.

He sidled up to my bar, grinning like the cat who swallowed the canary.

"Hello, Mr. Tate," I said, unable to keep a huge grin off my face.

"Hello, Ms. Parker. You're looking very lovely tonight."

I laughed and glanced down at my bar apron. He was a charmer. I had told him I was closing the bar and would be pretty late, but he showed up anyway. It sent a little shock of adrenaline through me that he was willing to come by so late.

"You're here pretty late. Don't you have a retreat to finish up?"

"I lied," he said and leaned on the bar so that his face was just a few inches from mine. "It was finished yesterday. I was trying to find an excuse to stay another day and see you again so I called a few business contacts in Wilmington and had a few meetings."

I grinned and finished pouring the last drink orders. Before I saw him walk through the door, I wasn't sure if I had enough energy to go to his hotel room for a bout of sex, even if it was the hottest sex I'd ever had. Now that I saw him in the flesh, looking so delicious, I knew I had the energy and more.

We made small talk while I finished closing the bar, restocking and cleaning, and then I did a quick cash out. Once I was done, I left the bar, switched on the alarm once everything was double-checked, and then locked the doors behind us.

The night was warm and the air still as we walked to his limo, which was parked on the street, the driver popping out when he saw us approach. He opened the door for me.

I hopped in and Beckett got in beside me. As usual, he sat close to me, helping me with my seat belt. I smiled at his chivalry. I wasn't used to it, but found it charming. He seemed to enjoy taking care of his date. Frankly, after a year dry spell, I enjoyed the attention.

"Will you come to my hotel for a while? The driver can take you back later, if you feel a need to go back to your place."

I hesitated. "I'd like that," I said, not committing to staying the night. I still felt uncomfortable staying the night. I didn't want Dan's parents to know I was with a new man. I knew that no matter what, it would make them think of Dan and make them sad.

So instead of staying the night the way my body wished I could, I went with Beckett to his hotel, with every intention of staying for a while and then going home before dawn, so Scott and Jeanne wouldn't know.

The best laid plans...

BECKETT RAN a bath for me complete with bubbles once we got into his hotel room and then he slowly undressed me and helped me into the warm frothy tub. I laid back, exhaling in pleasure, and then watched as he removed his clothes, hanging his suit up on the back of the door, and kneeling down beside the tub in his boxer briefs.

"You've worked a double shift today," he said and picked up a bar of soap. "Let me pamper you a while."

"I'm not arguing," I said and sighed while he began to slowly wash me starting at my hands and working his way up my arms and then down my body to my feet. By the time he was done, his fingers caressing me, slipping between my legs, sliding over my breasts, tweaking my nipples with his soapy fingers, I was relaxed and aroused at the same time.

He practically carried me to the bed and then made love to me nice and slow and deliberately.

I lay beside him, recovering, filled with euphoria and such a sense of release and relaxation that I fell asleep without even realizing how close I was. When I awoke, I gasped and glanced at the clock radio on the bedside table. Seven o'clock in the morning.

I bolted upright. "Oh my God," I said and slipped out of bed. "I have to get home right away. Scott's an early riser."

"Do you think he'll already be up?"

I nodded, panic rising in me at the thought Scott would wonder where I was. I rushed to the bathroom to quickly wash my face, and get dressed.

Beckett followed me and stood naked in the bathroom door, watching me.

"Why don't you stay for breakfast? There's no sense now trying to pretend you were home."

I stood beside the sink and considered. Scott was always up early. Sometimes six thirty at the latest. He'd be up when I arrived home. Maybe I could tell him I stayed at Leah's… But I didn't want to lie.

"I have to do the morning cash out. I need a change of clothes first, so I have to go…"

He made a sad face and shrugged. "We should have set the alarm. I'm sorry."

I dressed, and Beckett watched me. "I'll call for the limo."

I nodded and gathered up my things. "Thanks."

While Beckett used the house phone, I took one last look around to make sure I had everything and then went to the door. He came right over to me and pulled me against his body, squeezing me.

"Thank you for coming home with me," he said in a soft voice. "Don't worry about things. You're an adult. You have to live your life."

I nodded and stroked his shoulders. "I know. It's just hard to face them, knowing that they know I've been with another man."

"You have to move on."

I kissed him once more and then left, taking the limo back to the Lewis' house so I could have a quick shower and change my clothes.

When I arrived home, Scott was seated in the back yard, reading the morning paper with a cup of coffee. Jeanne was sleeping in as usual, so I slipped into my room, and then had my shower. I quickly changed into some fresh clothes and then went to the kitchen and poured myself a cup of coffee. While I was cutting up an orange, Scott came in and went to get a fresh cup of coffee.

"Morning," he said and smiled. "Looks like another great day in paradise."

"Sure does."

"Do you need a ride or are you walking to work?"

"I'll walk," I said and smiled. "I need the exercise. Besides, it's so nice this morning."

And that was it. He said nothing about the fact I didn't come home the previous night. He went back out to his lawn chair and continued to read.

I heaved a sigh of relief and then grabbed my sunglasses and bag and was off, walking the mile or so to the restaurant to do daily cash.

BECKETT

AFTER MIRANDA LEFT, I spent the rest of the day on my laptop, reading over briefs on upcoming projects, sending emails and speaking with my admin assistant about rescheduling all the meetings I had on my calendar.

I spent as much time with Miranda as I could. That night, I went to *Oceanside* again and sat at the bar while Miranda worked her shift, talking to her about everything and nothing, discovering more things we had in common as well as some things we didn't have in common.

"So tell me a bit about your father's side of the family," she asked while she poured a drink order.

I grimaced and gritted my teeth.

"I don't really like talking about them," I said, hoping to ward her off. "They're not the most law-abiding citizens, if you understand my meaning. Given your background, I doubt you'd approve..."

"Organized crime?" she said lightly, not meeting my eyes. I hoped the possibility wasn't a deal-breaker. She wasn't the kind of woman a man wanted to lose before he really even got her all to himself.

"Let's just say my uncle's involved in shady dealings in Hell's Kitchen and leave it at that."

"There are legitimate businesses there, but say no more," she said and nodded knowingly while she reorganized her work station. "I have a pretty good idea of what you mean."

"Hope that doesn't change things," I said, watching her face for a reaction.

She closed her eyes and shook her head. "Not at all," she said and finally turned to me, her eyes meeting mine. "I know it's possible to escape the influences of your parents, whether good or bad. Take my brother, for example," she said and I could hear a note of sadness in her voice. "He went the opposite way of my father. If there was a rule? He aimed to break it."

I nodded in return and relaxed a bit, commiserating with her about having family on the wrong side of the law, wishing I didn't have my uncle's skeletons in my family closet, especially considering that Miranda's family were all law and order types. My uncle was neck-deep in the Irish Mafia and I could only guess how many bodies were buried somewhere in the docks because of him and his fellow thugs. That they were using my father's business to launder money burned inside of me like a fire that wouldn't go out. One day, I'd get the business back and then I'd clean it up and make it what my father meant it to be.

"Do you have any days off this week?" I asked, hoping we could spend more than just an evening together, although that would be enough if that was all I could get.

"Tomorrow," she said. "After I do daily cash, I don't work at all."

I sat up straighter. "I just so happen to have the day off, too," I said with a grin. "Why don't we pack a lunch and take the bike over to the pier and soak up some rays. You know, last days of summer kind of thing."

"Sounds fabulous, but maybe we should ride further up the island," she said, her voice a bit hesitant.

"Sure, anything you want," I said, wondering why she was hesitating. "It's just that I like to watch the ships going out and coming back in."

She made a face. "I know most of the regulars around here. I'd rather go somewhere a bit more private. You understand."

It was then I did understand. Of *course*. She didn't want anyone who knew Dan and his parents to see her with some strange man.

"I understand completely," I said. I must admit that I felt bad that she didn't want to be seen with me. She'd mourned long enough, but I figured people were still possessive about her and Dan. Once she moved back to Manhattan, back to school, she would be free once more.

"I can pick you up at Oceanside or at your place," I offered, wanting her to call the shots so that she felt completely comfortable.

"Oceanside would be best. I'll make sure to pack a backpack with my stuff and we can go from there."

She still seemed a bit uncomfortable with me coming to the house. "I get it. You don't want your in-laws to know. I understand."

She lifted one shoulder in a shrug. "I feel a bit awkward about it. It has to bother them to think of me with someone new."

"Like I say, I understand. What time should I pick you up?"

"I'm usually finished by noon. I'll text you."

"What about tonight?"

"I'm busy all day."

"Will you come to my place after work?" I said, watching her face. "I promise to get you home before the sun rises."

"I'm closing," she said and shook her head. "I better go home one night this week and sleep or I won't be good for anything."

I let my shoulders sag, pretending to be more upset than I was, but then I smiled at her. "I get it. I'd sleep better with you beside me, but if you prefer to sleep alone…"

She leaned closer to me over the bar. "It's not that I don't want to be with you. I do. It's that I've been in late every night since that first night. I'm getting pretty exhausted. I need a solid night's sleep."

I mock-pouted. "What if I promised to give you a nice massage and let you sleep the whole night through without interruption? I hate not having you in my bed, now that I've had you there a few times..."

She laughed. "I like being there, but I highly doubt your ability to keep your promise, considering my past experience with you..."

I held my hand over my heart. "I promise, on my honor as a Marine, to let you sleep the entire night through. I won't wake you up until you want to be woken up."

She smiled at me, her green eyes twinkling. "All right, but if you break your promise, I won't be all perky and bright eyed for the day, let alone doing daily cash."

"I promise."

AND SO I had her back in my bed again for the night, and I kept my promise, allowing her to sleep the entire night through, despite the fact I woke up with a boner in the middle of the night, unaccustomed as I was to having a beautiful naked woman in my bed for the entire night. I usually kicked them out after the first or second time we fucked.

When I woke in the night and the first thing I felt was her naked skin, heard her slow deep breaths, and felt her warm flesh against me, I was immediately hard. I wished I could have woken her up for a nice slow fuck. Instead, I took in a deep breath and willed my erection to go away, thinking of the mud and sweat of hell week when I first became a Marine. That always worked to quell whatever enthusiasm I had at an inappropriate time.

When she finally woke up, after the clock radio beside the bed went off at six, we had an extra thirty minutes for a nice shower together and a fuck before she dressed. Then, she grabbed a quick cup of coffee and slice of toast from the tray of food I had pre-ordered the night before from room service, and was gone, taking the limo service to get to work.

I promised to pick her up after she was finished doing the daily cash out, and making the bank deposit for the day.

The only snag in a perfect day came when I went to pick her up at *Oceanside*. I got her text about a quarter after twelve.

MIRANDA: All done. Putting in an order for a knight on shining chrome to come pick me up for my day on the beach.

I laughed and texted her back.

BECKETT: My lady's every wish is my command. See you in twenty.

I finished packing my backpack with my swimming trunks, a pair of sandals, a t-shirt and floppy brimmed hat. I bought a bottle of wine from the hotel's off-sale and stole a couple of disposable plastic glasses from the hotel room. When I was ready, I brought along the spare helmet and drove down the street to a local tourist-trap beach store and purchased a big blanket.

Then, I drove down to Oceanside, and parked on the street across from the restaurant. I waited by my bike, watching the front door for her to come out, texting her to let her know I had arrived – as if the throaty growl of my bike's muffler wasn't enough.

BECKETT: Your steed is here, milady.

I waited, and then waited another five minutes, and then texted her again.

BECKETT: Hey, babe. I'm outside. Is everything okay?

Her response came a few moments later.

MIRANDA: Sorry... A bit delayed. Family matters...

I frowned and thumbed a text in response.

BECKETT: Dan's parents there? Do you want me to come back later?

MIRANDA: That might be best. I'll text you when the coast is clear.

BECKETT: *Okay. Your knight on a chrome ride will be waiting impatiently...*

MIRANDA: *I can't wait.*

So, I drove down the road that ran parallel to the ocean and parked at a small lot next to another restaurant and waited.

And waited.

About half an hour passed before I saw her walking down the street towards me, her backpack slung over her shoulders, her sunglasses under a wide-brimmed hat.

When she finally got to me, I opened my arms and pulled her into an embrace.

"Pesky in-laws wanting to hang out and talk?"

She laughed. "Yeah. I've been gone so much and Scott was curious about my whereabouts for the past few evenings. He tried to sound nonchalant, but he wasn't fooling anyone but himself."

I kissed her, pushing hair back from her cheek. "They just want to make sure you're all right," I said, trying to be supportive.

"I know," she replied and forced a smile. "It's just that I feel guilty..."

"You shouldn't," I said firmly, "and that's not just me being selfish. You said it's been almost a year."

"I know." She sighed and then smiled for real, the smile finally touching her eyes. "Let's go. I want some of whatever you packed for lunch."

"I didn't," I said and handed her the extra helmet. "I thought we'd do the tourist thing and buy something from a street vendor. You know – mystery meat and fries."

She laughed and hopped on the bike behind me, her arms threading around my waist. We drove up the island to North Topsail Beach and found a spot to park, not far from a nice restaurant.

There was small public beach with an abandoned lifeguard tower. Once I parked the bike, we walked up to a beach front restaurant and ordered a couple of burgers and fries. We bought a portable beach umbrella from a vendor at the side of the road and then we walked past the small row of dunes to a spot where we set up the umbrella and spread the blanket. Once settled, we ate our lunch, talking about the proximity to Camp Lejeune where I once was stationed when I was with Special Operations Forces.

There weren't many tourists around at that time of year and most of the beach front was private. Other than an older woman in a floppy hat walking along the edge of the surf looking for shells, we were alone. I took out my cell and put on some music, and we spent the afternoon in the warm sunlight, rubbing sunscreen on each other when the afternoon sun grew hot. When we got too hot, we ran into the surf and then laid on the blanket under the umbrella to get warm again. Luckily, some light clouds rolled in later in the afternoon and offered some respite from the incessant sun.

Miranda came back to my hotel room willingly every night for the rest of the week, and we made love twice or more, the two of us seemingly unable to get enough of each other. I was able to get enough work done on my computer each day while Miranda was working that I felt good about staying the extra week. By the time Saturday rolled around, I felt certain that we would continue the relationship once we were both back in New York. Although I'd be busy with Brimstone, and Miranda would be busy with classes, we would be able to continue to see each other.

Then reality struck home and I realized how unrealistic I was being.

Miranda still didn't know the truth and each passing day made it all the harder for me to even consider revealing to her how I got them.

On the Saturday night before I was returning to Manhattan, I suggested coming back the following weekend for a few days so we could see each other before her classes started and enjoy the last week of the summer holidays together.

She said she couldn't see me.

"I'll be in Arlington," she said. "It's the one-year anniversary of Dan's death. Scott, Jeanne and I will be driving up to Arlington for the memorial then on to Manhattan for the 21st. I have to check into my dorm at the New Yorker. Classes start on the 25th."

I knew then that I couldn't keep deceiving her. Even if I never outright told her a lie of commission, I was lying to her by omission. I *should* have told her that Dan died because of me.

I couldn't. No details of the reason I was there were supposed to be public nor the response team who came to rescue us. I'd already risked enough letting Brandon and Graham know.

Not being completely honest with Miranda weighed heavily on my mind. It was always there, from the very beginning, but I kept pushing it to the back of my mind, thinking I'd come clean later.

In the end, I didn't confess to her. Now I could see no way out. No matter what I did at that point, I'd hurt her. If I left her without an explanation, just left the package of letters behind, she'd hate me and feel hurt for a while, but then she'd move on. If I told her the truth, at least as much of the truth as I could, she'd hate me and feel betrayed.

I had to stop what I was doing. I had to stop the deception.

I'd done the wrong thing from the moment I found that package of letters in the brownstone.

There was no right thing to do at that point. I'd so thoroughly fucked everything up that there was no recovering from it.

All I could do was try to block any memory of Miranda and what we had together. I had a company in crisis and a family of criminals to watch over back in Hell's Kitchen. As much as I wanted to forget all that and immerse myself in Miranda, lovely Miranda, I knew she'd hate me – and rightfully so – when she found out the truth.

ON SATURDAY NIGHT, instead of going back to bed after Miranda took the limo service back home, I put on my sandals and walked down across the boardwalk to the beach. The moon was almost full and shone down on the ocean, highlighting the frothy surf. Above me were the stars, brilliant despite the moon.

I wished... I wished I'd done things right at the start of all this.

I should never have even considered seducing Miranda unless she knew who I was and why I was alive when her husband was dead.

I stood watching the surf for a long while, knowing full well that sleep would be a long time in coming.

I WENT for a long run the next morning, needing to work out some of my frustration. Then, before I left the hotel, I connected to a webinar being held for one of Brimstone's clients.

It was an important meeting but I barely heard a word. All I could think of was how Miranda would feel when she received my letter saying goodbye. I'd leave right after I dropped the letter off at Dan's parent's house.

I'd discourage her from contacting me. It would be better to hurt her now than have her learn the truth sometime in the future, when the mission was no longer considered classified.

"I'm a dick," I said when I called Casey during a break in the webinar, having a lapse in my resolve to never see Miranda again. "Tell me what I dick I am."

"You're a dick, Beckett," she said, her tone serious. "A total dick."

"You really mean that," I said when I heard her tone.

"I do."

I sighed heavily and ran a hand through my hair. "What should I do?"

I heard the rustling of pages on the other end of the call. "You already know."

"No," I said. "I don't know. If I tell her the truth, it will just bring up old pain, open an old wound."

"Better a cruel truth than a comfortable delusion," she replied.

"That's easy for you to say. You don't have to tell someone that you're a total dick."

She chuckled. "No, I had to tell you that *you're* a total dick."

"But you enjoyed it…" I sighed again and rubbed my forehead.

"Come on, Beckett. Tell her the truth. Fess up. You'll feel better for it. She'll either tell you to go fuck yourself or she'll give you another chance. This way, you're just being a big dick like every other jerk who fucks and runs the moment that they feel something actually human for a woman."

"Why don't you tell me what you really think?"

She laughed. "See you when you get back. Let's do a workout. Maybe I can knock some sense into you."

"Oorah."

"Oorah, yourself," she said and ended the call.

When the webinar was finished, I packed up my gear and drove down the strip to the Lewis house.

I knocked at the door and waited. She came to the door and when she saw me, I could tell she was surprised to see me.

"Beckett," she said. "You're here."

"I need to talk to you. I have something to confess."

She frowned. "About what?"

"Who I am. Can I come in?"

She opened the door hesitantly. I entered and glanced around at the house, which was a fantastic modern ranch style home.

"Is there somewhere we can be in private?"

She nodded without speaking and led me to the back of the house, down a long hallway with bedrooms on either side.

We entered a bedroom, feminine with soft colours and a very plush bed.

"What do you want to tell me."

I stood in front of her a few inches away and brushed a strand of hair off her cheek. "I haven't been truthful with you. I haven't told you everything."

"Tell me," she said, her voice low, and breaking with emotion, like she knew already that what I would tell her would be bad. "Tell me the truth. All of it."

Her face was pale, her eyes wide. I owed her an explanation for my behavior. I had to tell her the truth and bite the bullet, take my licks like a man.

"You better sit," I said softly.

She frowned at that but sat on the side of the bed. I bent down on one knee and took her hands in mine, looking at them while I tried to figure out the best way to tell her the truth. She had nice hands, her fingers fine, her nails short and well groomed. There was a faint indention on the middle finger of her left hand, from the ring she wore – Dan's ring. She'd recently taken it off and I realized she had finally stopped wearing it.

I glanced up in her eyes and despite the choke in my throat, I spoke.

"I should have told you everything right away. I fell a little bit in love with you from reading your letters to Dan." My throat was dry and I had to clear it before I could speak further. "When I met you, I fell even more. I wanted you for myself. I didn't want you to know how I got the letters because then you'd hate me."

Her face was unreadable. "Why would I hate you? You got them by accident, right? SNAFU?"

I shook my head, emotion welling up inside of me. I looked down, unable to meet her eyes. "I was there when Dan died."

I felt her reaction rather than saw it, in how her hand squeezed into a fist.

"What?" she said, her voice a whisper.

I nodded, holding her fist in my hands, wishing I could make her pain go away. I decided to tell her the whole truth, even the parts I wasn't supposed to tell.

"His team came to rescue us. I'm really not supposed to say

anything about it because we were testing some classified technology for the CIA when our MRAP – our armored vehicle – struck an IED."

"You were there," she whispered, her voice totally emotionless.

"Yes." I finally looked up and saw the shock written on her face, which was now flushed pink. "I got this," I said and pointed to the scar on my neck, "when the IED exploded and sent a piece of shrapnel into my neck. We were on our way back to our Forward Operating Base so we could take transport back home. Our GPS failed. We went through what we thought was friendly territory, but it wasn't. We accidentally crossed the border. That's why none of the details were made public. We were behind enemy lines in Iran."

"You were injured in an IED explosion."

I nodded. "Dan was the medic who saved my life. I was loaded onto his chopper. It went down in the dust storm moments later. Somehow, I survived and was taken to a hospital for triage. I don't have much memory of anything from a few days before to about a month after but he was killed in the crash. They tried to save him, but he was trapped. He must have brought your letters along with him and somehow they got mixed up with my things when they were able to medevac me out."

She frowned. "Why you? Why did you get his things? The letters were addressed to Dan."

I sighed. "My legal name is Daniel Beckett Tate-McNeil. In the aftermath of the crash, they must have thought the letters were mine. I only found them when I went through a box of my personal effects that had been sent back with me in July. They were in an old building I own. I went to check it out so I could sell it, because Graham died and I needed the money."

She sat in silence and then bowed her head, shaking it slowly. She fought tears, biting her lip, her eyes were brimming.

"I'm so *sorry*," I said, my own voice breaking. "I should have told you right away. I wasn't supposed to reveal classified information. But really, I didn't want you to hate me…"

Of course, it would hurt her to know the truth. What else could I expect? What kind of fool had I been, thinking I could tell her the truth and she'd still want me?

When she said nothing, I started to lose hope. Finally, she stood, her face red, her eyes teary.

"I'm *sorry*," she said and shook her head, holding out her hands to stop me when I tried to embrace her. I managed to pull her into my arms before she stopped me, but her body was stiff.

"*Miranda…*"

"I can't…"

She pulled away from me and as much as I hated it, I had to release her. When I did, she turned and left, leaving the bedroom and going to the front door, which she opened.

"Please leave."

I wanted to stay and comfort her but I knew I couldn't. I *shouldn't*. She wanted me to leave.

She knew the truth now. Her husband died because of me. She was a widow because of me. It wasn't some routing training action. It was a rescue.

I hadn't told her the truth from the moment I met her – I deceived her the entire time I was in Topsail Beach, about who I was and how Dan died because of me.

I could held her, kissed her, but I knew that what happened next had to be on her terms.

So I let her go.

I drove off, leaving Topsail Beach with a sick feeling in my gut, wishing I had the sense to do things right as soon as I arrived in town that first night instead of fucking everything up so thoroughly.

THE DRIVE HOME up the coast back to Manhattan seemed to take forever.

I almost turned back several times. When I stopped to gas up, I checked my phone, hoping beyond hope that Miranda had texted me, forgiving me for being such a dick, asking me to come back.

She didn't and I couldn't blame her.

How could I explain?

So my drive back to Manhattan was a long hot and thankless one and I arrived home feeling nothing but regret.

On top of that, the first few days back in Hell's Kitchen were just that – hell.

My business schedule was so busy with meetings and conferences for the next week that I hoped I'd be able to blot Miranda completely out of my mind, but I failed. A deep sense of regret filled me that I couldn't shake – not with exercise, not with bourbon – not with anything.

I met up with Casey for dinner after work on Wednesday. She wanted to meet at the gym but I was too busy catching up with work to take time off. I was planning on working late that night but agreed to go to our favorite restaurant for dinner before returning to the office to catch up on some paperwork. We met in the bar for a drink while we waited for a table.

"So fill me in," she said as she sipped her bourbon. "Tell me what you're going to do to make it right."

"I can't do anything," I said and downed my shot of bourbon. I sighed as the bourbon burned down my throat, needing the heat. "I fucked it up so totally, nothing can fix things."

"Nonsense," she said and punched me lightly on the shoulder. "Everything can be fixed, if you try hard enough."

I shook my head in doubt. "Not this. I'm the reason her husband died. He was killed in a horrible accident saving my life. I kept the truth from her while I pursued her, and finally succeeded in seducing her, fucking her brains out in my hotel room for ten days before letting her know the truth."

"Wow," Casey said and pulled back, giving me the evil eye. "You really did fuck it up."

"I did," I said and smacked my empty glass down on the bar. The bartender poured me another glass of bourbon. "There's no recovering from this."

Casey sighed. "Do you really like this woman? I mean really *like* her. Not does your *dick* like her. I mean *you*, Beckett. The man. Would you like a relationship with her?"

"I'm crazy about her," I said, totally honest. "If I could, I'd see her every day."

"Then, don't give up on her. Tell her how you feel. If she tells you to go to hell, take it like a man," Casey said, her brow furrowed. "Let the chips fall where they may. If she forgives you, you win. If she smacks you upside your head, you deserved it. If she doesn't smack you, I will." She grinned at that, but I didn't respond.

I stared into my glass somberly. "So I just walk up and ask her to forgive me despite the fact I deceived her for days and fucked her in spite of who I am?"

"Yep," she said. "Be a man, Marine," she said, growling like Master Sergeant Fillmore. I knew she was trying to lighten the mood, but it wasn't working.

I said nothing for a moment, wondering how I would do it. If I did it.

"Call her. If she won't answer the phone, leave a message or text her. Tell her you fell in love with her and let your heart guide you instead of your conscience. Ask for her forgiveness and then leave it up to her. If she can forgive you, maybe something more will happen. If not, end of story."

I nodded. "I will."

"Good," she said and drank down her own bourbon. "Now, that's enough about Miranda until you can tell me you came clean. Understood?"

"Understood."

THURSDAY CAME, and I woke up with a bad feeling in my gut. I sat up in bed and ran a hand through my hair, trying to clear my head and figure out why I was feeling so negative. Then I remembered the memorial service being held at Arlington. The one-year anniversary of the crash, Dan's death and nearly my own. There would be several memorial services held that day for the other fallen Marines. I never had the chance to attend the burial services, since I was recovering in a hospital in Germany and then in New York, but my uncle Colm told me about them, attending on my behalf.

Attending the one-year anniversary memorials would give me the chance to pay my respects to the families. If I couldn't face Dan's parents, I could at least attend the two other Marine's graves, pay my respects anonymously. My plan was to arrive early, visit the graves, then leave. Miranda said they would be arriving at noon, so I planned on going and leaving before 11:30 so I wouldn't bump into them.

I packed my uniform and dressed in my suit and tie, then drove my car down the coast to Arlington, Virginia, stopping along the way for a lunch break. I had a hotel reservation in Arlington, and intended to arrive in town, hit the rack early, and then get up early to get dressed in my uniform before making it over to the Arlington National Cemetery. I wanted to pay my respects to the fallen Marines and other soldiers I knew who died while on active duty or when they retired. There were a lot of names to see to, including those fallen who were buried in the main cemetery or in the Columbarium or Niche Wall for those who were cremated.

I spent a long time lying in my hotel room in the darkness, thinking back to when I was in Afghanistan and the vague details I could recall of the accident that injured me and took Lewis's life. My memory was pretty spotty on the actual event, but I remembered Afghanistan vividly. Hot dry days, the sand gritting between your teeth, the incessant sun burning your skin, the crunch of dirt under your boots. At night, the desert climate became cold. The desert air was clear at night and the sky was magnificent, the stars so incredibly bright you felt like you could reach up and touch them. How I longed to return with a telescope and spend time taking photos.

I could also remember a sense of accomplishment to our mission, when my Special Activities Division contact and I were going out on exercises with a team of Marines Special Operations Forces to test out the new coms Brimstone had developed under my DARPA contract.

When it came to the crash, I had only brief images of the IED aftermath and then the rescue and crash. The day it happened was like any other day in Afghanistan – cold at night, hot during the day, the heat and dust and sun making me long to get back to Manhattan and the familiar humidity. We were embedded with the Marines and were living in the same conditions with the same experiences, sleeping in tents, doing exercises night and day to test the equipment.

The day of the accident, we drove through new territory which was past a small settlement we'd already been through earlier in the day. A dust storm was brewing, and the first grains of sand gritted between my teeth. The first clue that we were in danger came when we found the main road blocked off by a broken down truck, the hood up like someone was working on the engine, and the doors wide open.

The Marines we were embedded with were familiar with all the tactics of the local insurgents and so we were on our guard, but this was supposed to be friendly territory. The driver at the head of our small convoy radioed back that the main road through the settlement was blocked so we would have to either go back or take a side road. I glanced at John and he shrugged. We'd been through several similar villages with no issues, and so we took the side road and that was our first mistake.

When our GPS malfunctioned, we should have turned back and retraced our route, but we didn't. We proceeded, taking a road the driver thought led back to civilization.

That was when all hell broke loose.

The ground underneath our MRAP exploded into a mountain of dirt and debris, the metal shrapnel flying, the concussion knocking me out.

After that, all I had were vague memories of a medic wearing goggles looking in my eyes, the *thwop-thwop-thwop* of the choppers that came to rescue us, then the crash, being thrown to the ground still strapped to a gurney, black smoke and cries of agony from other injured. The torn and bloody body of the medic on the dirt beside me. My next memory was waking up in a field hospital while I was wheeled into an OR for emergency surgery to remove the shrapnel that embedded itself in my neck.

Then, nothing until I woke up in a hospital in Germany, more overhead lights and more surgery, and then nothing again, until I was on the transport plane back to America for my long and uneventful rehab.

I didn't even know how close to death I was until I was back in the US in my local VA hospital in New York. It was all a blur to me.

What I did learn, a couple of weeks later, was that a member of our Marine recon team was killed in the initial blast and then two others, one on our team and one Navy Hospital Corpsman who came to rescue us were killed when our chopper went down in the dust storm that overtook us.

It was fully twelve weeks later that I was able to leave the rehab hospital, having learned to walk again after being in a drug-induced coma to relieve swelling on my brain. I'd been lucky that I had no lasting brain damage. Others in our group were not so lucky. Besides the dead, we'd had several members of the team suffering limb amputations and traumatic brain injuries in the chopper crash. My contact with SAD suffered some minor injuries and left the CIA soon after.

We'd strayed into Iranian territory, and had driven over an IED buried on the side road that we were forced to take in order to return to our Forward Operating Base. We'd had no issues in that area of Afghanistan, and so the roadside IED was unexpected. Our accident proved just how critical navigational and communications tech was to ground forces.

When I had mostly recovered, I returned to work, glad to be back into my normal life, but suffering from survivor's guilt. I had problems sleeping, of course, and had nightmares on a regular basis, but focusing on the business was a godsend. I spent some time reading what I could about the incident, but there wasn't much published because we were on a classified mission, since SAD was involved.

My name wasn't mentioned in what little press existed on the event. All that was mentioned was that two Marines and a Navy Hospital Corpsman were killed with several others injured. That was it.

I tried to put it all behind me and I focused on my business. Then Graham died in Malaysia, and I needed money to keep Brimstone going so I went to the brownstone to see what needed to be done to put it up for sale and that's when I found them. The letters.

I lay on the hotel bed, remembering everything – at least, as much as I could remember. There was just too much to deal with. Sue's death, my own injuries, Graham...

Truthfully, the only time in the past three years that I felt happy, truly happy, had been with Miranda. When we were together, no matter what we were doing -- eating pizza naked while watching television in my hotel room in Topsail Beach, sitting on the patio watching the surf, walking along the boardwalk, I felt – *happy*.

Like I could do that forever.

She was perfect for me. *Perfect.*

I couldn't imagine anyone else being as perfect as her. Besides Sue, I had never felt that way about a woman. Not in the three years since Sue died and not before her.

I felt such incredible guilt that I'd taken away Miranda's new husband and made her a widow. My mission killed Lewis. He died because of me.

How could I face her and tell her that?

In the end, I was a coward and it was hard for me, someone who lived through several tours of duty in Iraq and then in Special Forces in Afghanistan, to admit I was a coward when it came to facing the widow of the man who died to save my life.

I shouldn't have even been in Arlington to attend any of the memorial services. Maybe I needed to go to one of those group grief counseling sessions Casey kept talking about...

AFTER A FEW SCANT hours of sleep, I woke early and got up, showered, dressed in my uniform, and then made my way to Arlington National Cemetery so I could pay my respects before any of the families arrived. I'd stop, snap a few pictures of the headstones and plaques of the men I knew who were killed in action. Then I'd leave.

Miranda didn't need to see my face. She must hate me for what I did to her and seeing me again would only be adding insult to injury. I parked and began my walk through the grounds. Arlington National Cemetery is a beautiful location. The graves are marked by white headstones, row upon row that rest beneath trees, and the grass surrounding them is green and lush. Overhead that day, the sky was blue and it was peaceful as I wandered among the rows of headstones.

Using the App on my iPhone to locate the graves of several marines from my old battalion, I walked through the rows of headstones. While I walked, emotion built inside of me as memories of my time in Iraq and Afghanistan came flooding back. I found the names of several Marines who died during my first tour of duty during the surge and I bent down to touch their grave markers.

The Columbarium and Niche Wall were also impressive, with plaques on the wall, the whole complex feeling like a trip back to some Greek or Roman temple with the carved stone arches and walls. It was early, and I hoped to miss anyone who might know me – especially Miranda. As much as I would have liked to thank Dan's parents in person, I couldn't. I didn't want to hurt Miranda any more than I had already.

While I was standing in one of the alcoves, looking for Lewis's plaque, I heard some voices and turned to see, in the distance, Miranda with a couple who I assumed were Mr. and Mrs. Lewis. I quickly left the spot in the hopes that Miranda didn't recognize me for the brief moment she might have seen me.

I walked along the edge of the field, beneath the trees that grew on the perimeter of Arlington, hoping to make it back to the visitor parking area before anyone stopped me. I heard someone behind me and turned.

Miranda.

MIRANDA

THE WEEKS after Beckett left were hell.

I couldn't understand how I could be so damn wrong about him. He seemed like an honorable man. He was a Marine. He'd been decorated. He was a decent man, trying to build a business helping train Marines and make them safer on the battlefield.

How could he lead me on for so long?

He should have too me right away that he was the reason Dan died.

I cried my eyes out when I stopped being angry.

ON THURSDAY, we packed up the car and left for Arlington. We were staying at a hotel on the outskirts of the city, close to the cemetery. I dreaded seeing Dan's plaque on the Columbarium, because I'd know that behind it sat the urn with Dan's remains. It made me think of his death in that chopper in a desert storm. We had so few details of the mission because it was classified, but I knew he died in the crash along with two Marines.

Their families would be at the memorial and we planned on

meeting up with them for lunch. I was *not* looking forward to it – rehashing everything would open the old wounds again. After Beckett, I didn't need anything else to hurt.

I was numb all day, following Scott and Jeanne, letting them lead the way, make the conversation. I was mostly silent, looking out the window at nothing as we drove from Topsail Beach to Arlington, barely noticing the scenery. The entire trip, my mind went over everything I could remember that Beckett said to me, what we did, to see if there were any clues. He did repeatedly say, in a joking manner, that he couldn't tell me things. He said I shouldn't ask him about his work with the DEA. I was used to not asking questions, given Dan's work with Special Operations Forces, especially his last deployment, so I hadn't pushed.

"You okay, hun?" Jeanne said from the front of the car. "You've been so quiet since we left."

I nodded and forced a smile. "It's all just coming back to me. Plus, getting those letters…"

I turned away, my throat choking up. In truth, I thought maybe Dan had thrown the letters out, for they weren't with his belongings when they brought his remains back home. It hurt me a bit because he told me he kept them with him, inside his jacket, when they went on a mission – for good luck.

But in the aftermath of his death, in all the confusion around the event and the lack of details, I was too upset to think about it. The first month after his death I spent on his bed in the bedroom that Jeanne kept as it had been since he was a teen and when he first joined up. His Star Wars and Marvel posters were all there, beside the cork board where his ribbons from track and field in high school were pinned. His football trophies, his academic achievement certificate. He enlisted before he finished college, and trained as a Hospital Corpsman with the Navy. He received special training so he could become qualified for independent duty and was attached to Fleet Marine Force Recon. As a Fleet

Marine Force Warfare Specialist, he was invited to be a member of the Marines Special Operations Forces – a high honor.

He was so brave…

My brave warrior. I fell in love with him because of his strength and easy smile, his sense of humor and his love of life. He was an honorable man. A man like my father, who was willing to put his life on the line for his country.

I sighed and braced myself for the ceremony, and tried to put on a brave stoic face so I could meet the other families and offer my condolences for their loss. We didn't spend any time together between the initial funerals and today's anniversary memorial, but there was a common bond with the other families that could not be denied when you shared a loss with someone.

Our loved ones fought together and were injured or died together.

Only the families and friends left behind understood what it felt like to be in our shoes.

WE STAYED at a small hotel close to the cemetery, and had a quiet dinner in the hotel's restaurant. I didn't feel much like talking after dinner and spent the majority of my time reading an eBook on forensic science, trying to get my mind back into the world I'd left a year earlier when Dan died. It was futile. I read the same passage over and over again before finally turning the Kindle off and going to sleep.

In the morning, we all dressed and decided to make an early trip out to the cemetery before the memorial, because we wanted to be alone for a while before the other families joined us. We parked in the lot to the east of the Columbarium where Dan's ashes were kept and as we walked up to the stone arches, with row upon row of plaques marking the spots where the dead were interred, I saw a Marine in uniform. He was standing close to where Dan's remains were located, leaning against the wall, his hand on a plaque. He turned and even from a distance of maybe thirty yards, I recognized him instantly.

Beckett.

BECKETT

I TURNED to walk away but Miranda didn't stop. Instead, she came at me, her face flushed, her fists clenched. I turned back to her and held my hands up, wanting to apologize, but before I could she was right there in front of me, tears in her eyes.

I turned around to face her, bracing for her anger.

"Why are you here," she said and hit my shoulder. "I would think you'd avoid showing up to Dan's memorial."

I held my hands up defensively. "I'm sorry," I said. When she stopped hitting me, I took hold of her shoulders. "Really, Miranda. I'm sorry."

"Sorry isn't good enough," she said and wiped her eyes. "Why did you lead me on?" she asked, her cheeks wet. "Was getting laid so important that you'd *sleep* with me without telling me who you really were?"

I shook my head, struggling to find the words. "It was wrong. I was afraid if you knew the truth, you'd hate me. I have to go," I said and backed away. "Goodbye, Miranda. I'm sorry all this happened."

Then I turned and left.

"You're a bastard," she said, her voice low but not so low that I didn't hear it.

I said nothing, barely able to contain my emotions, walking fast, almost running away from her. My heart was pounding in my chest, my throat constricted.

I was a bastard by any definition of the term. What a fucking idiot I was to come here. How much more painful a day must I have made it for her? I thought I would get there early and miss the memorial, as it was scheduled for eleven o'clock. I never expected them to arrive earlier...

I drove off, my chest tight, my eyes blurry. I deserved everything she threw at me. I should have stayed and taken it like a man.

MIRANDA

WHEN HE TURNED and left me standing there, tears overflowing despite my anger, I yelled at him.

"You're a bastard," I said but he didn't stop or respond. I don't know what I wanted him to do at that moment – except explain. To make it all right so I could be with him.

I wanted to run after him and hit him, pound him. Mostly, I wanted him to be the man I thought he was – an honorable former Marine, DEA Agent, software engineer running his own company, who couldn't seem to resist me.

Instead, he seducing me all while knowing that Dan died because of him.

I turned and ran back to the car, closing the door and covering my eyes. Jeanne followed me, opening the other passenger door and slipping in beside me.

"What's the matter, hun? Who was that? Why are you crying?"

I shook my head, unable to speak at the moment. I wiped my eyes and stared off into the distance. Finally, I was calm enough that I could speak.

"That was the former Marine who left the package of letters in the mailbox," I said, my voice barely audible. "I'm just upset."

"Why did you hit him? Do you know him? Was he one of Dan's friends?"

I shook my head. "I don't really want to talk about it." I turned to her, my eyes blurry. "I'm sorry. I'm just very upset."

"Of course," she said and put her arm around my shoulders, pulling me closer. "You don't have to say anything. We're all upset today. It's a hard day."

I nodded. I wanted to go and see Dan's plaque, touch it. Seeing Beckett had ruined the day for me because it brought back how happy I was being with him, how much I enjoyed his company, how there was a part of me that I tucked away, back in the farthest corner of my heart, that hoped something more would develop between us.

We walked back to the memorial wall and stood in front of Dan's plaque, Scott talking softly about his earliest memories of Dan as a boy. How he always wanted to play soldier, right from his earliest days. How he was so proud of Dan when he joined up and then made Special Operations Forces.

I stood and cried my eyes out, and in truth, my tears were for Dan and for myself. I had hoped that Beckett was someone who could fill the hole in my chest left by Dan's death. Even though no one could ever replace Dan, there might be room in there for someone different. Someone new.

I thought Beckett was that someone. Everything seemed so great with him. It felt so damn easy.

I felt incredibly guilty that I was as upset about Beckett as I was about Dan.

"Let's go," Jeanne said and put an arm around my shoulder. Together, the three of us left the cemetery and went back to the hotel to get ready for our meeting with the other families.

I had thought I'd be able to say my goodbyes to Dan and while I knew that I'd never really get over his death or his loss, I could find someone else to fill part of the hole his absence left inside of me.

Now, all I felt was empty.

BECKETT

I DROVE BACK to my hotel room and removed my uniform, folding it back up and tucking it away in my suitcase. What a mistake, coming to Arlington. I really thought if I went early, I wouldn't run into her. Of all the luck to go early and find that they'd gone early as well...

I checked out of my room and drove back to New York, arriving much later that night, having stopped for a rest along the way in Philadelphia. It was dark and I went right into my apartment, removed my clothes, and threw myself in bed, having only eaten a hot dog I bought in a gas station on route from Philly. I tossed and turned, going over the scene in my mind's eye – her face as she came up to me, the tears in her eyes... I hurt her, badly, breaking it off via a letter after making plans for us to still see each other when she came to Manhattan.

For that, I knew she could never forgive me. Even if I told her the truth, she'd hate me every time she saw my face because it was my fault that her husband died.

How could she not hate me?

At 2:00 AM, after not being able to fall asleep, tossing and turn-ing, my guts in a knot, I texted Casey.

BECKETT: *Things did not go well.*

She could have ignored my text, but she didn't.

CASEY: *You really thought they would?*

I sighed and replied.

BECKETT: *I hoped.*

Her text took a few moments to arrive.

CASEY: *Hope in one hand, shit in the other. See which one fills up faster. What did she say?*

BECKETT: *She called me a bastard.*

CASEY: *Did you tell her you were critically injured and he saved your life? Did you tell her your mission was classified and you really were under legal obligation not to talk about it?*

I hesitated, feeling like such a dick because I didn't tell her anything.

BECKETT: *Yes. She was too upset and hit me. I realized at that point that there was no salvaging anything so I left.*

When she replied, I could almost feel her anger and frustration in her words.

CASEY: *Beckett Tate, do you know nothing about women? After all the women you've been with?*

I ran a hand through my hair and sighed.

BECKETT: *All I can do is move on and forget her.*

My cell rang. I checked the display. It was Casey. She must have grown sick of the texts.

"Look, Beckett, you have to give her the chance to get over the shock at learning how your life and Dan's were connected. You have to tell her the whole truth – all of it. Not only what happened in Afghanistan, but also about your injuries and rehab. Tell her about Sue. How after her death, you stopped believing that you would ever meet anyone and fall in love again? Tell her how you got the letters and what happened to you when you read them and started to learn about her. How you fell for her before you even met her, just from reading her letters. Tell her that when you met her, you were hopelessly smitten and while you fully intended to simply return the letters to the parents, you met her instead and fell for her. How each time you tried to come clean, you feared her response."

I took in a deep breath and mulled over her words. "That would make me look like a total coward."

"Beckett!" she said, almost shouting. "Of all the men I know, you are not a coward. You almost died testing equipment that is meant to save lives. You have survivor's guilt. You have PTSD even if you don't want to admit it."

When I didn't respond, she continued. "Am I right?" she said. "You fell in love with her and you were too guilty about surviving while her husband died."

"Of course," I replied, shaking my head. "How the hell else could I feel?" She didn't say anything for a moment. "How do you know all this, anyway?" I asked, grudgingly admitting she was right.

She laughed lightly. "Because I know you, Beckett. I freaking know you better than you know yourself. You're in love with this woman. Tell her everything. Give her the chance to forgive you. Maybe you're the first man who made her feel alive again. Maybe she fell for you, too."

I stared up at the ceiling, my cell in my hand, and considered.

"I'll take your advice under serious consideration," I said, trying to sound officious.

"I'm not joking, Beckett. Give her time, but don't give up. If you love her, that is."

I sighed once more. "I will."

"When?"

I rolled my eyes. "When I get the chance."

"Do it," she said, her tone impatient. "You of all people should understand that there's no time to waste. Tomorrow is never certain. Do it today."

"I'll think about it."

The line was silent for a moment and then I heard her yawn. "You okay?" she said finally.

"I'm good," I replied. "Thanks, Case. I mean it. You're always there for me."

"I am. You better appreciate me."

I laughed but I was serious. "I do."

"Goodnight, Beckett. Get some sleep. Everything looks better when the sun's shining."

"Goodnight."

I finished the bottle of bourbon that remained from a party I'd had a few weeks earlier – before Graham died.

Before my life started to go to shit.

Finally, when the room spun from too much alcohol, I was able to fall asleep, passing out sometime after three.

THE NEXT DAY, I was pretty hung over and feeling incredibly sorry for myself, but I had to go into work and try to get caught up on more pressing matters than my hangover, such as how I was going to fund the next project while I waited for the brownstone to sell. While I was stirring a raw egg into a post-drunk concoction Casey swore got rid of hangovers, my cell buzzed, indicating I had an incoming text. I checked my messages and saw that my uncle had texted me, inviting me over to the pub for dinner. The youngest brother of three, he liked to have me over so we could catch up on family matters.

After a long day at work, I went to my fitness club for a workout and then after a quick shower, I made my way to Colm's restaurant in Hell's Kitchen, the home of the local Irish-American community. Colm was my kind of man – he'd fought with the Irish Defense Force back in the day but got out of Ireland as soon as he could, bringing his wife and kids with him and enough money to start a restaurant. He was perhaps the only man in my family with whom I could identify. He and my father were very close when they were kids.

My grandfather was an engineer back in Northern Ireland. My father carried on with the family's interest in engineering, but wanted to become a rich entrepreneur, with his eye on starting a company that would be passed down from generation to generation. Like Brandon, he wanted to create a business empire. Growing up in the mean streets of Northern Ireland, even if your father was one of the more fortunate ones due to his career and IDF membership, was still one of deprivation and feeling like you were hamstrung from following your dreams.

My father followed his dreams in the USA, but unfortunately, his dream of founding a business empire that he could pass on to his son didn't pan out. I didn't get his business when he died. His older brother Donny did. Donny, the thug. The lowlife in the local Irish Mafia. How I hated him...

Colm was sympathetic, but shrugged his shoulders. There was nothing he, as the youngest brother, could do. Donny was the head of the family now. He was also involved with very scary men. I wasn't afraid of them. I'd looked death in the eye many times when I'd been in the Marines and deployed in Iraq and Afghanistan. They were scum compared to the heroes I fought beside and the religious zealots who tried to blow us up.

Colm was someone I could respect. He in turn respected my desire to join the Marines, and we spent some quality family time talking about Afghanistan whenever we got together. Fighting was something we had in common despite being separated for all those years after my mother and father divorced and I moved down to New Orleans and then California with her and her new husband.

I drove my car over to the restaurant in Hell's Kitchen. Despite the fact Colm wasn't involved in the mafia, and tried to run a clean ship, he still had to face its reality so there was a security guy standing outside the back entrance, smoking a cigarette.

The man saw me and nodded, familiar enough with my face that he let me in without stopping to check my ID.

I went in through the kitchen, where the line cooks were busy with the night's menu. My stomach rumbled as I smelled the food being cooked. The first seating for dinner was already under way, and the scents wafting from the kitchen as I passed by made my mouth water. I popped into the office and saw Colm's daughter Dana sitting at the computer, staring at a spreadsheet.

"Hey, cousin," I said and pecked her on the cheek.

She smiled when she saw me. "Daniel! It's been so long. How are you? You missed the last family supper."

I stood in the doorway and glanced around, noting the Irish calendar on the wall, and a very ornate cross over the desk. Colm was a staunch Catholic. *Jesus, Mary and Joseph* was his favorite curse.

"How am I?" I said and ran a hand through my hair. "Well, my business partner died a few weeks ago. I've been trying to deal with it. I'll be at the next family supper."

"Sorry to hear that," she said and nodded her head. "You need your family. My dad misses you. You're like a son to him."

"He's been a great uncle," I said.

She smiled and then I left, going to the bar, which was pretty empty, with only a few guests seated at small tables. I went up to the bar and said hello to Dana's husband, who was bartending.

"Hey, Mike," I said and we shook. "How are things?"

"Great to see you," Mike said. "What can I get for you? Colm's out picking up something. He'll be back soon."

I sat at the bar and watched the news, sipping my glass of bourbon in wait for Colm to return. While I waited, I assessed my life.

All in all, it was pretty good, despite my recent loss of Graham, and the financial insecurity that resulted. Sure, I'd had my own degree of tragedy – my parents' divorce, the loss of my father, Sue's death, my injury, Graham's death... In fact, I'd had a lot of tragedy if you sat down and thought about it – which I tried hard not to do if possible.

Then there was the fuckup that was my relationship with Miranda – the one woman I'd met since Sue's death that I would even consider being with long term.

Maybe I *would* go with Casey to a VA grief counseling session one of these days…

FINALLY, Colm showed up and gave me a bear hug when he saw me at the bar.

"Daniel," he said, his face beaming. "You've finally come by to see your old uncle. It's about bloody time."

"It's been too long."

He sat beside me at the bar and nodded to Mike. "Pull us some Guinness," he said despite my protest. I really didn't like stout but it was an Irish thing.

Mike poured us each a glass of stout and we toasted each other.

"So Dana tells me that you lost your partner, Graham? Tell me."

I nodded and proceeded to tell him about Graham being killed while over in Malaysia, due to a suicide bombing in a crowded market square.

"I'm selling the brownstone to help with finances until I can find another partner or investor."

"Go to *Donny*," Colm said and frowned. "I know you don't like the way he runs the business, but it's your money, or it will be one day."

I shook my head. "Gonna keep my hands clean," I said firmly. "I'll make it work."

We chatted for a while and then went into the dining room for dinner. Much beer was consumed, and we were treated like kings by the staff.

I left much, much later that night after a few more shots of Irish whiskey and a few more toasts to everything and everyone Colm could think of.

I flopped into bed and tried to sleep, but thoughts of Miranda kept me awake. Instead, I took out my collection of photos and, like a pathetic stalker, I stared at them and remembered our time together.

One of the happiest times in my recent life.

I fell asleep with her picture in my hand, the flatscreen TV on the wall across from my bed droning the latest news.

MIRANDA

THINKING about Beckett sent me into a funk.

I had hoped that because I had so much to do before classes started on the 25th, I would have barely any time to think about him and the whole mess in Topsail Beach and at the memorial, but I was wrong. I went around with a sick feeling in my gut and a sense of loss I hadn't felt since Dan died. All I could think of was Beckett and why he'd kept the truth from me. He didn't exactly lie. He admitted that Dan saved his life, but he didn't tell me that Dan died because of him.

The first few days back in Manhattan were exhausting as I got moved in, and my room set up. I was glad that I had a few days to get things all in order before classes started on Thursday. Leah was going to study at Columbia and she had a space in the student housing there, while I would be going to CUNY and had a room in The New Yorker, which was student housing specifically for John Jay students.

I had a single enhanced room, with my own washroom and tiny bar fridge along with a single bed, desk and wardrobe as well as a window overlooking the street. The cost was high, but I had a combination of scholarship and savings that allowed me to live there for the year. I'd be so busy during that week, getting back into the whole student life, I wouldn't have much time to think.

Before he died, Dan had joked that we used to sleep on his tiny bed in his mom and dad's house in Topsail Beach or in my tiny bed in residence. One day, when we had the money, we'd rent an actual apartment in Queens, closer to my granddad's and I'd take the train in to school. But that was a year or more down the road, when I finished my degree and joined the FBI. Dan was supposed to be in for three more years, and then he'd get out and do his certification to become an EMT. My income with the Bureau and his as an EMT would be enough to get a big enough apartment that we could have a king sized bed instead of the twins we were used to.

So, while the paperwork and moving and everything else kept me busy, not to mention the start of classes, my nights were still hell.

I laid awake for what seemed like hours each night, thinking of Beckett and why he didn't tell me everything right away. Was it because he was involved in some undercover work with the DEA? Assuming that he was in fact working with the DEA… At that point, I had no idea what to believe.

When Leah and I got together after classes for a slice of pizza, we sat in the park with our slices and drinks and of course, I went over it all again.

"I suppose I'm driving you crazy with this," I said, laughing ruefully.

She smiled and then rolled her eyes in an exaggerated manner. "What? You driving me crazy talking about Beckett again? *Never…*"

We laughed, but there was an ache in the pit of my stomach that no amount of pizza or Rocky Road ice cream could assuage.

"Are we going to try to find an MCMAP class somewhere to take?" she asked as we walked down Fifth Avenue.

I shook my head. "It would just remind me of Beckett."

"And how he had his nice big strong hands all over your body..." Leah said and wagged her eyebrows.

I nodded. "We had great sex," I said softly. "Lots of great sex. I thought I could get used to it."

"Talk to him. He left his number on your phone..."

I turned to her and made a face of disbelief. "You seriously think I should talk to him after what happened?"

She shrugged. "He must have had a reason."

I shook my head.

We walked in silence back towards the subway. "Call him," she said again. "Give him a chance. He seemed like a really great guy. Brandon thinks the world of him."

I exhaled. There was a part of me that wanted to know what he meant by that remark about bad news. There was a part of me that wanted everything to be good and for us to be together. I hated that part of me, because I deserved honestly and to be treated with respect.

I didn't think I could trust Beckett because he didn't come clean right away.

"I don't know, Leah," I said and stood beside the stairs to the subway. "Would you?"

She nodded vigorously. "I'm seeing Brandon again."

"He didn't lie to you."

"Look, Miranda, it's up to you, but if you like him, if you really like him, give him a chance. It would be a gas if we were to all get together and do things. Have dinner. Go dancing. Beckett seemed to like to dance..."

I sighed. As much as I had hoped we could get together once we returned to Manhattan, and for me to prepare dinner for him at his apartment like he suggested, I was afraid of what he'd tell me.

I hugged Leah and we parted ways.

I STARTED BARTENDING the following weekend at my grandfather's pub in Queens. To mark my first day back, I invited Leah to come and sit at the bar while I bartended. She said of course, and so I looked forward to seeing her and chatting on my first shift. It was great to be back, and I was so glad I was going to see Gramps again, after a year away.

When I arrived, the place was just as I remembered it from over a year earlier, when I was last there before going to Topsail Beach to marry Dan and live with Scott and Jeanne for a few weeks. The pub was comprised of one long narrow room with a huge wooden bar with polished brass fixtures. Behind the bar was a wall-length mirror and glass shelves on which were stacked glasses and bottles of liquor. A dozen stools sat under the lip of the bar. It was still pretty early, but the place was half-filled with patrons, most of the cops who came in from the local precincts.

Gramps was standing behind the bar, leaning over and speaking with two patrons, a white bar cloth in his hand. He was mid-sixties and looked like an aging Robert Duvall, with a bald head and eagle eyes. He glanced my way when I entered, and his face lit up when he recognized me.

"Mira!" he called out and put down the cloth, opening the bar hatch and coming out to give me a big hug. "I am so damn glad to see you, you can't know. It's been hell not having your smiling face here this past year."

I hugged him back and we kissed each other a couple of times, laughing and smiling. I was truly happy to see him again.

"Gramps, I'm so sorry to have stayed away for so long, but I'm back now."

Gramps led me to a table in the corner, out of the way of the other patrons, and we sat down. The cocktail waitress came right over. She was new so she didn't know me, but Gramps must have told her about me coming.

"Is this your granddaughter?" she asked and gave me a smile.

"Your grandfather has been talking about you non-stop since the summer when I started working."

I glanced at Gramps and smiled. "I missed him and I missed this place." I turned to her. "Are you working tonight?"

She nodded. She seemed pleasant enough and if Gramps liked her, she was all right in my books. He had a very good sense about people, having been a cop for his entire career.

Before my shift, we had dinner, the two of us eating heaping platters of corned beef and fries at a local deli down the street like we used to before I left for Topsail Beach a year earlier.

"So how are you, sweetheart? Ready to start your new life?"

I nodded, forcing a smile. "Yes," I said and lied.

I was ready, but my heart still ached out of disappointment. I hoped I'd be seeing Beckett once I returned to Manhattan and that he'd be part of my new life. Now, that was likely not going to happen.

We had a nice meal, catching each other up on our own news since the last time I visited at Easter. Then we walked back to the pub and I took my place behind the counter. A few hours later, Leah showed up and sat at the bar, and spent the next hour regaling me about her first week of classes and the hot business school grad she met in a seminar. I laughed, amazed that she was such a flirt and always meeting new men wherever she went.

About 9:30, Steve from Topsail Beach walked into the bar and made a big to-do about seeing me and Leah.

"Well, looky here," he said and came up behind Leah, grabbing onto her shoulders and squeezing. "Fancy meeting you here," he said and winked at me.

"How did you find this place?" I said to Steve, frowning.

"Oh, Mira," Leah said and turned to me, a look of guilt on her face. "I forgot to tell you that I met up with Steve and told him about tonight. I thought it would be fun for the three of us to spend your first night back bartending together."

I forced a smile I didn't feel and wiped down the bar. "Wasn't that thoughtful?" I said, trying not to sound too sarcastic.

It wasn't that I disliked Steve. It was that he'd been a bit too protective of me. He took his big brother role a bit too seriously for my liking.

We made small talk for a while about his decision to transfer to Columbia and Leah and Steve had a few drinks while I bartended.

Then, out of the blue, Leah brought up Beckett.

"I'm trying to convince Mira to give Beckett a chance," she said and pointed her glass to me.

I made a face at Leah, wondering why she'd bring Beckett up. She must be feeling the couple of beers she already drank.

Steve and I were work friends – nothing more. He wasn't a confidant. I didn't want to talk to him about Beckett. The very fact he knew about it made me really uncomfortable.

"Why?" Steve said, shaking his head. "What's so great about him? He seemed pretty rough to me. A biker. Had this swagger and cocky attitude. Not your type," he said to me.

"He's not rough at all," I said, suddenly feeling all protective about Beckett. "He's a former Marine. He's a business man."

"He's hotter than hell, Mira," Leah said, raising her eyebrows. "You have to admit it. Plus, he was clearly hot for you."

I felt my face heat, and turned away, pretending to do something behind the bar.

"Are you seeing him now?" Steve asked. I turned back and saw his jaw was clenched.

"No," I said. "We're not seeing each other." I turned to Leah and made a face intended to shut her up about Beckett. She seemed immune to my signals.

"You could be if you just called him up," Leah added. "You have his number."

I shook my head and turned away again. "Not going to happen."

"Why not?" Steve asked, his eyes narrowing. "Did he hurt you?"

"He broke her heart," Leah said. "Seduced her and Ididn't tell her about Dan and—."

"Leah!" I frowned at her. "That's personal."

Leah looked all surprised "We're all friends," she said, glancing between Steve and me.

"This is private," I said with as much emphasis as I could. "End of story."

Steve nodded. "I get it. He broke your heart and you don't want to talk about him. I could have known he'd hurt you when I saw him the first time. He was just way too pushy."

I rubbed down the bar a bit too hard, trying to keep from responding too emotionally. He was wrong. While Beckett was pretty clear that he wanted to spend time with me, and then once we were together, he wanted to be with me and have me as much as possible, he wasn't pushy. At least, not pushier than I wanted him to be.

I wanted him, too.

I wanted to spend time with him. I wanted to be in his bed. I did nothing with him that I didn't want to do and very enthusiastically.

The rest of the evening went more smoothly, with Steve and Leah complying with my request to not talk about Beckett. Instead, Steve told us about his first week at Columbia and how different it was to be in Manhattan rather than Wilmington. How he made out in the subways and learning which train to take and where to transfer.

When I was off shift, the three of us left together and took our own trains home. It was logical for Steve to go with Leah, since they were both in student residence at Columbia and so I went on my own back to my place at The New Yorker.

When I got into bed, I lay awake for a long time, thinking about my life now that I was back in Manhattan. Part of me was happy to be back – the part of me that was able to blot out my thoughts of Beckett. It felt good to be finishing my Masters and I looked forward to my internship with the FBI after Christmas. I was glad Leah and I were still friends and had got together several times since we both returned, despite having busy schedules.

But I felt this gnawing emptiness in my gut. A pervasive sadness about Beckett. Everything seemed easy and exciting with him. I was so comfortable with him, no matter what we were doing.

Sex was really great with Beckett.

My body and heart ached, and both felt so empty and in need of the feel of his skin beneath mine. His eyes staring into mine.

I turned over and wiped the tears out of my eyes, trying to blank my mind of everything so I could sleep and forget about Beckett. I had to contact him and try to find out what he meant or I had stop thinking about him. One or the other.

This indecisiveness was hell.

LATER THAT WEEK, I met with Leah and we sat having a beer at a local pub. I frowned when she told me she and Brandon had seen each other for dinner and then went back to his place.

For hot sex, of course.

"Look," she said and leaned in closer to me. "I asked Brandon about Beckett, and he said that Beckett really liked you. *Really* liked you. He said that you were the first woman Beckett seemed to actually like since his girlfriend died. There are reasons he can't see you. That's all Brandon said, but he said Beckett was a totally honorable guy."

"His girlfriend *died?*" I sat in shocked silence. Then I remembered that he told me he had a sad story he didn't want to talk about. "He said something about having a sad story, and that he was almost married but fate intervened, or something." I shook my head in disbelief, a small twinge of sadness for him. He knew what it felt like to lose someone you loved. Someone you thought you were going to marry and live with forever.

But he obviously didn't understand how it felt to be lied to.

"It doesn't matter anyway. If he was so honorable, he wouldn't have seduced me while not telling me how he knew Dan."

"Brandon said there were reasons," Leah said with a shrug. "He's pretty closed up about personal stuff, but Brandon does know that Beckett lost his girlfriend three years ago during an accident while they were snorkeling off the coast of India. She was stung by some kind of poisonous fish and died in front of him."

I frowned, my throat tightening at the thought that Beckett saw his girlfriend die right before his eyes. "That's terrible," I said, my gut twisting. "That still doesn't explain why he didn't tell me the truth about Dan."

Leah shrugged. "All I know is that Brandon thinks Beckett has survivor's guilt and works super long hours to try to deal with it. His business is all about developing better technology to prevent combat deaths. He lost a lot of friends over there. His own injury was like a catalyst."

I knew that, as a Marine, Beckett would have seen terrible things in combat. It still didn't explain why he deceived me.

"I guess Beckett spends a lot of time at this club his uncle owns. Brandon's meeting me there on Saturday. If I see Beckett, do you want me to say anything?"

"*No*," I said, frowning at the thought. "He had the chance to explain things many times. He didn't. End of story."

Leah shrugged. "Brandon seemed so sure that Beckett was still crazy about you."

We sat in silence, and I tried to figure out why Beckett wouldn't have just contacted me if he was still 'crazy' about me.

"Why don't you meet us at the club on Saturday night?" Leah said and jabbed me with her elbow. "Brandon said Beckett really fell hard for you. He stayed an extra week because of you and hoped to see you again when you returned to Manhattan." She wagged her eyebrows meaningfully.

Beckett *had* stayed an extra week to be with me. A week that was the most wonderful I'd spent in a very long time. A week that made me think we were going to be a couple, once I returned to Manhattan.

"Give him a chance," Leah said, "if it's driving you crazy."

"I don't know…"

She shrugged. "It's up to you but I'm meeting Brandon at the club around nine. You could come and see him and then at least you'd know…"

I sighed and drank the rest of my beer. I couldn't imagine just showing up and seeing Beckett. It wasn't like me to do something so ballsy. I was the type to slink away and lick my wounds in private, to put on a brave face when in public, and not admit I had been hurt.

Going to the club with Miranda and Brandon would be really ballsy of me. What would I say to Beckett?

I could imagine him seeing me with them and leaving. That would hurt even worse than if I never saw him again. But Brandon said Beckett really liked me. He had a girlfriend who died? He had survivor's guilt? Then I thought back to my oath to seize life by the balls for a change. *Carpe diem.*

Going to the club on Saturday night would be ballsy, that was for sure. If Brandon was telling the truth, I figured I should give Beckett a chance.

ON SATURDAY, after dithering for hours trying to talk myself out of and into going with Leah, I got dressed in my tiny one-bedroom apartment in The New Yorker, standing in front of my mirror, adjusting my dress, which was far too revealing of my ample boobage.

Leah sat on the bed and watched. She had dressed and came over to my apartment so we could take the train together.

"We won't be leaving together," she said and cocked her head to the side to examine me in her critical way. "Not if you wear that dress."

I frowned at her. "A dress isn't going to win a man's heart." I adjusted the bodice once more.

"It can do wonders," she said and twirled a lock of her hair. "Brandon said that he couldn't get my dress off his mind after we met. You might be surprised at how memorable a revealing neckline can be to a boob man."

I laughed and adjusted my bra so that I wasn't spilling out.

"I think men are far more interested in what's underneath," I said wryly. "Or at least, that was always my experience..."

"That too, but men are visual. They like to look almost as much as they like to touch."

I nodded, remembering how Beckett liked to sit on the edge of the bed and just look at me in my lace bra, thong and heels. I'd make sure to wear some high heels, on the off chance that things worked out between us.

I had my doubts. Brandon seemed so certain that Beckett really liked me and had been moping around since he got back from North Carolina. I hoped he was right.

He said that Beckett hadn't been with any one woman more than once in the past three years – not since Sue died. Beckett was with me for ten glorious days in Topsail Beach. He stayed an extra week to be with me.

That had to mean something...

Finally, I was ready. After a last minute brush of my hair and reapplication of my lip gloss, we collected our bags and left for the train. The sun had set and the lights were bright as we walked to take the train to Hell's Kitchen. From there, we'd go to The Irish Club where Brandon and Beckett were having dinner and would stay for drinks. Brandon told Leah that Beckett's uncle owned the restaurant and nightclub, famous among the Irish crowd. I was nervous, and not entirely certain the night wouldn't end in disaster, but Brandon had been adamant that Beckett had reasons for not revealing how he got the letters. Reasons to do with his work in Afghanistan.

The only thing I could think was that they were black ops reasons. Dan had been involved in classified actions. I knew not to ask about them.

Maybe it was the same with Beckett.

I HAD no idea what to expect as we finally arrived at our stop and walked the remaining couple of blocks to the restaurant, which was really nice, the front of the old red brick. Even at nine, the street was busy and people strolled hand in hand along the walk, enjoying the warm night, the antique street lamps hanging outside the restaurant adding a nice atmosphere.

"I'm nervous," I said as we stood at the entry.

"*Carpe diem*, sister," she said and grabbed my arm. "Your very words."

"Famous last words, more like it," I said with a laugh that I didn't feel.

"Come in," she said and pulled me towards the door. "Give the man a chance. He really likes you, Mira. Trust me."

I allowed Leah to pull me inside the darkened interior. A hostess greeted us and we said we were meeting friends in the nightclub. She pointed the way to the bar and we went through a doorway. Once inside, I spotted Brandon and Beckett immediately. At that moment, I felt like a total idiot for coming. I almost turned away, deciding to run instead of facing Beckett. but it was too late. Beckett looked so handsome in a dark suit, white shirt and grey tie. My heart did a flip, and my gut felt tight as I saw him with a pretty cocktail waitress leaning over him, smiling at him. He seemed distracted and didn't see us at the door.

"Come on, sister," Leah said and pulled my hand, squeezing it to encourage me. "*Carpe diem.*"

Then Beckett glanced over at the door and saw us. Our eyes met across the room and I thought, *oh fuck. Now you're in for it, Miranda...*

Those blue eyes felt like they pierced right through me and I knew I wanted to forgive him, but most of all, I wanted to know why I had to.

So instead of bolting like a frightened deer, I stood firm and waited for him to come to me.

BECKETT

It rained all week, the water soaking me as I ran at dawn, trying to get enough exercise in so that I slept at night instead of lying awake, thinking of everything.

Everything, like Miranda Parker. Widow of Hospital Corpsman 1st Class Daniel Lewis.

It was crazy – I'd only met her six weeks earlier. How could she occupy so much emotional real estate in so short a time?

As Casey reminded me, I read her letters, all three dozen, and felt like I knew her far better than you normally would get to know a person in that short amount of time. Her letters were personal and intimate, revealing who she was and how she felt.

The truth was that I wanted someone like her to love me the way she loved Dan.

The way Sue had loved me.

Miranda didn't know me, but I was familiar territory. Military. A law enforcement type. We seemed simpatico and shared a similar sense of humor. Sexually, we were definitely compatible. She really responded to me. She was a hot and eager lover.

I considered texting her several times, but then I thought – no. It would just prolong the pain. Se couldn't look at me without bringing it all up again – the death of her new husband. The trauma of the news, his body torn up in the accident, burnt beyond recognition.

Most of all, the fact that he died while rescuing me.

I ached to have her forgive me. To take her in my arms and kiss her, hold her. Make love to her.

In my crazy romantic fantasy, she'd forgive me, and we'd fall into each other's arms and would spend the rest of our lives making each other happy.

That was most likely a combination of bourbon and wishful thinking.

I ARRIVED BACK at my apartment, and shook off the rain before taking the elevator up to my loft on the seventh floor. The old building was a beauty, and was one of the first to have a working elevator in it. My loft was Spartan, with very Zen décor and wall-to-wall windows looking out over the city.

Miranda said she'd be living in residence in the New Yorker. We couldn't spend time there – she'd have to come to my place. A place that hadn't seen a single woman walk through the door in years other than Sue, with the exception of a designer who deco-rated the place. And Casey.

I wanted Miranda there, in my bed, sitting at my table for a meal. I could picture her cooking at the counter in my kitchen, the two of us sharing a glass of wine while she prepared her famous *linguine agli scampi* like she promised.

That wasn't going to happen.

I had to forget about Miranda.

I SPENT the day at the office, catching up on work I'd let slide since the retreat. Usually, work filled my time and distracted me from other more difficult issues, but for the past week, I'd been unable to focus. That afternoon was no exception, and I found myself going over everything again, pulling up the pictures I took of Miranda while we were together. Selfies of us arm in arm, smiling like life was our bowl of cherries.

Maybe Casey was right. I should tell her the truth – as much of it as I could – and let her decide whether to see me or hit me again and walk out of my life.

It was really her choice to make. I wanted to see her again. There was no doubt about it. I couldn't stop thinking of her. I felt this huge hole in my chest at the thought that I'd blown it with her but could see no way that she could forgive me.

I sighed and left the office earlier than I planned, deciding that I'd go home, have another shower, and go to my uncle's club for dinner with Brandon. By all rights, if I had played my cards right instead of fucking things up royally, I'd be bringing Miranda and the four of us could spend an enjoyable evening together.

Instead, I'd be the third wheel, alone with my bourbon, which had become too much of a good friend, helping me fall asleep at night.

I MET Brandon at my uncle's restaurant and we had a nice dinner, lavish food and service, followed by a few drinks with my uncle. His sons, who worked at the restaurant in the kitchen and bar, stood around and we caught up on family news.

"What are you two doing now? Going out to find some pretty girls, I hope…"

"We're staying. Brandon's meeting his new girlfriend," I said and poked Brandon good-naturedly. "I'm living the single life."

"When are you going to bring a girlfriend?" Colm said, leaning over the top of the banquette at our table. "I've never seen you with the same girl twice."

"He's not the type to have just one woman," Brandon said with a grin.

"That's not right," Colm said, shaking his head. "He had a girl once." He met my eyes. "He was ready to marry her."

I glanced away, not wanting to be reminded of just how close to marrying Sue I had come.

"He found a little filly he liked down in North Carolina," Brandon said and gave me a meaningful look.

"Long distance romances don't work," Colm said, wiping his hands on his apron.

"She lives in Manhattan," Brandon said. "When he was in Topsail Beach, they were quite a thing."

I frowned at him and shook my head. "We're not a thing anymore," I said quietly.

"You sure *are* a thing," Brandon said. "She's crazy about you. Leah told me. From what I can tell, you're crazy about her."

"Bring her here for dinner," Colm said, nodding. "I want to meet this girl. Who is she? What does she do?"

I gave Brandon a shut-the-fuck-up look, but he seemed to be enjoying my pain.

"She's going to work for the FBI," Brandon said and smiled. "She's a really beautiful girl with long auburn hair and big green eyes. She looks like she stepped out of a travel brochure for Ireland."

"FBI, huh?" Colm said. He raised his eyebrows. "So she's a smart girl. Bring her by, introduce her to your family. I'll make a proper Irish feast for her."

He squeezed my shoulder and nodded like it was settled.

Finally, after a bit more ribbing from my uncle and cousins, Brandon and I left the restaurant and went to the bar on the other side of the building. It was only nine, so we were early. The larger crowds didn't come until ten. We took seats in an alcove that overlooked the dance floor, and ordered a couple of drinks from the waitress who came to take our order. I knew her from having spent a good deal of time at the club. Christa leaned over my chair and spoke to me about her father, who was a friend of Colm's.

It was then I saw Miranda and Leah standing in the door to the club.

"Oh, *God*," I said and stood, feeling numb when I realized she'd come with Leah.

Miranda stood in the doorway, staring at me. She was beautiful, her curves nicely emphasized by her little black dress and heels, her long auburn hair shining in the overhead light.

My throat choked up immediately, but this was going to happen whether I wanted it to or not. I knew I had to go and speak with her.

So I did.

I buttoned my suit jacket and stepped down off the dais and crossed the dance floor to where she stood, her hands at her side, her brow furrowed.

"Hey, Beckett," Leah said and wagged her eyebrows. "Look who I brought along…"

I nodded at Leah but my focus was completely on Miranda.

"Miranda…" I said and stopped a foot away from her. "I…" I was at a total loss of what I could possibly say to her.

MIRANDA

I TURNED AND LEFT, unable to talk to him.

I went out the doors and raised my arm to flag down a cab, in tears.

"Why are you leaving?"

I turned to her, frowning, my nose running. I rubbed my eyes with the backs of my hands, not caring if my mascara smeared.

"I can't do this. I have to go."

Finally, a cab stopped at the curb. I opened the door and sat in the back seat. Leah stood blank-faced, and stared at me.

"Do you want me to come?" she asked. "I have to get my bag if so…"

I shook my head and closed the door. I turned to the driver and gave him directions to take me to my dorm at The New Yorker.

I cried my eyes out on the trip there, but didn't care. The poor driver probably didn't know what to say, but I felt his eyes on me in the rear view mirror.

I arrived back at my dorm and threw myself onto my bed, crying my eyes out until I finally fell asleep much, much later.

WHEN I WOKE EARLY the next morning after only a few hours of sleep, I checked my cell and saw that I had about twenty messages waiting. Most of them were from Leah, but several were from Beckett.

I deleted all those messages unread and thumb typed a text to Leah, assuring her I was fine and that I'd spill all over coffee and bagels at our usual Sunday morning brunch spot. Then I had a shower and tried to wash the tears out of me.

I pulled on my jeans and a t-shirt and grabbed my sunglasses. My eyes were still a bit red and my nose looked like Rudolph on a good day. I walked to the subway and took a train to Central Park West and the little deli where Leah and I used to go before Dan died.

"Hey, sweets," she said when she saw me. She stood and gave me a hug. I sat down, my latte already waiting. "You look like shit."

"Thanks," I said with a sardonic laugh. "Just what I needed to hear."

"Tell me what you're thinking," she said and narrowed her eyes. "Beckett was really upset that you left. He wanted the chance to talk to you."

I frowned. "I could't do it."

"I think you're being too hard on him," she said. "I stayed behind last night and talked to him and Brandon. He was really, really upset, Mira. I mean, heartbroken."

"Sure he was. His supply of free pussy was cut off," I said sourly.

She made a face. "Come *on*," she said, her voice dismissive. "He could have any woman he wanted. Not only is he a freakin' Norse God, he's rich as sin. And smart."

"He lied, Leah. Some things are unforgivable."

"You lie all the time. We all do. White lies meant to make things easier for us and everyone else. Your sister asks if the dress makes her ass look big? You don't say yes. You say how great the color looks on her skin. The neighbor asks if you think his bug-ugly baby is cute? You nod and smile."

I scoffed. "Lying about Dan is a bit different than a white lie about a dress."

She shrugged. "Only in degree. Not kind. The intention was the same. Look," she said and leaned forward. "He got your letters, and fell in love with you after reading them and seeing your pictures. He told you that Dan saved his life. He just didn't tell you about the crash."

"He has *pictures* of me?" I said, shocked, not letting the words *fell in love with you* hit my brain just yet.

She made a face and covered her mouth. "Oh, you didn't know?" She shrank down in her chair. "There were a few pictures of you in with the letters. He kept those." She smiled sheepishly.

I sighed heavily. "So the moment he walked into the bar that day, he knew exactly who I was. He knew Dan was my husband, and he knew I was a widow. Most of all, he knew that my husband died because of him."

She nodded. "He went to Oceanside to ask the manager for Scott and Jeanne's address so he could go and shake their hand, thank them for Dan's sacrifice, give them the letters but when he saw you, he was struck. He couldn't stop himself. He wanted to get to know you. He said he went off the rails at that point."

"He sure did," I said, huffing. I remembered back to that night and how hot he was, and how fun he was. How sexy he was. How persistent he was.

How much I enjoyed him.

I enjoyed the fact that he was really trying hard to amuse me and get me to have a drink with him. There was no mistaking his interest and his attraction to me. After so long without much in the way of male attention – other than from men I had no interest in – it was a real ego boost. Plus, he was really, really sexy and good looking.

We *did* hit it off right away.

Was that because he already knew who I was? Or was it plain old sexual chemistry?

From the moment I met him until the day he left, everything was so easy. So *good*.

Not just good. *Hot*. When I was with Beckett, I was ecstatic. I laughed, I smiled, I had many, many great orgasms. With Beckett, I felt like someone who had been starved and was finally sitting down to eat a four course gourmet meal.

"Give him a chance. He's not a bad guy, Mira. Really. Brandon thinks the world of him."

"Convince me why I should give him a second chance."

She nodded, happy to do so. She held up her hand and ticked off each finger. "One, he was a Marine. Which means, like, he's super strong, loyal, patriotic, dedicated and mentally tough. Two, his company makes high tech communications equipment to help soldiers on the battlefield and train them to use it. He could do anything else with his smarts, but he chooses to give back. Three, he's really impressive, with a degree in symbolic systems or something from Stanford. That means lots of brains. Four, he's heroic. He went to Afghanistan to test the technology which is intended to save lives and almost died. He almost died, Mira."

"Dan *did* die."

There. I said it. That was what I couldn't get my mind around. "Beckett was there when Dan died," I added, my voice catching. "He was the reason. Dan went in to save him."

"They were both doing their *jobs*," Leah said and folded her arms, staring at me. "That's what Brandon said. He wasn't supposed to tell me but they were doing classified stuff. That's why Beckett couldn't tell you the truth."

"He could have told me," I said, not willing to accept that. Not just yet.

"*No*," she said, her voice insistent. "Technically, he's not allowed to because he was with the CIA on some kind of clandestine operation. Who knows what kind of trouble he could get into if people knew he told Brandon? And if Brandon told me, and I told you?"

"He *could* have told me that he was there and that's why he got my letters."

"Look, Mira. There's a reason the Navy didn't tell you or Dan's family what happened to Dan. They were in *Iran*," she whispered and leaned forward. "I'm not much into politics, but seriously, Mira. That could cause an international incident."

I shrugged, avoiding her eyes. "So what?" I said, doubtfully.

"According to the State Department, Iran is deemed a state sponsor of terrorism. The US has sanctions against Iran. I know because Brandon told me and I looked it up. Iran would be really pissed if they knew the US military was inside their country. I mean, they know the US already goes in and stuff. But they're not supposed to. That's what."

She took my hand and squeezed. "Look. Beckett couldn't tell you because then you'd want to know details about Dan's death. Am I right?" she said and peered into my eyes.

I said nothing and glanced away. Of course, she was right that if I knew who Beckett *really* was, I would have asked him about Dan. How he died. What happened – whether Dan suffered.

We ate our bagels in silence, but I felt Leah's eyes on me. She was so willing to forgive Beckett for lying. I was usually a pretty lenient person but when it came to lying...

"I can't stand lies."

She shook her head adamantly. "He didn't lie. He just didn't tell you. A lie of omission rather than commission."

"They're supposed to be better somehow?"

She nodded. "Of course. He didn't tell you a direct lie. He just never told you every detail."

When I didn't reply, she put her cup down. "Look, Mira, you should be glad to have met him. He fell in love with you from a distance and then fell harder when he met you in person. From what I could tell, you fell pretty hard for him as well. What would you have thought about him if he flat out told you that Dan saved his life in the accident? That he wanted to thank you and Dan's parents and that's why he was there?"

I shrugged one shoulder. It would have been different. I still would have been attracted to him. In fact, I might have been more willing to stay and have a drink with him that first night so we could talk about the accident. Maybe everything would have come out the same.

"I don't know..." I said softly. "How can I ever trust him again?"

"He told you the truth about everything else, right? Did he tell you about his reprobate Irish mafia family members?"

I nodded. "Yes."

"His father's death and the fact his uncle took the business?"

"Yes."

"He told you about his work and his education, his mother's family..."

"Yes."

"He told you everything except about the classified operation he was on with the CIA when the accident happened that he shouldn't have told me and Brandon about and that I shouldn't be talking about?"

I sighed, but said nothing.

"Am I right?" she said, leaning forward, her eyes expectant.

"You're right."

"Okay, then," she said and sat up straighter, her chin tilted up as if she'd just won a point. "Give him a chance."

I sat thinking about that night in Beckett's hotel room when I first saw the horrible scar on his neck and freaked. How it brought back memories of learning that Dan died in a helicopter crash. How I had to leave because it was all still too raw.

How must Beckett have felt, knowing that his injury was what got my husband killed? For just a brief moment, I put myself in Beckett's shoes.

A *very* brief moment.

He must have felt so … guilty.

"So I just text him and suggest we get together and talk?"

"Why not?" she said, as if it were so simple. "Were you happy when you were with him? Did he treat you well? Other than not telling you classified info that he wasn't allowed to tell you anyway?"

I didn't respond, not certain I wanted to admit that I was happiest when I was with him – the happiest I had been in a long time.

I sighed heavily and dramatically. I really was confused about what I should do. Part of me thought that I could never forgive his lies of omission. Part of me wanted to fall into his arms and let whatever would happen between us happen.

To hell with second-guessing everything.

"I'll think about it," I said and finished my coffee.

"Fair enough. You know what they say – you don't regret the things you do as much as the things you didn't do. Give it a try. That way, you won't always be wondering what if."

I nodded. That was enough talk about Beckett for now. I wanted to wipe my mind of the events of the past six weeks. I had to think about my year at CUNY finishing my Master's and doing my internship with the FBI. I had a paper to write. I had research to conduct. I had a job and would be working three shifts a week.

I had a date with Gramps on Tuesday night for dinner and then a shift in the bar. Working at his bar would give me extra pocket money and help him out. I knew that bar like it was the back of my hand and so I felt honor-bound to work again, even though I probably had enough money saved from my year and from Dan's life insurance to support myself nicely. Luckily, they were only six hour shifts.

"You working this week?"

I nodded. "Having dinner with Gramps and then pulling the early shift on Tuesday."

"Talk to him. See what he says about Beckett."

"I will."

We parted company after paying our bill and I walked back to the subway and to my apartment in the New Yorker.

BECKETT

ON MONDAY, after my Saturday night from hell and my reunion with Miranda, and Sunday spent regretting everything I had done and didn't do in Topsail Beach, I went through my usual routine of going for an early morning run as the sun was rising. After I showered and dressed in a navy business suit, I went in to Brimstone and read through my email, went over a few briefs my staff prepared for me on plans to replace the work that Graham once brought into the company.

I had lunch with Brandon, and spent the afternoon meeting with a few clients of mine to discuss future projects, including further development of training videos for private security operators overseas. I was so busy, I didn't think once about our precarious financial situation, but I did find my mind wandering to Miranda and how she was doing. I wondered whether she had been able to get over the shock of learning that Dan died while on a clandestine or "black op" that took him into enemy territory to rescue me.

How would Dan's parents react to learning the truth? As far as they knew, he was on a routine training mission. They didn't know it was black. I couldn't imagine that she wouldn't tell them, and I expected they'd be upset and want to speak with someone in the military about it, just to confirm facts. It could get me in trouble, but love does that to you – messes with your ability to reason.

I let my attraction to Miranda get in the way of my faculty of reason.

I'd never done that before, priding myself on being calm in the face of danger, cool in a crisis, and making sound decisions – business or personal. I'd done everything wrong with Miranda right from the get go.

That was going to change.

From now on, I was going to do what Brandon suggested. Instead of letting Miranda go, I was going to fight for her. She was the best thing that happened to me in a long time and I wasn't going to let her slip away due to my inaction.

I remembered Miranda talking about her grandfather's bar in Queens that was frequented by the cops in the precinct – *The Harp and Keg*. On a whim, I decided to go and speak with him. He sounded like he really cared about her and they were very close. I don't know what I thought meeting him would accomplish, but I wanted to explain myself to someone in the family.

Did I deserve a second chance with Miranda?

If he kicked me out on my ass, I'd have my answer.

THE HARP *and* Keg was a small bar in the middle of a block in downtown Queens, New York. It screamed Irish Pub, with the Guinness Logo in the window, and thick wooden floor boards, a long burnished wood bar with polished brass fixtures. A mirror ran the length of the bar and a few dozen bottles and glasses glittered in the light from the overhead lamps.

I spent a lifetime avoiding my father's side of the family due to their not-so-law-abiding careers as small time hoods, and here I was in love with an Irish beauty, with the lovely auburn hair, hazel-green eyes and freckles. Miranda looked like an Irish maid from some medieval era in her wedding photos, with flowers braided in her hair. I focused on the Cajun side of my family – my mother's side, learning a bit of patois and French, learning how to cook Cajun jambalaya, spending time down in the gulf. Here I was back in Manhattan, living in Hell's Kitchen, for Christ's sake, in love with an Irish American who could be a model in travel brochures for the Emerald Isle.

I went inside and took a stool at the bar, checking out the place, noting the beer on tap. An older man who looked to be in his late sixties came over, his bald head shiny in the overhead light of a Tiffany lantern.

"What can I get for you?" he asked, his eyes assessing me. He probably wondered why someone like me was there, with my longish hair and scruff, despite my business suit.

"I'll have whatever's on tap, thanks," I said and nodded to him in greeting.

He pulled a glass for me, his skill obvious. It must have been Miranda's grandfather.

"Haven't seen you around before," he said and placed the glass in front of me.

I gave him a bill. "Keep the change. You're Miranda's grandfather," I said, taking a sip and watching his reaction.

He glanced up at me quickly. "That I am. How do you know Miranda?"

"We met in Topsail Beach while I was there for a retreat."

He nodded. "You former military?" He scanned me, his eyes narrow.

"Marines," I said and nodded. "Special Operations Forces. I left a few years ago and started a company. I provide security technology for businesses that operate in war zones." I pulled out my business card and handed it to him.

"Beckett Tate, CEO, Brimstone Solutions, Inc. That's quite the title. How do you know Miranda? She never mentioned you."

It was at that point that I faltered. I looked away from his too suspicious eyes.

"Well, sir," I said, my voice low. "That's why I'm here. I fell in love with her when I was there earlier this summer. I believe she felt the same about me, but we parted on bad terms. I wanted to make sure she was all right."

"She's fine," he said, but he took in a deep breath. "However, I did hear some talk from her best friend about her having her heart broken by some young man she met. The way I heard it, this young man lied to her about some really important details. You want to give me the details so I can decide whether to buy you a drink or punch your lights out?"

I nodded and took in a deep breath.

Then I told him the whole damn truth.

No embellishments. I told him material that could get me in real trouble if it was known, but he was an ex-cop and understood about the need for secrecy.

He leaned against the bar, listening, while I told him about my trip to Afghanistan with the CIA, to test a new comms system that used our tech, and how we'd gone into Iran and hit a roadside IED. How Dan's unit was dispatched to rescue us. That he saved my life and lost his own, dying in a terrible fiery crash when the chopper went down in a sandstorm.

I explained how my things and his things became mixed up in the aftermath and Miranda's letters were sent to me by mistake, because my given name was also Daniel. How I discovered them nearly a year later, read them, and was captivated by the beautiful young woman who wrote those letters.

I told him about learning that the letters belonged to the Navy Hospital Corpsman who died saving my life. How, against my better judgement, I found myself traveling to Topsail Beach with the plan to return the letters to the Lewis family and shake their hands, to thank them for their son's sacrifice.

I told him about falling in love with Miranda and how I kept intending to tell her the whole truth, but felt I couldn't because the story they had been given about Dan's death and the story I knew to be true were different. How I felt I couldn't reveal the truth, no matter how much I wanted to be with Miranda.

I felt so much guilt over still being alive while Dan was dead.

I even told him about Sue and how close I had been to marrying her before she died horribly before my eyes.

"I'm in love with Miranda, Sir," I said. "I think I fell in love with her on letter three, but when I saw her in the bar that day? Goner."

He was pretty silent the entire time, not passing judgement. He didn't comment, and he didn't change his expression, which was neutral the whole time I spoke.

When I finished talking, when I said everything I could think of, it felt so much better, but then I had this terrible sinking feeling that even given the fact I'd come clean, he would kick my ass out of the bar and tell me to never see his granddaughter again.

If he did, he had every right. I'd kick my own ass out if I'd heard my story coming from someone else's mouth.

Finally, he put his cloth down and leaned on the bar, his steely blue eyes level with mine.

"You sure as hell screwed up."

I nodded, exhaling, and took a sip of my Guinness. "That I did."

He sighed and continued to wipe down the bar. "I'm having dinner with her tomorrow night before her shift. I'll see what she tells me. I'll see what she says about you and how she feels. That's all I can promise."

"Of course," I said. "Thank you for listening."

I stood and looked around the bar, trying to imagine Mira here, standing where her grandfather stood, pulling glasses of Guinness for the patrons, laughing at their jokes and miserable attempts to pick her up.

I felt a stab of regret in my chest at the thought I'd lost her.

"Thank you, sir," I said and tucked my hands into my pockets. "Really."

"For what?" he said a bit gruffly. "I haven't promised you anything."

"For listening."

He nodded. "*Semper fi*," he said and waved me away.

"*Semper fi*," I replied.

Then I left, feeling somewhat better that I'd spilled my guts to him, hoping beyond hope that it might help in some small way.

Realizing that it was probably a false hope, but I needed something to keep me going.

MIRANDA

ON TUESDAY, classes went quickly, and when I was finished for the afternoon, I went back to the residence to get ready for dinner with Gramps and then my shift at the bar.

All the time I was on the train, I thought about Beckett and how he'd knelt at my feet, my hand in his, his face so honest and open – in contrast to how easily he'd hidden the truth from me about his role in Dan's death.

I arrived at the bar and hugged Gramps, glad to see him. He was my only family left in visiting distance. I needed family at that moment more than anything.

"So, sweetheart," Gramps said when we were finally alone, seated at a table in the back of the bar after the waitress took our dinner order. "How are you doing? I got this phone call from Jeanne about you…"

I sighed and folded my arms on the table, not sure I wanted to go through everything with Gramps, but he asked.

"What did she tell you?"

He shrugged. "Only that you met someone and there was something about letters from Dan."

I nodded, thinking of the letters that were now folded up and packed away in the bottom of my desk drawer at the residence.

"He was a soldier who was there when Dan died. He got my letters by accident and returned them. Dan saved his life."

"That was nice of him."

"He didn't tell me exactly who he was and spent a couple of weeks seducing me."

Gramps frowned. "Did he succeed?"

I nodded again, not meeting his eyes. "Yep."

He sat back and took a drink of his coffee. "There must have been a reason he succeeded. Tell me about him. Do you want me to do some sleuthing about him?"

I shook my head. "I already know a lot about him and his family. He told me pretty much everything except that he was there when Dan died."

"He was in Dan's unit? How did he get Dan's letters?"

"It's a long story," I said, not wanting to go through all the details. "He was the reason Dan died. Dan's unit went in to rescue him after their vehicle hit an IED and Dan's chopper crashed in a sandstorm."

Gramps nodded and exhaled loudly. "I thought it was a routine training mission."

"So did we all. Apparently, the military didn't tell us the classified stuff." I took a drink of the coffee that the cocktail waitress put in front of me. When she left, I turned to Gramps and leaned in a bit closer, keeping my voice low so that no one else could hear what I was saying.

"Dan always carried my letters in his jacket when he was on a mission – for good luck." I frowned, because of course, they didn't give him luck in the end. "I guess when his chopper crashed, the letters got mixed up with the other soldier's things and they were sent back to him by accident."

"And you liked this man?" Gramps asked, his eyes narrowed.

I nodded, because I really did. "He was fun. We hit it off right away."

"So what's the problem?"

"The problem," I said and closed my eyes, taking in a deep breath, "is that he didn't tell me who he was right away."

"He never told you?"

I shook my head. "He told me everything only after we'd been together for several weeks. He was on a clandestine operation that went behind enemy lines in Iran. And I could get this man in trouble by revealing that, so forget I told you."

"Ahh, it becomes clearer now. You can't forgive him?"

I glanced at his face. "You think I should?" I was shocked that I even had to ask that question. "He knew more than we did – Dan's family – about Dan's death. He seduced me even so and never told me who he really was and how he really got my letters until after the fact."

Gramps rubbed his chin, his expression thoughtful. "He should have told you right away, no doubt about it. He was smitten when he met you. Probably tongue tied."

"No, he could never be tongue tied, Gramps. He was smooth as a baby's ass and made me laugh, flattered me, joked with me and charmed me."

Gramps laughed. "I really can't blame him for being smitten with you," he said and smiled affectionately. "You're beautiful and smart. A chip off the old block, if you ask me."

My mouth hung open in shock. "I'm surprised you're not going to go and punch him out for lying to me."

He took a drink. "He should have come clean right away. He didn't because he was probably thinking with his heart, not his head."

"His heart?" I said with a snort, unable to believe Gramps was being so lenient with Beckett. "More like his private parts."

Gramps laughed. "Oh, sweetheart, men always think with *them*." His eyes twinkled. Then, he became serious, his smile faltering. "Look, I'm just an old fighter pilot and cop," he said. "What do I know about you young people today? But something tells me that he fell for you and just couldn't find the right time or way to tell you the truth. If he was really on a clandestine operation, he probably felt he couldn't tell you. You of all people should understand that."

I sat back in my chair and stared at him, dumbfounded. "I can barely believe what I'm hearing. You'd forgive him?"

He took a drink. "I would. He read the letters you wrote to Dan and saw your pictures, and probably couldn't help but fall in love."

I stared at him in silence. "I never mentioned the pictures."

He froze and then, smiled to himself. "Damn," he said, then looked at me with a sheepish grin. "Losing my touch."

"You *talked* to him?"

"I did," he said and tried to hold back a guilty smile. "He came here and spoke to me last night. Told me everything."

"Gramps!" I said and sat there, totally blown away. "You should have told me! You *two*..."

He couldn't suppress a huge grin. "The boy's in love, Mira. Totally smitten. Total write off."

"I can't believe it," I said, angry that Gramps knew the whole story and never told me. "You should have called me right away and told me Beckett had been by to speak with you. Did Beckett think he could enlist your support to win me back?"

"I think he wanted to make sure you were okay, and explain himself to someone."

"You should have called me right away!"

He shrugged. "He made me promise not to tell you. Said he wanted to leave things up to you. I agreed it was your choice. Your move. Look," he said and leaned closer to me. "In general, I think it's best to be totally honest and upfront about things. Usually, I'd kick his ass out of the bar if he'd done something to hurt you, but the boy is clearly in love and clearly feels terrible about what happened. He said he fell in love with you after reading your letters to Dan and then when he met you, it was game over."

"He said he was in love with me? He told you that?"

"I believe his words were to the effect of *I'm in love with her, Sir. I think I fell in love with her on letter three but when I saw her in the bar that day? Goner.*" Gramps smiled and took another drink. "Kinda hard to argue with a man who confesses his love for you."

"Dan died because of him."

"Dan died doing his job," Gramps said, his voice soft.

The waitress put our food down and we were silent for a moment.

"He loved his job. That's what you always told me when I said he had a dangerous profession," Gramps said. "He was a hero."

"He was," I said and my eyes teared up, my vision blurring.

"If you ask me, so was Beckett. He almost lost his life trying to test equipment that was intended to make combat safer for our soldiers. I checked around after he came here and talked to a few friends I still have in high places. I believe Beckett has a few medals to show for what he did."

I didn't say anything. I wiped tears off my cheeks with the back of my hand and tried to get ahold of myself. I had to work in thirty minutes and wanted to be in control over my emotions.

"It's up to you, of course," Gramps said and handed me a tissue. "You have to decide whether to see him again. I liked him, if that means anything."

"His family is in the Irish Mafia."

"He told me that, too. I checked his uncle out. Don't worry," Gramps said. "Apparently, Beckett is keeping tabs on his uncle for the DEA."

"He told me he was an undercover DEA Agent. I wasn't sure whether to believe him." I wiped my eyes with the tissue and blew my nose. Then I looked back at Gramps. "You like him? You think I should give him another chance?"

He shrugged. "I like him, but it's not my choice. You have to decide whether to give him another chance. Or not. But I know Marines. Top notch men and there are not too many good men around these days. That's all I can say about it."

I sat in silence and pushed my food around on my plate. Usually, I'd have been all excited about eating the meat pie that my Gramps's kitchen was so famous for, but my appetite had gone completely.

We didn't talk any more about Beckett or Dan or the whole mess. Instead, Gramps caught me up with the news of the bar and what had been done to renovate it in the year since I left. He told me about his friend from the NYPD who died a few months earlier, and I recalled the man from my time working there. He even caught me up with news of my mother, who was living up north with her new husband. She was apparently trying acupuncture to cure her pain and had gone off her pain meds. I hoped it was true because they made her a zombie.

"You should go up there and visit," he said. "I know she misses you and feels as if she's been absent from your life for too long."

"She has," I said, an old sore spot in my chest hurting. "I'll think about it."

"Don't let things go too long. People die, sweetheart. You know that only too well."

I forced a smile and nodded. He was right. I should patch things up with my mom, if she was making a real effort to go off her meds.

As to Beckett, I couldn't at that moment consider forgiving him, but if Gramps was so willing to give him a pass, maybe I had to seriously consider it.

I'd give it some time.

I SPENT a long time that night at the pub thinking about what my grandfather said about Beckett.

He said he knew Marines, and they were honorable and strong, heroic and loyal. I knew Gramps was right.

I tried to think of what I'd tell Leah if it were her in my shoes and I knew the whole story. I'd probably tell her to give him a chance.

Just the way she was telling me to give Beckett a chance.

"So," Gramps said before he left for the night. "How are you doing, kiddo? Going to forgive him? Give him another chance?"

I smiled. "I'm thinking seriously about it." Then I put down my bar cloth. "Why do you care? It seems like you like him."

He shrugged. "He came clean to me. I checked out his story and it was all above board, far as I can tell. Besides," he said and leaned in, pinching my cheek. "I'm an old romantic at heart. I want to see you happy."

I smiled and said good night, watching as he left the bar. As I helped close up for the night, I remembered him and my grandma together. They'd been inseparable before she died a few years ago from early onset Alzheimer's. Now he was all alone, with nothing but me and his bar as far as close, reliable family went.

If he felt so certain about Beckett, maybe I had to trust his instincts. Of all the men I knew, his were instincts I trusted more than anything.

BECKETT

THAT THURSDAY AFTERNOON, I got a strange text.

PHANTOMJOCK: Make your move.

I read the message over and frowned. *Phantomjock?*

Then I remembered that Miranda's grandfather had been a Marine fighter pilot in Vietnam, flying the F-4 Phantom in combat.

What did he mean, make my move? He must have spoken to Miranda about me on Tuesday... Was he encouraging me to try one more time?

I thumbed a text back.

BECKETT: Thank you, sir.

Then I sent Miranda a text.

BECKETT: Meet me for coffee. Or lunch. Or dinner. Your choice of time or place. Let me explain.

I sat back and waited for a response, not sure whether she'd agree.

Finally, later that evening as I sat alone in my office, working late again as usual, I got a text.

MIRANDA: Why should I? You lied to me. How will I know what to believe?

She was right. I almost lost hope at that point.

BECKETT: *You're right. Let me at least explain what happened. You deserve to know.*

There was a long pause, and I half expected to never hear from her again. An hour passed. Then two.

When the end of the usual business day came, I had given up all hope.

Then, I heard my cell ding, indicating a new text message.

I grabbed my phone and checked.

MIRANDA: *Not promising anything but I do want to know exactly what happened. The military never gave us any details. You were there, so you can tell me what happened and why my husband had to die.*

That hurt and I felt a sick sensation in my gut. I closed my eyes and tried to stop from overreacting.

BECKETT: *Where do you want to meet?*

There was a pause. Finally, she replied.

MIRANDA: *Tomorrow at your uncle's restaurant. It's not too far from my apartment. 1:00.*

Even though it was only so I could fill in the blanks about Dan's death, I felt relief. At least I'd be able to come clean.

BECKETT: *Thank you. Meet you at 1:00.*

I sat back and ran my hands through my hair. I couldn't afford to get my hopes up too much. I'd have one chance to apologize and try to at least answer her questions about how Dan died and why.

MIRANDA

THE REST of the night passed slowly, with me tending bar, and watching the clock, hoping the hands would turn a lot faster than they were. My co-bartender Curt let me go fifteen minutes early, so after I cashed out, I left the bar and took my usual route down the street to where I caught my train.

The streets were pretty empty, and as I walked, I thought about the next day and hoped that Beckett could say something to me that would convince me I could forgive him. At that moment, I was startled when I passed a darkened doorway and of all people, Steve stepped out in front of me.

I stopped up short and gasped, then covered my mouth when I realized it was him.

"Steve," I said and exhaled loudly. "What are you doing here?"

Of course I already knew what he was doing there. I had hoped he wasn't really interested in me, but I'd been fooling myself, hoping he'd eventually get the message.

"I just wanted to make sure you got home safely," he said and held out his arm like he was a gentleman helping me onto a cart in some Victorian romance. Even from where I stood, I could smell the liquor on his breath. He'd been drinking. From the way he swayed, I could tell it was a lot.

"I'm fine," I said and frowned, not taking his arm. "I've lived in Manhattan for years and know how to look after myself."

He shook his head. "It's midnight, and it's dark. There are all kinds of strange people on the street. How do you know that one of them wouldn't hurt you?"

I pointed to the subway entrance down the street and kept walking. "That's my subway stop. I'm not afraid because I know the trains and don't feel unsafe. Not at this time of night. Manhattan's always busy. The city that never sleeps, right?"

He shrugged. "It's pretty deserted around here. If someone wanted, they could force you into a back alley and assault you. I wanted to make sure you were okay. Leah told me you were working late tonight so..."

"Thanks, but really," I said and started down the steps. "I'm fine."

He caught up with me and took hold of my arm. "Hey, not so fast," he said and smiled, his grip on my arm a bit too tight. "Have a drink with me before you go home."

I frowned and tried to pull my arm away. "It's late," I said, my voice low. "I'm tired and you've already had enough."

His grip lessened but he didn't let go. Instead, he stroked my arm and then took hold of my shoulders. "I know that Beckett guy broke your heart," he said. "I'm here for you, if you want to spill. You can cry on my shoulder."

I made a face and pulled away, but he wouldn't let go. "I'm fine, Steve," I said and laid my hand against his chest. "I don't need a shoulder to cry on, thanks."

"Come on," he said and pulled me closer, his grip tight as if he took my hand on his chest as an invitation for intimacy. "I know that he hurt you. Leah told me everything."

He tried to push my head onto his shoulder like he wanted me to cry.

"Steve," I said and then he tried to kiss me, one hand on my jaw, his lips missing my mouth and mashing against my cheek only because I tried turn my head away.

"I care about you, Miranda," he said when I finally was able to pull out of his arms. "I've been there for you all summer, and when I saw you with him, I knew he'd break your heart..."

I stepped away and wiped off my cheek, which was wet from his sloppy kiss. "I'm fine," I said.

"How could you sleep with a jerk like him?" he said and stepped closer to me, running his fingers through my hair. "Someone who could never appreciate you like I do."

I glanced around and wanted to run, but he was blocking my way to the entrance. Then he grabbed my arm and pulled me into the narrow alley between the two buildings. I struggled with him, but he was much stronger and managed to pull me into the alley a few feet.

"Steve, *stop*," I managed to say, my voice hoarse with shock and fear.

"*Hey!*" I heard someone shout. When I turned, I saw Beckett standing at the entrance of the alley. He rushed over and grabbed Steve by the collar and pulled him away from me. "Leave her the fuck alone."

Beckett shook Steve and Steve didn't resist. Beckett had about fifty pounds on him and was a few inches taller.

"*You* leave her alone," Steve replied, his hands on Beckett's, which were almost wrapped around Steve's neck. "You broke her heart."

"Get the fuck out of here," Beckett said, his fist rearing back, "before I punch your lights out. I could report you for assault..."

"Don't," I said and put my hand on Beckett's arm. "Let him go. I just want to go home."

Beckett glanced at me, his eyes narrowed, and then he turned back to Steve, shaking his head. Finally, he let go, and stepped back, blocking Steve's access to me. "Go the fuck away before I change my mind."

"*You*," Steve said and pointed at Beckett. "You're a fucking horndog. You don't deserve her."

Beckett nodded. "No, I don't," he said and adjusted his jacket, which had become bunched up during the altercation. "But I'd never force her to do anything against her will."

"Yeah, well, she'll be sorry if she picks you."

"Get the fuck out of here," Beckett said. Steve finally complied and staggered off down the street.

Beckett ran his hand through his hair and then turned to me, shaking his head. "I'm so *sorry* that happened to you."

I stood there with my eyes filled with tears, relieved that Beckett stepped in and upset that Steve seemed so tone deaf to my rejection. He *scared* me. I didn't really think he'd rape me, but he was drunk and was willing to force me into the alley and try to kiss me despite my saying no.

"Thanks," I said, my eyes filled with tears of fear and shock. "Why were you here?"

"I sensed you were in danger," he quipped, smiling softly, running his hand over my hair. "It's one of my super powers."

I couldn't help but smile back, although I hid my smile behind my hand.

"Actually, Leah told me you were working late and I wanted to make sure you got home safely," he said, a guilty look on his handsome face.

I sighed. "That's what Steve said."

He closed his eyes. "I'm not Steve," he said, his voice low. Then he reached into his jacket pocket and pulled out a tissue. He handed it to me. "I'd never force you to do anything."

I nodded and took his tissue, using it to wipe my eyes. "I know. You'd just lie to me."

"I didn't *lie*," he said, his voice sounding frustrated. "I just didn't tell you the truth."

"There's a difference?" I said, but couldn't help smiling.

He glanced at my face and smiled back when he saw mine. "There is," he said. "It's subtle."

Of course at that moment, I broke down in tears, overwhelmed suddenly by everything. I held the tissue against my eyes and cried, my arms wrapped around myself. It all became too much – Steve, Beckett, the anniversary of Dan's death…

Beckett took me in his arms and I didn't resist. I wasn't afraid of him or his touch. It was comforting.

"I'm so sorry, Miranda," he whispered, his face next to mine, his lips near my ear.

"I'm so glad you're here," I said and slipped my arms around him.

"So am I," he replied and squeezed me. "So am I."

We stood like that for a moment and I realized how easy it would be to just go on from there, to invite him up to my apartment and to fall into his arms. When I felt his body pressed against mine, when I felt so warm and safe in his arms, I knew how I felt about him.

I wanted him despite everything.

I glanced up and our eyes met and in his gaze I saw such tenderness and concern. It made my breath catch in my throat.

He bent down to kiss me just as I was leaning up to kiss him, and when our lips met, I melted into his arms, a thrill coursing through my whole body. The kiss was passionate, almost desperate, and my arms slid around him, squeezing him, my body pressed tightly against his.

He took my hand and pulled me to his car, which was parked just down the street.

"Come with me," he whispered when he opened the passenger door. I stood still for a moment, but when I saw the expression on his face, I knew I wanted to go with him.

After what happened with Steve, I didn't want to be alone.

I sat in the seat and fastened my belt while he got in the

driver's side. As soon as he started the car, he took my hand and kissed my knuckles tenderly.

"Come to my place," he said, his eyes meeting mine. Then he quirked a smile. "We could go to your place, but you said you had a single bed…"

I leaned my head back against the headrest and sighed. "You're assuming an awful lot, Beckett."

"Say the word and I'll take you home."

I said nothing, staring in his eyes, knowing that I wanted him. I wanted him to wipe thoughts of Steve away with his kiss and his touch.

So I said nothing.

Finally, he drove off and we zipped through the almost deserted streets to his place in Hell's Kitchen.

We didn't talk while he drove, and it was as if we both were afraid to say anything in case whatever was happening between us stopped. When we finally arrived at his building, I let him lead me up the stairs to the front entrance and into the elevator. He pulled me against his body the way he had that first night at the Yacht Club and we kissed, deeply, my heart racing, my body warming at the thought that finally, it was clear to me how I felt and what I wanted.

When we entered his penthouse apartment, I barely saw the place, despite my curiosity, for he wasted no time pulling me into his bedroom. He sat on the side of the massive king sized four poster bed and pulled me into his arms, my body between his spread legs, my arms around his shoulders.

We sat like that for a moment, his face buried in my neck and I closed my eyes and gave into my desires. At that moment, I knew I still wanted him and had wanted him even though he deceived me. I was so afraid after Dan died that I'd never meet another man who would make my pulse quicken and my heart squeeze the way it did with Dan, but I had.

Beckett made me feel that way again and it felt so good. It felt like I was finally living again. Until Beckett, I'd just been existing.

He pulled off my shirt, revealing my bra. He buried his face between my breasts, kissing the skin on them before pulling down one cup to reveal my nipple. He sucked on it, tugging gently on it with his teeth and I gasped with pleasure.

Then I was lost in the sensations of his mouth on mine, his tongue on me, his fingers and hands insistent, hungry, his eyes feasting on me once I was fully naked and lying back on his bed.

"Oh, God, Miranda," he whispered. "I thought I'd lost you forever," he murmured against the skin on my neck. "I couldn't stand it. Not after I met you. Not after we were together, but I didn't know how to make it right."

I kissed him, my emotions too high to speak. He made desperate love to me then, both of us so aroused and needy that I came so quickly, barely after he entered me and began to thrust and he wasn't long after, groaning when he ejaculated, my name on his lips.

WE LAY ON HIS BED, arms around each other, and recovered.

"I don't know what I would have done to stop him if you didn't come along," I said, when remembered how I got there. "I was afraid I'd actually have to use some of that MCMAP training I received from Devil Dog and you."

Beckett rose up on his hands and leaned over me as I lay beneath him. He grinned, and I knew he was remembering back to our encounter in the gym during the fitness class. His eyes twinkled and he smiled back.

"Glad to be of service, *sha*," he said and bent down to kiss me. "Anytime." He pulled back and looked into my eyes, and then his voice became serious. "I couldn't stand to think that he hurt you."

"You were there like my own personal superhero," I said and smiled, trying to lighten his mood.

He grinned. "I told you I had superpowers." He kissed me again and before I knew it, he was leaning down, arousing me once more with his mouth and fingers. "I meant it."

Then he showed me what he meant.

EARLY THAT MORNING while Beckett still slept, I crept into the ensuite bathroom with my bag and called Leah.

"You'll never guess what just happened," I said, keeping my voice low.

"What?" she said, her voice excited. "Did Beckett come by and sweep you off your feet?"

I laughed. "Yes. Twice. After he almost punched Steve out, that is…"

"*What?*"

I told her what happened and she was practically speechless while I spoke, except for a *no way* now and then.

"I am so sorry," she said, and she sounded really sad. "I had no idea Steve would be like that. He seemed so harmless to me. I thought he was just being protective."

"He saw me as rightfully his and pulled me into a side alley, trying to kiss me and who knows what else he might have done."

"Oh, *God*," she said and gasped. "He wouldn't have hurt you, would he?"

I sighed. "Who can say? I can't believe he would, but he was drunk and could have if Beckett hadn't come by."

"Thank God he did."

"Yeah," I said, remembering the relief I felt when I saw Beckett. "Thank God."

Leah spoke again, her voice soft. "So you two are back together? Tell me you're back together."

"We're back together," I said and smiled, barely able to believe it. "I forgave him for lying to me."

"He didn't lie," she said. "He just didn't tell you everything."

"That's what he said." I laughed softly. "You know that he actually went to the bar and spoke to Gramps about me?"

"He told us that last night," Leah said. "He is so in love with you, Mira. Poor bastard."

I smiled to myself but didn't say anything but inside, I said *I love him* in my mind.

I felt so guilty even thinking it, but it was true. I realized that I loved him.

"I'm glad you're giving him another chance."

"I am, too," I said finally and rubbed my eyes. "I have to have a shower and leave. We'll talk later."

"I'll be waiting for your call, sweets. I'm so glad, hun. I know he'll make you happy."

I ended the call and sat there in the bathroom, the biggest grin on my face.

BECKETT

MIRANDA HAD ALREADY SHOWERED and dressed by the time I woke. She bent down over me as I lay in bed and kissed me, smiling when she met my eyes.

"You're a sleepyhead," she said and snuggled against me.

"I haven't been sleeping well and I guess I was exhausted. Plus, you wore me out," I said with a laugh. "How come you're dressed? Are you going to deny me an early morning delight?"

"I am," she said and tried to sneak away when I grabbed her. "I have to go back to my place and get my stuff. I have an early class."

"Damn," I said and let her go with extreme reluctance. "What about lunch?"

"It's still on," she said and stood by the side of the bed. "There's still a lot I want to ask you."

I nodded. "I'll tell you anything you want to know. Now, let me get dressed and I'll drive you to your class."

She shook her head. "Nope," she said. "I'll take the train. I'll meet you at your uncle's place for lunch. We can talk then."

"Please," I said, getting out of bed. She held up her hand to stop me.

261

"Really," she said, her voice insistent. "I have a morning routine and have to keep to it. You stay in bed. I'll see you at lunch."

I sighed and gave in, kissing her again before she left. I stood at the door, my sheet wrapped around my waist, and watched her leave the apartment.

Once she was gone, I dressed in my sweats and went for a run just to bleed off some of the energy I felt after my night with Miranda. I didn't want to get ahead of myself but I felt elated that she had come home with me, made love with me.

After my run, I could barely eat my breakfast, my hunger dampened, but I knew I had to get something in me if I was going to last the morning. I had several meetings, and was glad that my mind would be occupied so I wouldn't dwell too much on the time and my meeting with Miranda.

Finally, the clock read 12:30 and after I finished up my meeting with one of my staff, I took my car to Colm's restaurant. As I stepped into the cool interior of the building, I wondered what questions she'd ask and how she'd respond.

Miranda sat alone at a round booth at the side of the restaurant. I went over and bent down to kiss her cheek. I sat beside her, close, and wrapped my arms around her, kissing her deeply. She kissed me back and at that moment, I felt so incredibly relieved.

"Ask me anything. I'll tell you everything."

"Tell me *why*."

I inhaled and folded my hands on the table. "We lost our GPS and strayed into enemy territory," I said, staring at the salt shaker, remembering back to the day. "We'd been out testing the comms tech Brimstone developed with a DARPA contract and—"

"No," she said and held her hand up. "Tell me why you didn't tell me who you were right away."

I closed my eyes. That *why* was harder to explain. It was easy to explain why Dan came to rescue us. It was far harder – practically impossible – to explain why I didn't tell her who I was right away.

"I was afraid that if I had told you the truth, you would've hated me. I didn't want you to hate me."

"Why would I hate you?"

"He died because of *me*," I said, my throat constricted. "His team was dispatched to rescue us. He came with me in the chopper. I was his patient," I said.

She took my hand and entwined her fingers with mine and that gave me strength.

"When we crashed, he wasn't strapped in yet, and when we hit, he was caught beneath the airframe..."

I heard Miranda's intake of breath. "Did he die quickly at least?"

I said nothing. I'd lied to her too many times. "I'm so sorry," I said, not wanting to tell her how he screamed in pain while the other members of the team tried to rescue him, and how they finally freed him after he'd suffered horrific burns, ripping off his clothes to apply bandages and tourniquets to stop the bleeding because of amputations caused when the rotor blades cut him.

She covered her eyes with a hand and I heard her sob. My eyes blurred, remembering the ghastly scene. I pulled her into my arms and remembered the scene that replayed over and over in my mind every day since then.

It was the only thing I remembered from the week before the accident to three weeks afterward. It was the one thing I couldn't forget, even if I tried.

"I'm so sorry," I said, my voice breaking.

After a moment, she seemed to get ahold of herself. Finally, she glanced up, her eyes wet. She reached out and touched my cheek, her gesture so tender. My throat closed up with emotion.

"Dan was a medic," she said softly, smiling through her tears. "Rescuing you was his job." She squeezed my hand.

"I wasn't even in the Marines at the time," I said, barely able to speak. At that moment, a huge weight of guilt lifted off my chest.

"I was a civilian contractor. I was just there to test some new technology that Brimstone developed for the military."

She held my eyes. "He was doing his job. He *loved* his job."

I nodded, and wiped my eyes. "He shouldn't have died because of me."

She smiled faintly, her own eyes wet. "No one should die," she said softly, "but we all do. My father died taking down a racketeer. It was what he loved to do. Dan died being a medic. It was what he loved to do. You could have died. You almost did. Thank God Dan was able to save your life or the mission would have been a total loss."

I couldn't speak my relief was so great. She was so accepting of what I told her. Her husband died when he came to save my life.

She didn't hate me.

"I feel responsible."

She shook her head, still holding onto my hand. "It was an IED. The insurgents who set it are the ones responsible. It was the sandstorm getting into the engines that brought down the chopper..."

"If I hadn't been there..."

She took both my hands in hers. "If my father hadn't gone to work that day. If you and Sue hadn't gone snorkeling."

"You know about Sue?" I said, shocked at the mention of her name.

"Brandon told Leah. From his lips to my ear."

I pressed her hands against my forehead, biting back emotion, barely able to believe she was so forgiving. So understanding.

The past weeks had been emotional for me, filled with wild swings from happiness and pleasure to the pits of guilt and regret, after I found her letters and met her. I never thought it would be possible for her to understand or accept my story – especially not after I had seduced her and not been honest about my identity.

"Dan's dead," she said, her eyes sparkling with tears. "I wish he'd never died and that you and I'd never met, but he did and we did. I'm alive. So are you. I'm so glad that given what happened, I finally met you. I love you."

I kissed her hands, one after the other, squeezing them in mine. "I love you."

"We're alive," she said, her voice filled with emotion.

"We are," I replied, taking her face in my hands. "We have to live."

She nodded in reply and smiled, the tears spilling onto her cheeks.

Then I pulled her into my arms and she wrapped her arms around my neck. Finally, our lips found each other's, our mouths joining in a deep passionate kiss.

THAT WAS the way Colm found us when he came barging to our booth moments later.

"There you are," he said, standing with his feet spread, his hands on his hips. "Are you going to introduce me to your lady friend?"

He had the biggest grin on his face, which mirrored mine and when I looked back at her, I saw a smile on Miranda's face as well.

I stood up and pulled Miranda up with me. She adjusted her dress and wiped her tears with the back of her hands, grinning like a kid caught stealing candy.

"Uncle Colm, this is my lady friend, Miranda Parker. Miranda is a student studying forensic psychology and plans on a career with the FBI," I said and turned to her, barely able to stop from grinning like an idiot. "Miranda, this is my Uncle Colm, my surrogate father. He makes the best damn Cottage Pie in Hell's Kitchen."

"Hell's Kitchen!" Colm said in mock insult. "In all of Manhattan. Speaking of which, I have your lunch all ready. Cottage Pie with stout."

"What do you think?" I asked, looking in Miranda's eyes.

She smiled. "Sounds fantastic."

I took Miranda's hand and we sat back down in the booth, side by side, my arm around her shoulders. Then, Colm and the waitress brought a spread of food, including my uncle's famed Cottage Pie, and tall glasses of dark brown stout.

"Will you join us?" Miranda asked, gesturing to the empty seat beside her. Colm glanced at me and I shook my head almost imperceptibly. I wanted to be alone with Miranda.

"No, no," he said and shook his head. "Thank you for asking. You two have a nice lunch alone. I've got work to do."

Colm left us and went behind the bar. As Miranda and I turned to our plates of Cottage Pie, I glanced over to where Colm stood behind the bar. He had poured himself a glass of soda and raised it. *Sláinte!* he mouthed and took a sip.

I raised my glass of beer, holding it up and toasting him silently.

I took a sip and turned to Miranda, who was staring at her plate. She was smiling softly, and at that moment, I couldn't really believe my luck at meeting someone like her.

"I honestly didn't believe you'd ever forgive me," I said. "Why? Why did you?"

She looked at me, her eyes meeting mine. "Life's short. People die. We have to keep living, even when bad things happen. Not telling me who you were from the beginning was wrong but I don't think you meant to hurt me. You're a good man with a good heart and you deserve a second chance." Then, she raised her glass of Guinness. "To life," she said softly, nodding to me.

I raised my glass in return and met her eyes. "To life."

We each took a sip and then I put down my glass and took her glass out of her hand.

Then, I pulled her into my arms and kissed her, pulling her closer, closer, unable to get enough of her and barely able to believe my luck that she was willing to forgive me.

If she could forgive me, maybe I could forgive myself.

EPILOGUE

Miranda

We spent the first weekend that we were reunited mostly in bed at Beckett's penthouse apartment. Beckett cancelled his appointments and we sat with his uncle Colm and talked about the family and Dan, answering Colm's questions about how we met and what my family did in Topsail Beach.

When we went to Beckett's apartment later that night, after dinner and drinks, I barely got through the door before he had me naked and in bed with him.

We didn't leave his apartment for the next two days, except when Beckett went to get fresh cream for our coffee and bagels from a deli around the corner.

"We'll be like John Lennon and Yoko Ono," Beckett said with a laugh, as we didn't even bother to get dressed on Sunday, and ordered in because his fridge was bare. We didn't even want to get dressed.

Those first few days were spent going over everything that each of us could remember about our shared past. He told me about his

DARPA contract to develop a new comms system, about how he was working with Special Activities Division and so his presence in Afghanistan – and especially the breach into Iran – was classified. How he had very few real memories of the events surrounding the IED and crash except for seeing Dan's face and the immediate aftermath of the crash when Dan's teammates tried to rescue him. He told me about his long recovery back in a VA hospital in New York.

I told him about the first months of my life after learning that Dan had died, and after the funeral. How I had fallen apart and spent the first couple of months staying at home, sleeping all day, watching old movies at night.

"You felt guilty that you survived," I said simply, understanding how hard it was for those who lived to accept it.

He nodded. "Friends wanted me to get grief counseling, but it seemed like I was the lucky one so I had no business being depressed."

We held each other and talked in quiet voices about how lonely we'd both been in the months after our loved ones died – both of us losing our fathers, and both our romantic partners.

Beckett felt as if he failed Sue, being unable to save her life, despite getting her to the nearest hospital in record time but the sting had been too close to her heart and there was nothing anyone could do.

I was unable to go to school that fall and winter, taking a year's leave of absence to recover.

We shared how we each coped with our losses in the aftermath of the crash, Beckett learning how to walk again, and me learning how to live again.

We were each other's best medicine.

FOUR WEEKS LATER, I had a short break in my school schedule so we took a drive down the coast to Topsail Beach, deciding to take a long weekend so Beckett could meet Scott and Jeanne and thank them for their sacrifice, as he had wanted to do since he found the letters.

The weather was warm and sunny, and perfect for our weekend away. We stayed at the Yacht Club, in the same hotel room, and spent three glorious days doing nothing but walk on the beach, lie on the beach, eat our lunches on the beach and then late at night, we took a blanket down to the edge of the dunes and lay back, watching the stars.

One of Beckett's interests, I discovered, was astronomy, and as we lay on the blanket staring up at the sky, he pointed out Cetus, the sea serpent, which has the star Mira.

"When I read about Dan's death on a forum online, it listed you as Mira, not Miranda and so I thought you were named after the star."

"You asked me about it, if I recall," I said.

"I did," he said and I could see his cheek rise in a smile as he lay beside me. "I was already infatuated with you from your letters and your photos."

"My photos?" I said, pretending not to know.

He turned over and faced me, resting his head on his hand. "You included some polaroids of yourself in with the letters. When I returned letters, I kept the photos."

I turned over and faced him, keeping my face unreadable. "You did?"

He reached into his pocket and pulled out his wallet, opening it to remove one of the photos. It was dark, and I couldn't see, so he took out his keys and shone a tiny LED flashlight that was attached to his keychain.

The photo was of me, wearing a floral sundress sitting on the patio at *Oceanside*. I was smiling, my cheeks sunburnt after a long day on the beach, nose covered with freckles.

"I fell in love with you, looking at this photo and reading those letters," he said. "Your dimples, your freckles… I had no hope after I saw you in person that first day."

I smiled. "When I first saw you, I thought you were a biker. In other words, not on the menu, given I intended to join the FBI. Instead, you were a veteran, and a business man. I'm so glad you found those letters," I said and cupped his cheek. "I fell in love with you, too, but I felt so guilty about Dan that I didn't admit it to myself," I said and looked deep into his eyes. "But I couldn't stop thinking of you, even when I thought we'd never be together again. I realized I loved you when I thought of you going to my grandad's to talk to him about us. It seemed like such an old-fashioned thing to do that I realized you didn't do it to hurt me. In truth, I haven't been this happy for so long."

"I love you," he replied. Then we kissed, deeply, passionately.

When he pulled back, he stroked my hair. "I know this is sudden but life's too short and too precarious to waste any more time. Let's live together, Miranda. I want you to move out of your room at The New Yorker and live with me."

I smiled, imagining waking up with Beckett every morning.

I kissed him again and then we lay back in each other's arms, watching the stars overhead. The past year had been tumultuous for us both, filled with loss, pain and a very slow recovery, but it seemed that we both had finally found what we needed, in each other's arms.

THE END

ABOUT THE AUTHOR

S. E. Lund is a writer who lives with her family of humans and pets in a century-old house on a quiet tree-lined street in a small city in Western Canada.

She writes erotic, contemporary and paranormal romance.

You can find her on social media:

Join the S. E. Lund Mailing List and get free eBooks, updates on new releases, upcoming sales and giveaways as well as sneak previews before everyone else.

She hates spam and will never share your information!

Join here:

http://selund.com

For more information:

www.selund.com
selund2012@gmail.com

ALSO BY S. E. LUND

Military Romance / Romantic Suspense

THE BAD BOY SERIES

Bad Boy Saint: Book 1

Bad Boy Sinner: Book 2

Bad Boy Soldier: Book 3

Bad Boy Savior: Book 4

PARANORMAL ROMANCE:

THE DOMINION SERIES

Dominion: Book 1 in the Dominion Series

Ascension: Book 2 in the Dominion Series

Retribution: Book 3 in the Dominion Series

Resurrection: Book 4 in the Dominion Series

Redemption: Book 5 in the Dominion Series

www.ingramcontent.com/pod-product-compliance
Lightning Source LLC
Chambersburg PA
CBHW050718180626
46814CB00002B/488